About the Author

David Liston was born and educated near The Oval cricket ground, in South London. After leaving the local grammar school, he spent forty years in the stockbroking industry, first as a successful Fund Manager and then as an Equity Research Analyst, where he covered the Food and Drink sectors. Besides food and drink, David's interests include sport — mainly cricket and golf — and global travel.

After retirement, an Open University course in Creative Writing and enrolment in the Writer's Village led to David entering a number of short story competitions, and eventually, to this book.

Loose Ends leans heavily on his experiences in the financial world and his travel interests.

David now lives in Buckinghamshire with his wife Linda, in an area of outstanding natural beauty—a far cry from his youth amongst the council estates of South London.

Loose Ends

David Liston

Loose Ends

Vanguard Press

DEDICATION

I dedicate this book to the memory of Dr John Yeoman, who sadly passed away in July 2016.

After a lifetime of teaching and writing, John Yeoman created the *Writers Village*. He was an inspiration to me and writers worldwide. I shall be forever grateful for his guidance.

DEDICATION

ACKNOWLEDGEMENT

In completing *Loose Ends*, my first book, I wish to acknowledge the help of several people. This includes Wallace Wormley, who was my first unofficial proof reader and who helped to highlight for me differences in the use of English between the USA and Great Britain; to my Australian cousin, Neil Brown, who enthusiastically read every chapter as it emerged, and to my wife, Linda, my editor-in-chief, who made sure that the pace of the story never stalled.

VANGUARD PAPERBACK

© Copyright 2023
David Liston

A CIP catalogue record for this title is
available from the British Library.

ISBN 978 1 80016 701 8

Vanguard Press is an imprint of
Pegasus Elliot Mackenzie Publishers Ltd.
www.pegasuspublishers.com

First Published in 2023

Vanguard Press
Sheraton House Castle Park
Cambridge England

Printed & Bound in Great Britain

MAIN CHARACTERS
(In order of appearance)

Brian Jenkins: Investment Strategist

Miriam Snape: CIA operative

Patrick Covington: Head of the PMC Hedge fund

Emilio Jimenez: Covington's Head of Security, son of Henrique Jimenez

Ron Mathis: Colleague of Brian Jenkins, at the PMC Hedge fund

Jeremy Crichton-Smith: Works at the Financial Securities Authority (FSA)

Covington's thug/ruffian: Burgles Brian Jenkins's flat and follows him to Hawaii.

Kylie Griggs: Friend of Brian Jenkins

Gregor & Charlie: Two servers at the Kona Inn restaurant in Kona, Hawaii

Juan Luis Santos: Computer hacker, worked on rigging South American elections

Mateo: Friend of Santos

Matt Booker: CIA agent

Helen Thompson: Socialite, works for MI5 with husband, Joe

Joe Thompson: Husband of Helen, also works for MI5

Miguel Jimenez: Runs a hotel in Kona, Hawaii, son of Henrique Jimenez

Pika: Friend of Miriam in Hawaii, obtains everything through black market sources

Pablo Segura: Grandson of The Professor, security guard at PMC Hedge fund

Sam Johnson: CIA operative, language specialist

Antonio Segura (The Professor): Friend of Henrique Jimenez; manufactures drugs

Detective Sergeant (DS) Mortimer: City of London. Police officer
Henrique Jimenez: Father of Emilio, Miguel and Francisco, member of
    the Mexican Government
Emily Winterburn: Swiss Secret Service
Franz Josef Haas: Covington's lawyer in Switzerland
Herr Fischer: Covington's banker in Switzerland
Frank McCarthy: Senior FBI Agent in Washington, friend of Miriam
FBI Agent Reed: Based in Hawaii
Daphne Mitchell: CIA operative
Felipe Gonzales: representative from the Mexican Embassy

CHAPTER ONE

Brian Jenkins was lost in his troubled thoughts when the captain's cheerful voice came over the intercom.

'We have now started our descent for Kona and should land in twenty minutes. The weather is a balmy 86 degrees and the winds are slight. Thank you for flying with Hawaiian Airlines and enjoy your stay on the Big Island.'

These words gave Brian no comfort.

Only three days before, he had been at his desk in Canary Wharf, the heart of London's financial centre. Now, he occupied the window seat in row 4 of the Hawaiian Airlines B712 aeroplane, on the other side of the world. He thought he needed to disappear fast, but was it *too damn fast?*

He realised his information could put some nasty people away for many years, but who to tell? People he considered trustworthy were not what they appeared.

His London flat had been broken into and ransacked, but he had stopped the thief getting what he wanted. Brian had a friend at the Financial Services Authority (FSA). They met to discuss Brian's suspicions. But was he a friend and was the fact that they met only the day before the burglary merely a coincidence? Brian had his doubts.

Brian had only recently joined his firm and had not met many people, except Ron. This meant Brian could not turn to his colleagues for help. Besides, it looked as if his office might be the headquarters of the operation. The hedge fund he worked for was unregulated, like most in London, and judged itself beyond the law. They paid well; no wonder, given the risks employees were asked to take.

Still, the high salary he received enabled him to buy this air ticket.

A woman's voice broke into his contemplation.

'Have you been to the Big Island before?'

'What? No,' he said, brushing the hair out of his eyes as if it irritated him.

'Bert and I used to come over here every year before he died,' she said.

Brian ignored her.

'Even though he died three years ago, I still come back.'

Annoyed at being disturbed, he turned towards his co-passenger. She looked like a small crow, frail and beaky nosed. Her hair was dyed red but with grey roots showing. She'd never see sixty again, he reflected, but she smiled and her blue eyes gleamed brightly.

'That's nice.' He forced a reply.

'Cabin doors to manual,' the instruction came over the intercom.

Brian turned towards the window again. The lady fell silent as the plane continued its descent.

What am I doing in Hawaii? He raised his eyes in anguish. *How will this help solve my problem?*

In an effort to escape, he'd assumed he needed to get as far away as possible. He'd taken a dog-leg journey from Heathrow to Honolulu, through Pittsburgh, San Francisco and now onto Kona. Five airports in twenty-five hours with no luggage to delay him, just a backpack. Still, he was unsure whether he had been followed.

His thoughts raced. *It was just after nine o'clock on Thursday morning I left the office to meet Jeremy at the FSA. But he proved no use. I told Jeremy I possessed evidence my boss might be committing money laundering through one of the firm's leading clients. He took a few notes and said somebody would be in touch. He just told me to act normal and that I would receive a text giving me instructions. What text?*

***

THE PREVIOUS THURSDAY, 3RD APRIL 2008
LONDON 23.00 (GMT+1)

Brian worked late that Thursday, preparing for a talk he was due to make to his new firm's clients. It was very late, and tiredness began to overcome him as he worked on his PowerPoint presentation. He knew he should close for the night, as his eyes felt very heavy.

Because of his tiredness, Brian hit the wrong key and the screen in front of him disappeared. He panicked at the fear of losing all the work on which he had spent hours disappearing into the ether. He hit various keys in random succession, and thankfully, the screen came back to life.

Initially relieved he could recover his work, Brian realised he had entered a part of the system unknown to him. As far as he could see, the information in front of him related to the client account ledgers and had nothing to do with his role in the organisation. Intrigued, he delved deeper. All too soon, he realised the confidential nature of the information he viewed. Not only that, but the plethora of payments in and out of the firm's accounts suggested this was illegal.

In another part of the office, a security official became alerted to the fact that somebody was accessing information from the accounting systems.

Brian knew he had no time to look at this right now, so he took a USB stick and downloaded the information to review it at home. He wished he'd brought his laptop in to the office, which would allow him to view the information on his way home. But he knew there were specific restrictions on members of staff prohibiting them from using their own computers in the office to support the privacy levels.

He left in a hurry, retrieving his mobile phone at the front desk as he departed.

***

Friday's morning meeting went like a blur. Brian had other matters on his mind. But he remembered his finishing words to the traders.

'World markets are becoming more volatile and rising steeply at the moment, but they are being driven by small speculators. They always buy at the top and are always wrong. Global equities will turn and we will enter a bear market, but we don't know when and we don't know what will trigger the reversal. Our new strategy is to position portfolios by shorting 10% of funds on each market surge. Go to it.'

His boss, Patrick Covington, looked on as Brian gave his message. The firm's main fund, PMC Hedge fund, was named after Covington's firm, PMC International. This stood for Patrick Michael Covington. The fund had risen up the league tables to become the best performing hedge fund in the past few months. This had happened since Brian's arrival from the Swiss asset management company, where he worked before being poached. He had been offered the role of Chief Strategist at an exorbitant salary, which he couldn't refuse, even though he was sorry to leave Zurich.

The PMC Hedge fund was attracting enormous amounts of additional money, as a result of Brian's successful strategy. Covington had arranged for him to make a presentation to the firm's new clients. It was the first such presentation PMC had organised.

Patrick Covington was looking displeased. Was it about the bearish message Brian gave the traders? Or because of the information he was being given by the man dressed in a plain, dark suit? Brian recognised him as one of the firm's security officials. At PMC International, only security guards wore suits in this modern office; the traders dressed casually; smart, but casual.

Brian wanted to find out what had displeased his boss. But before the morning meeting started, he phoned a friend of his at the FSA and arranged to meet him for a coffee.

***

When he returned to the office, Ron Mathis, one of Brian's colleagues, nudged him as he walked through the door.

'Covington's after you. There's blood on the tracks.'

Brian's meeting with Jeremy left him feeling disappointed, and now he was worried.

Calmly, he walked over to Covington's office and tapped on the open glass door.

'In here!' Covington said curtly. 'Shut the door.'

Nervously, Brian closed the door and stood in front of his boss.

'Were you working late last night?'

'Yes sir. I was preparing for the presentation next week.'

'Did you see anyone else in the office?'

'No, I don't think so.'

'Either you did or did not; which was it?'

'No, I didn't. Why?'

'There's been a serious breach of security protocol and right now you are the only person I can find who was here when it happened.'

'But it wasn't me, I can assure you.'

'Okay, we'll leave it there, but let me know if you remember anything else.'

With that, Brian left his room and sat at his desk.

'What was that all about?' Ron asked.

'Apparently, there's been a breach of security and he wanted to know if I was responsible.'

'And were you?'

'Don't be stupid.'

'You know what he's like about security. He won't let us bring our own laptops into the office for fear we'll download proprietary information, and we have to turn our mobiles in at the desk on our arrival.'

Just as well I phoned Jeremy before entering the office, Brian thought.

They looked up as Covington stormed out of his office and into the elevator.

Brian stood up and said to his colleague, 'Ron, I have to go to a meeting. I'll be back later.'

But Brian did not return to his office.

17

Just after eleven o'clock in the morning, Brian exited Ealing Broadway underground station. He stumbled up the steps and shielded his eyes from the bright sunlight. He was on his way to retrieve the USB stick from his laptop. It was only a short walk from the station to his first-floor flat opposite Ealing Common. Along the way, he kept on bouncing into people going in the opposite direction.

'Sorry,' he said.

'Sorry, forgive me,' he said again, as he pinballed off another bunch of pedestrians, whilst only just avoiding a lamp post.

Gathering pace as he walked, a youth in a black hoodie with arms wrapped around his chest bumped into Brian.

'Sorry mate, didn't see you.'

A cry rang out. 'Stop him! Burglar!'

Brian looked up towards the person who'd shouted; it was the caretaker of his block of flats. Brian turned around and caught the hoodie person breaking into a run.

'Right!' he said to himself. 'I've got you!'

Brian was over six feet tall, with long legs, which were used to running at pace. He played as an inside centre for Ealing Rugby Club and he brought his experience to bear.

His eyes were now fixed on his enemy, only thirty yards away, running fast. But Brian was faster. Twenty yards, now ten yards; Brian kept gaining. Now close enough, he launched himself at the hoodie with a flying rugby tackle.

There was a loud thud as the hoodie hit the pavement, followed by an explosion of air from his lungs as Brian wrapped his frame around the thief. As he flattened the wretch, a large knife fell on the pavement together with a laptop he carried inside his sweatshirt. The hoodie recovered disentangled himself, picked up the knife and disappeared at pace. Meanwhile, Brian collected the laptop, not caring that the hoodie made his escape.

He looked back to his block of flats and saw the caretaker standing by the front door, trying to stem the flow of blood from a gash in his forehead.

Brian bounded up the stairs to his flat. The front door lay battered and unhinged. His flat was even more untidy than usual. He went straight to the back of the airing cupboard to look for the USB stick where it was hidden. It was still there.

This episode frightened Brian. It was only last night that he had downloaded the information and then this morning he'd spoken to Jeremy. Now, somebody had tried to recover what Brian had taken. He was lucky he'd come home when he did.

The knife the hoodie carried scared him. Clearly, whoever was behind it would stop at nothing to retrieve the data. Brian was worried his life might be in danger. He panicked.

Brian made sure the caretaker was in no further danger then he threw a few clothes as well as his laptop into a backpack and took a taxi to Heathrow. With no actual idea about where he should go, he tried to make his escape as complicated as possible. The next British Airways departure was to San Francisco via Pittsburgh. The BA flight was not full, but passengers were boarding, so he bought a ticket, heading directly for the gate.

As he settled into his club class flatbed seat, his mind still raced and his thoughts ran round in circles. He had been to San Francisco many times before on company business and they knew him well at the Mark Hopkins Hotel, but the city was too big. He sensed he needed to be somewhere less crowded, where he could keep better control of his surroundings.

As Brian exited the terminal at San Francisco, he saw an advert for Hawaii. This was better, but he did not want to be in Honolulu. Maybe he should go to one of the smaller islands. After a restless night, he finally settled on the Big Island as his ultimate destination. It ought to be far enough.

***

Hawaiian Airlines flight 288 landed at Kona Airport after its short hop from Honolulu. The sun shone in a cloudless sky, but it didn't help Brian's mood at all. After exiting the plane, he walked directly to the Hertz rental desk, not knowing where he might stay that night. If he was being followed, he admitted to himself, no hotel would be safer than any other. But he needed the flexibility to move freely if required. He needed wheels.

'Don't you have a return ticket or even a confirmed address on the island?' the attractive receptionist asked. Her eyes widened in disbelief. Or maybe suspicion?

'I am so sorry,' she said, looking to the far end of the room, as if seeking help, 'but I cannot rent you a car.'

Brian turned away in frustration, only to see the little old lady with the beaky nose standing in the queue behind him.

'Can I help?' she asked with a sweet smile on her face.

Brian nodded, 'I can't rent a car because I don't have anywhere to stay yet,' he admitted.

'That's easy,' she said. 'I can give you a lift into town. Why don't you stay at my hotel tonight? Then, if you don't like it, you can find somewhere else to stay and you can rent a car later.'

Brian returned her smile and brushed the hair off his brow with slight embarrassment.

'It's very kind of you.' He blushed.

'No problem; in return you can carry my suitcase. It's heavy. I'm Miriam, by the way.'

Brian looked at the suitcase beside her, which was virtually as large as Miriam and almost certainly weighed more.

'I'm Brian,' he said. 'Are you staying here long?'

She nodded whilst completing the paperwork, so she could rent them a car.

On the short drive to Miriam's hotel in Kailua-Kona, Brian felt his mobile vibrate. He looked at his phone and it showed the call came from Kylie Griggs, a friend from London. Not a girlfriend, just a friend. Somebody he had run into at business meetings. But why did she try to contact him at this time of day? If it was five o'clock on Saturday evening on the Big Island, it was four o'clock Sunday morning back home.

He would call her back after he had checked into the hotel.

***

Brian thought back to when he had met Kylie. He had been at a seminar and wanted to ask the presenter a question. Brian raised his hand to request the microphone. It annoyed him when a female voice asked the same question he had considered.

He looked towards the sound of her voice. She was young with long blonde hair and looked smart.

After the question had been answered, the audience stood up to leave or go to the back of the room for refreshments. Brian noticed she chose to stay for a coffee.

'Hello,' Brian opened, smiling his shy grin. 'You asked the question I intended to ask.'

'Sorry,' she replied. 'I didn't mean to spoil your moment.'

'No, I didn't mean it like that. Few people think the way I do.'

'Oh, really? And how do you think?'

Brian realised this conversation wasn't going the way he'd hoped. He felt himself blushing.

The girl noticed this and smiled.

'I'm sorry,' she said. 'I'm teasing you. I thought it was your chat-up line.'

'No, it's all right. I'm sorry if you assumed I was chatting you up; it wasn't the case.'

Brian recognised he was digging himself in deeper.

He took a large breath and said, 'I have to go back to the office, but here's my card. Maybe we can have coffee and a proper conversation another time.'

Since then, they had met for several coffees. He found her intriguing. Kylie's mind was razor sharp, and she appeared to know Brian's thoughts before he did.

They discussed various topics, all about global economics and the geo-political outlook for major countries. Brian had never chatted her up or asked her on a date. Their relationship was purely platonic, but he looked forward to their meetings and it gave him a sounding board for his market theories.

Kylie never disagreed with Brian, but she suggested various alternatives. This helped him revise his thinking. He enjoyed discussing economic theories with Kylie. It was like two grandmasters discussing chess openings. There was never any correct move but alternatives could be just as effective.

***

A blast of the car horn brought Brian back to the present moment. 'Why did she call him?'

Miriam had glanced over when Brian looked at his mobile and this made the car swerve as she momentarily lost control. Another car, overtaking closely on the outside, got too close Miriam responded in a fit of pique. The blast of the car horn let him know it.

She looked at Brian and raised her eyebrows. Her naturally inquisitive mind would not be happy until she understood his story

As they drove along I-19, passing the Old Kona Airport State Recreation area, Miriam kept going on about the hotel. She told Brian how lovely it was. How close it was to the beach, that it was run by a Mexican family, with a fabulous restaurant nearby and a night club next door.

'It has everything. You'll love it.'

Brian was certain he wouldn't.

CHAPTER TWO

Later that afternoon, Brian was sitting on the hotel veranda by the pool drinking Dos Equis beer. He had picked up a copy of the newspaper, *USA Today*, and was skimming through the financial pages, but his mind was still in turmoil.

The hotel had accommodation, although it was on the same floor as the lobby and had little space. The sheets looked as if they needed cleaning and the room had no air conditioning. In fact, the entire place looked tired and in need of renovation. However, the staff were friendly, and when Miriam came outside to the pool area, they fawned over her, much to her animated delight.

'Now, boys, enough!' she said, laughing. 'It is lovely to be back again, but you have other guests. Don't they, Brian?' She laughed again, nodding in his direction.

He smiled self-consciously and raised his beer bottle to acknowledge her remark.

Miriam walked over to Brian and touched his knee.

'Brian, I'm hungry!' she said. 'Are you?'

He nodded in a noncommittal way.

'Well, let's go eat. There's a lovely place on the beach, a short walk from here.'

They left the hotel and crossed the road to the Kona Inn Shopping Village.

'Along here is my favourite restaurant in the entire world,' Miriam announced.

They walked through the shopping village along the boardwalk. Brian and Miriam looked an odd couple. She was a little under five feet, a dolled-up version of Grandma from *The Waltons*: petite not to say skinny, with dyed red hair cut into a bob. He stood over six feet tall, was thick set with dark brown moppy hair, dressed in a brown leather jacket and jeans. Definitely not a local.

Miriam casually slipped her arm into his and continued talking as they strolled along, like any other couple, until they reached the restaurant.

'It has the most marvellous views. You can see the sunset on the beach. Bert and I used to sit here forever, drinking our Mai Tais, watching the sun go down into the ocean. Time seemed to stand still. Then he left me.'

Miriam's face seemed to go grey as she recalled her husband's passing.

Brian felt uncomfortable with the way he had behaved. Here was this little old lady being friendly, looking for company maybe, but essentially helping him and all he could do was to reflect on his own problem.

He shook himself and resolved to put on a more positive attitude for the rest of the evening. Tomorrow would come all too soon, and he accepted he must face up to whatever it might bring. But tonight, he could enjoy Miriam's company, and perhaps she would enjoy his.

Brian realised that, whilst she lost him in his thoughts, Miriam had not stopped talking.

'...and the fish here are all caught locally, so it is really fresh. You'll love it,' she concluded.

He nodded at her and smiled. As they entered the restaurant, a rather camp server danced over to greet them.

'Ah, Mrs Miriam, so nice to see you,' he said as he welcomed her with the broadest smile, flashing every one of his ultra-white teeth. 'And you have brought a friend,' he observed, grimacing towards Brian, of whom he clearly did not approve.

'Yes, I have,' Miriam said, not revealing his name, to Brian's relief.

'Would you like your normal seats?'

'That would be lovely, Gregor.'

The server preceded them as he led the way through the restaurant, onto the deck outside where the sun was already setting.

'Gregor? Is that his actual name?' Brian asked Miriam as they exited the restaurant to a wonderful view overlooking the sea.

'He likes to think he is a Russian revolutionary.' Miriam said.

Brian and Miriam laughed in unison, and for once, he began relaxing in Miriam's company.

'I'll call the server over for you,' Gregor announced with a flourish.

'And he can start by bringing us two Mai Tais.' Miriam said as Gregor waltzed back towards the restaurant.

Miriam's attention now turned to Brian, and her face took on a more serious expression.

'Now, Brian, you have said little, but it's obvious you're a man in turmoil. Tell me your problem,' she said in a matter-of-fact voice.

'I don't want to burden you with it,' he said with sad eyes. 'Why don't we enjoy the evening. That sunset looks fabulous.'

Miriam gave an enormous sigh.

'That telephone call while we drove over here, was that your girlfriend?'

Brian didn't respond straightaway. He sat there looking at Miriam, trying to read her face while considering what to say.

'Yes,' he finally replied. 'We broke up. Very messy.'

The server brought two Mai Tais to their table and came back with two menus.

Brian thought it strange that Miriam had said nothing, especially considering how chatty she had been until then. He took a sip of his Mai Tai.

'Mmm, that's nice. I've never had a Mai Tai before. I'm more of a beer man, myself.'

Miriam seemed pleased with the change of subject. The smile returned to her face again.

'It's not just any Mai Tai, it's a Kona Village Mai Tai. It has a blend of three types of rum, light, gold, and dark. Most other Mai Tais only have light and dark rum. This is the best.'

Miriam leaned over and seemed to fumble for something in her handbag, which rested on the floor beneath her seat. When she returned to her normal sitting position, her expression had changed again. Gone was the sweet little old lady. Instead, she became an unfamiliar person, with an aggressive attitude. Her brow was furrowed; her eyes no longer gleaming brightly, but shining fiercely in anger. Her voice was almost unrecognisable. The chatty tone had vanished, replaced by a thin, whispered, steel-like pitch.

'Right, Brian, underneath this table, I have a gun aimed at your dick. Unless you tell me precisely what is happening here, I will let you have it. Your manhood will disappear in a flash. So level with me!'

Brian's mouth flew open, his jaw dropped, and his eyes almost popped out of his head.

'I told you.' He stumbled over his words. 'I-I've broken up with my girlfriend and I had to get away. It was very messy.' He stuttered in shock at what was going on in front of him.

Miriam's face told him she did not believe a word he had said.

'Come on, Brian, you're not running away from your girlfriend. If you were, you could've gone anywhere much closer to home, not to Hawaii. Not to the other side of the world. I switched on CNN and saw your face on the television. I didn't have the sound on, and by the time I turned it up, the story had moved on. But it was your face. Somebody is looking for you and it's not your girlfriend, at least not on that story.'

'Shit, I don't know, Miriam, that's the truth. Don't shoot me!' Brian gabbled loudly now, looking alarmed and incredulous. Luckily for Brian, Miriam believed him.

There was nobody else out on the deck that might hear them, but the servers realised something was wrong. Gregor came out in a flash, worried that the stranger might harm one of his favourite customers.

Miriam reassured him that there was not a problem, and in a level tone, asked if the server could take their order. Gregor asked one of his most senior servers to look after them. Charlie was a native Hawaiian, with greased black hair, dark, swarthy features, and strong shoulders. He had recently taken part in an Iron Man contest and Gregor thought he could be certain to handle the situation if the stranger cut up rough.

Over the meal, Brian told Miriam his story.

'I work for a hedge fund in London. I'm the investment strategist.'

Miriam raised her eyebrows and smiled, recognising his seniority.

'I recently discovered that we have some clients who are dangerous and that my boss runs a money-laundering operation for them.'

'So, why didn't you go to the police, or the SEC?'

'Financial Securities Authority,' Brian corrected her. 'I have a friend—or I considered him a friend, in the FSA, but now I'm not so sure. Truth is, I don't know who to trust, and I needed to get away so I can think out the whole nasty business. But you're right, I need help.'

Miriam said nothing. She settled the bill, and they left the restaurant, waving goodbyes to Gregor and Charlie, who still had concerned looks on their faces.

As they walked back to the hotel, Brian felt relieved that she knew his story.

As he recalled the events of this evening, though, he thought something was not right.

Brian put his arm around Miriam's shoulder. She looked up at him and smiled, but the smile disappeared when she realised he was pulling her in tight, stopping her from getting away, hurting her.

'Miriam, why did you have that gun in your bag?'

'I always keep a gun in my bag,' she said. 'After all, I'm only a little old lady and I need some protection in times of trouble.'

'But the way you questioned me, your entire attitude. Little old ladies just don't talk or act like that. If I didn't know better, I'd say that you were no stranger to violent behaviour.'

'Well, you've got me there. Did I tell you that my Bert was a detective?'

'No, you must've missed out that bit. Who did he work for, the FBI?'

'No, the CIA and sometimes we worked together on cases.'

Brian whistled. 'Wow! I didn't see that coming.'

They walked on silently for a few moments, with Brian digesting this latest piece of information. Then Miriam spoke again.

'What about your girlfriend?'

'What girlfriend?'

'You know, the girl who phoned while we were driving over.'

'Oh, her,' Brian paused. 'She's not my girlfriend. She's only someone I've met a few times at conferences.'

'Does she often call you?' Miriam continued with her gentle interrogation.

'No,' Brian said, frowning. 'This is the first time.'

'But she has your personal number, not your business number,' Miriam pressed further.

'Well, yes, I might've given it to her one time,' Brian replied, blushing.

'Brian, this is important. At what time did she phone you?'

'You remember, about five.'

'And what time would it have been in the UK?'

'Let me see… about four in the morning?'

'On a Sunday morning, doesn't that seem strange?'

'Well, I guess.' Brian felt himself being backed into a corner.

'OK, let me piece these facts together,' Miriam said. 'You've had a problem, and you needed to leave the country. This woman, who may be a friend—'

'A business associate,' Brian corrected her.

'OK, a business associate, but someone not close to you phones you at four o'clock on a Sunday morning when good people should be asleep.'

'OK, that is strange,' Brian acknowledged.

'And coincidentally, I see your face on CNN. Do you get the link, Brian?'

Brian nodded glumly.

'You need to phone her back to find out what she wanted.'

'It'll be early morning now. I'll call her when we get back to the hotel.'

'No, you won't. Not tonight.'

Not for the first time in their brief relationship, Miriam confused Brian.

'But you said…'

'If you phone her from your mobile, or from the hotel, someone can track your whereabouts by GPS. You need a phone that is untraceable. We'll sort that out in the morning.'

As they exited the Kona Village Shopping Centre, events across the road stunned Brian. There were four or five police cars parked in the front of their hotel, with blue lights flashing.

Miriam pulled Brian behind some bushes so the police couldn't see them.

'Do you think they're looking for me?' Brian asked.

'I'm not sure. I'll go over there and find out.'

'But if they are, the hotel staff will remember that I was with you and you'll be in danger.'

'Well, in that case, I'll have to lie and say that you went off somewhere. Anyway, we need to find out and I'm more used to this kind of situation than you.'

In the light of Miriam's most recent comments, Brian had to agree with that summary.

A few minutes later, Miriam returned.

'It's all right, you can come on over.'

'What was the problem?' Brian asked.

'Apparently, there was a man with a knife holding up the front desk, but they pressed the panic button and the cops came running.'

'Nice neighbourhood.'

'The strange thing, though, is that the cops said he couldn't have been a local person as he would've known they don't keep cash on the premises.'

'Did they catch him?'

'No, he got away, must've realised they had called the cops.'

'They were lucky he didn't use the knife,' Brian ventured.

'Well, sometimes shit does not happen.'

They walked into the hotel. Brian took out his room key and was about to insert it in the lock when Miriam grabbed his arm. She looked up at him and placed a finger against her lips.

Brian looked at her curiously.

'Kiss me, Brian.'

'I will not,' Brian said in anger.

'I said kiss me!' She grabbed his neck and forced his lips onto hers. As they kissed, Miriam turned the key, opened the door, and they fell into the room. There was nobody there.

29

***

In the office at the back of the desk, two of the hotel staff were looking at the CCTV monitor and they caught Miriam kissing Brian.

'Looks like Miriam has pulled again,' one said to the other.

'That gets you off the hook this time, *hombre*,' the other giggled.

'It wasn't my turn, that was last time and anyway you're younger than me. You know Miriam likes them young.'

'She sure likes them young,' the other agreed.

***

'What was that all about?' Brian asked, picking himself up from the floor and holding out his hand to help Miriam up. He noticed she was holding her gun.

'Well, it was only in case somebody had been in the room and I hoped we might surprise them.'

'It sure surprised me.' Brian admitted. 'Anyway, it doesn't look like anybody has been here.'

'Are you certain about that?' Miriam asked, holding up his backpack. 'Didn't you have a laptop in here?'

Brian grabbed the backpack and recognised that his jumble of clothes was just that, a jumble. There was nothing missing. He smiled back at her. Then he reached underneath the mattress and pulled out his laptop.

'Look, I'm not completely daft.'

'Well, that's as may be, but you shouldn't stay in this room tonight. You'd be safer with me.'

Brian raised his eyebrows and gave Miriam a silly grin, but she was deadly serious.

'Pack your stuff and come up to room 211. Don't make a noise.'

Miriam left and Brian put his gear together, shutting the door quietly behind him.

Miriam had gone up to her room in the hotel lift, whilst Brian took the stairs. When he reached Miriam's room, he tapped on the door. She opened it and let him in.

'Did anybody see you?' she asked.

Brian shook his head and looked around the room.

'Wow, this is much better than my broom cupboard,' he said.

'Do you want a coffee?' she asked.

'Actually, I wanted to get some sleep. I've been travelling for two days and what with all the tension, I am absolutely exhausted.'

'I thought we'd watch some television,' Miriam remarked.

This confused Brian again.

'Well, I've switched the TV onto CNN. I wanted to see if they showed that picture of you, and this time I would like to hear the sound.'

Brian admitted it was an excellent plan and sat in an armchair whilst Miriam sat on the edge of the bed. After half an hour, there had been no sign of Brian's face on the news channel.

However, what interested Brian most was that the Dow Jones Index was down by over 400 points over the week. There was some concern in the news anchor's voice, but Brian smiled as he remembered his recommendation to the traders in his office.

Not long after, Miriam looked over at Brian, who had fallen asleep with his head slumped into his chest, holding his cup of coffee precariously on his knee. Miriam removed the cup and got a blanket from the cupboard, which she wrapped around him. She kissed him gently on his forehead.

'Sweet dreams,' she said and climbed into her giant king-size bed.

CHAPTER THREE

The midday sun shone in Bogotá, itself a rarity. Even though the temperature was only 18ºC, at 8,600 feet above sea level in the middle of April, it felt pleasant, made fresh by the recent rain shower.

Juan Luis Santos sat on a rickety stool in a tiny courtyard in the old town. As he leaned over his iPad, the yellow trumpet, or Brugmansia tree, gave just enough shade for his eyes to focus on the small screen in front of him. Santos wore a white sweat-stained tee shirt, over crinkled white linen trousers. On top of his shaved head, he wore a Panama hat with his eyes protected by black- framed sunglasses.

Technically, Santos was convicted of crimes against the state. But his friend Mateo arranged a deal with the mayor to keep him alive. Mateo and Santos grew up together in Medellin in the early 1960s, a town that was associated with the drug cartel run by Pablo Escobar. Although Mateo and Santos had gone their separate ways as men, they never forgot their childhood friendship.

A year ago, Pablo Escobar's cartel ended when his last lieutenant was executed. Juan Diego Arcila Henao was killed in his Jeep as he left the parking lot of his home in Cumana, Venezuela.

Santos was afraid he might also be a target of *"Los Pepes"*, the sworn enemies of Escobar. But they did not link Santos to the drug activities of the Medellín. His misfortune was to be a technological wizard, responsible for organising "dirty campaigns" by hacking on behalf of the cartel. Latterly, the Medellín had proved small fry for Santos as he turned his talents to arranging political victories throughout South America.

These days, Santos and his team of hackers stole campaign strategies and manipulated social media to create false information. He installed spyware to help the favoured candidate. Typically, the candidate was merely the frontman, never the dealmaker. Mostly, Santos received his commissions from a Floridian-based political consultant, believed to be associated with the CIA.

Each job became more highly paid than the last one, culminating in the most recent election of a senior politician in the Mexican Government. The Floridian contact had nothing to do with this job, but the man who hired Santos knew him by reputation. The contract was on behalf of a multimillionaire, with a trophy wife, who operated one of the largest hotel chains in the world. He could afford the best, and Santos was the best.

The Mexican client duly won his place in the government. As Santos celebrated, knowing that his Swiss bank balance would benefit, he accepted the need to disappear.

Mateo was as shady as Santos many years ago, but now the people of Bogotá loved and trusted him, as he sought to eliminate the corrupt society of modern Colombia. When Santos needed to disappear, Mateo arranged a deal with the mayor to have him arrested for unstated crimes against the city of Bogotá.

Now, a door opened and an unshaven, overweight man entered the courtyard. His visitor was not tall and wore a dark suit, with an unbuttoned shirt collar and a tie knotted halfway down towards his enormous stomach. Sweat poured from his head. The visitor held his dark blue trilby hat in two hands at his waist, concealing the gun inside. He smiled, but his eyes resonated fear.

'How are you, my friend?' Santos asked as he rose to his feet and towered over his visitor.

'Better than if I was not your friend.'

The two men laughed at this feeble excuse for a joke as they hugged and patted each other on the back. Then the visitor stood ramrod straight and looked at Santos with eyes that did not see. There was a dull thud, and he crumpled to the ground at Santos's feet.

Santos had felt for the gun, held by the caller. It was an old trick, but one that he had seen before. He was much quicker than his guest and had taken the gun and used it before his visitor had been aware of what was happening.

Santos turned round, put the handgun in his pocket and retrieved the iPad. The message he had seen on the screen was still there.

The next man to enter through the door will try to kill you.

He did not know who had sent the message. Initially, Santos did not believe it. This place was a fortress, well-guarded and in a quiet corner of the old town. The mayor suggested it when he arrested Santos. He recognised Santos was toxic and that many groups in Colombia wanted him dead. But Mateo and the mayor determined Santos would serve his six-year term and remain alive.

Santos cried out.

'Guards, guards! Somebody tried to kill me!'

Nobody answered.

Santos's mind raced. He must get out of here. Santos opened the door through which his visitor had entered. There was nobody there. The guards had disappeared. He ran down the hall in terror, scarcely missing one guard lying on the floor. As he stepped over him, Santos noticed the bullet hole in the back of the head. Shot execution style.

Another guard lay prone around the corner, his gun ready to fire, but it was too late. Yet another guard lay dead across the corridor, twenty metres down. His rifle strung across his chest.

It was clear to Santos that the man who came to see him was a puppet. Santos thought he looked nervous but assumed that was just because of his own reputation as a hard man. Santos had had many men killed as part of the service to his clients, many of whom he had placed in positions of power.

As he turned another corner, Santos came face to face with a man who held a gun towards him. Could it be the murderer?

'Juan Luis Santos?' the man challenged.

'Who wants to know?'

'Matt Booker, CIA. Are you Santos?'

'Yes.'

'Thank God! We need to get you outta here,'

'Out of Bogotá?'

'Out of Colombia. We have to take a plane from El Dorado.'

'But I have no identification. Not even a passport.'

'Which one would you like? The mayor gave me a selection he held for you.'

'The mayor? What does he know about this? Where is he?'

'Too many questions, Santos. You must trust me now, and when we have time, I will answer your questions.'

Santos decided he had no choice but to trust this man from the CIA, who spoke with an American accent.

The two men exited the front door and leaped into a silver Ford Taurus. The American turned on the ignition. A screech of tyres heralded their rapid departure to the airport. Almost immediately, a black Mercedes GL450 turned the corner toward them.

Six men in the Mercedes pointed their guns at the Ford. A hail of bullets was let loose as they approached each other at over 100 kilometres an hour.

Santos ducked below the passenger air bag as the American swerved to avoid the Mercedes and the bullets speeding towards them. The Ford swerved violently as they turned a sharp corner and headed for the airport. Santos heard the screech of tyres and brakes as the Mercedes tried to reverse its direction to follow them. At this point, the American thought they would be caught in the 21 minutes it took along the Avenida Carrera to the Avenida El Dorado.

The American took out his phone. Santos just looked on in astonishment. This was crazy, even by his own standards.

'Hi, it's Booker.'

Somebody answered.

'We have unfriendlies on the Avenida Carrera in a black Mercedes. It would be nice if they could be diverted.'

Somebody replied.

'Thanks.' Booker put the phone back in his jacket pocket.

A few minutes later, they heard an explosion and saw a plume of smoke rise high above the buildings.

Booker slowed the car down to within normal speed limits as they approached the airport. Traffic was always busy in this area, even on Sunday afternoons. The car stopped in a no parking zone by the entrance to Departures and the two men got out. Santos looked at Booker questioningly.

'Someone will be along later to retrieve the car.'

'And my luggage?'

'In the trunk.'

'You seem to have thought of everything.'

'So it would seem.'

Santos and Booker entered the departure area and went towards a check-in desk, where Booker spoke to what appeared to be one of the airline personnel.

'Where are we going?'

'Istanbul.'

'Why Istanbul?'

'You have no contacts there. Nobody will look for you in Turkey.'

The airport official directed them to a door on the far side of the departure area, marked "Emergency Exit". Once through the door, they were in a long and wide corridor with no outside view. Overhead signs directed them to Business Flights. As the two men turned a corner, they came upon an empty airport personnel transporter. The key was in the lock.

'Your friend has been as good as his word.'

Santos looked at Booker questioningly. He had no clue what was happening.

Booker jumped aboard, closely followed by Santos. They threw the luggage onto the back seat. Santos was impressed that Booker seemed to know where he was going. The corridor appeared endless, but at least they were riding, not running.

Soon the end of the corridor came into sight and they could see a desk, behind which was another door. A grey-haired, partly balding man sat behind the desk, wearing a white, crisply ironed shirt. When he stood up, he walked in front of the desk to reveal light grey tailored trousers and black patent leather shoes. He looked elegant.

The man held out his arms to Santos, who ran over to greet him.

'Juan Luis, it's good to see you.'

'What is happening, Mateo?'

'He will explain, but you must move fast. You are not safe in Colombia.'

Booker intervened and pulled Santos away from his friend and shoved him towards the door.

'Go, go,' Mateo said. 'The plane is ready; the engines are running.'

Booker opened the door and the three men ran outside to the waiting Gulfstream executive jet, used regularly by the CIA for rendition.

Santos stood at the top of the steps on the plane and turned round to his friend.

'Cuidate mucho,' he shouted as he waved goodbye. 'Take care, my friend.'

Booker pushed Santos onto the plane, but as he did so, a shot rang out. Booker turned to look at Mateo and saw a bullet hole in the middle of his forehead. Mateo crumpled to the ground as his face shattered. He had been a good friend.

On board, Santos was distraught at the thought that his friend, who had only been concerned about saving his life, had cruelly lost his own.

More shots rang out, blistering the aircraft, but the plane was soon hurtling along the runway and racing to the sky. Santos's enemies would not get him today.

The Gulfstream V (or G-five), is a long-range private jet, capable of flying at 0.85 Mach, or 650 miles per hour, at over 50,000 feet. It has a range of 6,750 nautical miles, which is the same distance as Bogotá is from the air base at Adana in southern Turkey.

The atmosphere on-board the aircraft was very tense as the pilots attempted to make sure they left Colombia safely. The CIA, historically, had been reluctant to visit Colombia. Apart from the high level of anti-American feeling in the country, it always appeared that the local rebels, the FARC, were well equipped with arms. *Too well equipped!*

Matt Booker stood behind the pilots in the captain's cabin, agreeing the route to Turkey. They would fly over Venezuela, across the North Atlantic, then through the Mediterranean, towards Cyprus and onto Adana, in south west Turkey. The overall flight time would be approximately 15 hours. On the assumption there were no problems, they would arrive at Incirlik Airport, Adana, just after four in the late afternoon local time. From there, they would take a ten-hour drive to Istanbul.

Booker returned to the main cabin to make sure that Santos was safely in his seat. He settled down with his back to the captain's cabin, seated diagonally across from Santos. One of his colleagues, acting as steward during the flight, brought some sandwiches and water. Another colleague, seated at the rear of the aeroplane, looked out of the window, but remained alert for an emergency.

Booker removed his jacket, exposing his shoulder holster and gun. He had explained to Santos that he would have no problem using his gun in the event of him causing trouble. Santos appeared to drift off to sleep. Booker closed his eyes. He hoped it would be an uneventful flight.

CHAPTER FOUR

SUNDAY 6TH APRIL 2008
LONDON (03.00 LOCAL TIME)

The mist over the River Thames was thick. Kylie Griggs could barely see Tower Bridge, less than two hundred yards away, as she stood on the tiny balcony of her apartment at Butler's Wharf.

Kylie had only returned home a moment ago, but it was already three o'clock in the morning. She had attended a dreary dinner party with friends. Helen and Joe were lovely, but they insisted on matchmaking her with potential husbands. They didn't see why, at thirty-four years old, with her long blonde hair and fabulous hourglass figure, she couldn't attract a man, any man. Kylie kept on saying that her job was too stressful and all she wanted after a long day's work was the comfort of her flat. They didn't appreciate the pleasure she got from kicking off her Louboutin heels, or Lou-be-Lous, as she would call them. Next, she would discard her fashionable Stella McCartney work clothes and immerse herself in a hot bath. Afterwards, she would put on her red fleece nightdress and comfy slippers while she lazed on her sofa with a large glass of red wine.

This evening had been the same as all the others and the latest offering, a real upper-class fool, was ghastly. She arrived by taxi, but "the fool" insisted on driving her home. When they reached her building, he leaned across to kiss Kylie, but she recognised what was coming and was well prepared. The passenger door opened before he realised and she slipped out onto the pavement, leaving him sprawling over the seat, tasting the leather upholstery.

Kylie laughed as she walked over to the security entrance. She laughed when she heard his tyres screech and his exhaust roar as he sped away, no doubt cursing her as he left.

Before going to bed, Kylie dreamily turned on the television, and as she often did, switched on CNN. That was when she awoke, jolted by the picture of a man she met recently at an investment conference. She did not believe the story being related. She needed to contact him now.

Kylie knew he gave her his business card and was certain she underlined his mobile telephone number. Of all the men Helen had set her up with, this man was not one of them, but she admitted to herself that she did quite fancy him. Convinced she hadn't thrown away his card, frustrated because she couldn't find it. But where did she put the damned card?

Kylie turned out all the drawers of the furniture in her flat, throwing the various contents on the floor. She would clear it up tomorrow, or whenever. Kylie remembered the conference she attended, dressed in that stunning yellow-and-black outfit, a recent purchase. Kylie had only worn the suit the one time. Where had she put it? She remembered how she spilt red wine on the lapel as she laughed at one of his jokes. What was his name? She must have sent it for dry cleaning. No, not yet. It must be in the pile of clothes in the bathroom.

Rushing into the bathroom, Kylie found the suit, and yes, there was his business card, tucked into a pocket, along with a tissue, a lipstick and some used cocktail sticks.

Kylie looked at the card. Brian Jenkins, yes, that was his name and there was his telephone number. Kylie found her mobile phone amongst the mess of clothes by her bed and dialled his number.

There was no reply.

'Come on Brian, pick up your phone.'

At that point, Kylie realised the time and thought he must be asleep. She made a mental note to phone him later that morning.

***

Kylie came to with a loud ringing in her ear. After a while, she realised it was the land line phone beside her bed. She picked it up.

'Brian?'

'Morning, Kylie. Who's Brian?'

Kylie recognised Helen's voice, the friend who invited her to dinner last night.

'Oh, nobody.'

'Well, it must be somebody. You don't simply wake up and the first thing you say is a man's name. Not a man that I am acquainted with, by the way.'

'He's only someone that I know vaguely. I remembered before going to bed last night that I needed to call him today.'

'Sounds interesting. Tell me more.'

'There is no more to tell, Helen. Why did you call so early?'

'It's not early. It's almost midday and we're off to the pub. I only wanted to hear how you got on with Jeremy last night. He drove you home. I wondered if he was still there,' Helen said, sounding very interested.

'No, he is not still here. I left him kissing the passenger seat if you must know.'

'Oh, Kylie,' Helen said in a flat tone.

'And don't keep trying to match me up with people, Helen. I love you and Joe dearly, but I don't have to like your friends.'

'That's not a nice thing to say, Kylie. After all, we are only trying to make sure you're happy. You sit all alone in that apartment of yours. You might go for days seeing nobody.'

'Yes, wouldn't that be nice, me and my friendly bottle of red wine?'

'Kylie, be serious.'

'I am serious, Helen. Now leave me be. I need to tidy up after throwing out the contents of my drawers, trying to find Brian's telephone number last night.'

'Oh, so he is *not* just a nobody, then. I'd love to meet him.'

Kylie put the phone down.

'So would I,' she said.

Kylie wandered aimlessly round her flat. Picking up clothes here, redistributing them there. She was concerned about Brian and picked up her phone, pressing the redial button. Still no answer. Kylie threw the phone down on the sofa in annoyance.

Out on the balcony, Kylie saw the fog had disappeared and that the sun was out. The Thames was busy with pleasure boats going right and left as they took passengers on sightseeing trips. Looking over her balcony, she saw several people milling about on the embankment before they entered the restaurants on the ground floor. Kylie smiled to herself as she considered the location of her flat. It was so central to the City where she worked. The flats at Butler's Wharf had a gym plus swimming pool with restaurants of the quality of Pont de la Tour and Stone's Chop House. These she could reach without going outdoors. She had everything she required of her living accommodation. And then there was the Thames; the magnificent River Thames right next to Tower Bridge. What a view, especially on such a lovely spring morning.

Kylie stood there, taking a deep breath. The air was so fresh and the scent so beautiful. What should she do today?

Kylie considered staying home, on her own, sitting on her balcony. She stretched and smiled as the thought enveloped her body.

She tried Brian again. Still no answer. This time, she left him a message.

'Brian, it's Kylie, Kylie Griggs. Look, Brian, I need to speak to you. It's urgent, so call me back as soon as you get this message.'

After she ended the call, Kylie paced up and down her flat. Onto the balcony for a glimpse of the Thames, then back inside again. She sat on the sofa, switched the television on, and almost straightaway, turned it off again. She stood up and walked into her bedroom, redistributing clothes along the way.

'Oh, this is no good,' she rebuked herself.

Kylie accepted she needed company, somebody to take her mind off Brian. However, the only friends who would be in town at the weekend were Helen and Joe. Helen said they would be off to the pub and that meant only one place, The Dove by Hammersmith Bridge.

Kylie had met Helen and Joe at The Dove three years ago when she had gone to watch the boat race. She went with another gormless George, whom she had met at another friend's party. She realised as soon as she saw him again that it was a mistake, but he had asked her along to watch the boat race and she agreed to go.

Why is it that public schoolboys can be so dim and yet totally arrogant at the same time?

Anyway, she remembered trying to get away from him after he made a pass and then she bumped into somebody. That was when she met Joe.

'I'm terribly sorry,' she said, blushing. 'Please forgive me.'

'Nothing to forgive,' Joe said, smiling. 'Are you here for the race?'

'I thought I was.'

'Oh, trouble on the boyfriend front?' Joe noted quickly. 'Come over here and meet my wife, Helen. We'll protect you.'

And that's how she met Joe and Helen. They told her how they had found The Dove one year; when they came to watch the boat race and became Sunday regulars. Helen was an excellent cook, but she loved the roast lunches at The Dove.

'It's my day off,' she would say, 'and I don't intend cooking on my day off.'

After the gormless George experience, Joe always enquired about her attempts at finding a boyfriend; somebody sensible and intelligent; somebody she could have a conversation with and who would not always want to grab hold of her well-formed breasts. Then Helen decided that if Kylie couldn't find a suitable man for herself, she would act for her. She became Helen's project.

Kylie took a taxi, as she usually did in London, which dropped her off by Hammersmith Bridge. From there, it was only a short walk down some steps to the pub. She realised that Helen and Joe would be out on the riverside terrace on such a fine day. As she approached the pub, she spotted them clearly, but she dreaded the fact that last night's upper-class idiot, the abominable Jeremy, had also turned up.

She considered turning round and going back to her flat, but too late, Helen had spotted her and was waving her arm frantically.

'Well, this is nice, isn't it,' Helen said as she greeted Kylie with kisses on her cheeks, 'and Jeremy is here too? Isn't that nice?'

'Nice,' Kylie repeated in a flat tone.

Jeremy stood up and tried to kiss Kylie on her cheek, but a deft sway left him kissing air, just as he had kissed his leather seat last night. Joe was up at the bar getting refreshments. He guessed correctly that Kylie would have a large Merlot.

'Now, come and sit here, Kylie,' Helen said, patting the seat of the chair next to her. 'I want you to tell me all about Brian.'

Jeremy nodded his agreement to this suggestion as well.

'There is nothing to tell,' Kylie said, with a sigh. 'He's only somebody I met at a conference a short while ago.'

'And?' Helen said, waving her hands in encouragement. 'Go on.'

Kylie resigned herself to the fact that Helen would not shut up until she said something useful.

'Well, if you must know,' she conceded, 'I need to get a message to him, but he won't answer his phone.'

'Well, that is a coincidence,' Jeremy said. 'I'm trying to contact somebody called Brian too. What's his last name, Brian what?'

Signals blazed in Kylie's mind. She didn't trust Jeremy.

'Oh, nobody you would know.'

'Try me?'

'Brian Jenkins.'

She hadn't intended on saying his name, but there it was out in the open now and she could do nothing about it.

'No, you're right, that's not a name I'm familiar with. My man is Brian Fuller,' Jeremy said, looking at the pub signage. 'What does he do?'

'I'm not really sure,' Kylie replied.

'You must know what he does, Kylie,' Helen interjected, 'if you need to give him a message.'

Then she paused briefly.

'Unless it's personal,' she said.

Kylie was getting annoyed now.

'Oh, drop it, Helen!'

Helen did not like to be told off, and she turned her head to look at the river in a huff.

Joe returned with Kylie's drink.

'Joe, you're an angel,' she said.

Helen returned to the conversation.

'Kylie, you can see we all want what's best for you,' she said.

Joe nodded, so too did Jeremy, although Kylie did not understand why.

'Helen, you are one of my best friends and I love you dearly, but you must let me do things my own way.'

'Well, I suppose so,' she said grumpily.

But as she said this, the smile returned to her face, and she continued.

'Jeremy said that he had tickets for the O2 on Friday for Robbie Williams. He's one of your favourites, Kylie.'

'Oh, Helen,' Kylie said. 'I swear that one day I'm going to kill you.'

Kylie laughed, and they all joined in.

The rest of the afternoon passed peacefully, with no further mention of Brian. Time seemed to slip away whilst Hammersmith Bridge gleamed as the sun dipped into the Thames.

Kylie looked at her watch. It was nearly seven o'clock. She couldn't believe they had sat there for so long. Kylie had even begun to like Jeremy's sense of humour, just a little.

She realised that there was still much preparation to do for work tomorrow, so she bade farewell to her friends and made to leave.

***

Kylie walked back up the steps to Hammersmith Bridge, where she hailed a taxi to take her back into the City. Two hours later, her mobile phone rang.

'Hello?' Kylie said cautiously.

'You didn't think it was Brian this time, then?'

'Who is this?' she demanded.

'It's Jeremy.'

'Jeremy, I have nothing to say to you.'

'But I have something to say to you.' He paused. 'It's about Brian.'

'Are you still with Helen and Joe?'

'No, I left them at the same time as you. I returned to my flat in Chiswick, debating whether I should tell you about Brian.'

45

'What about Brian?'

'He's having problems.'

'How do you know?'

'Let me come over to your flat and I'll tell you.'

Kylie wasn't certain about Jeremy's motive.

'Where are you?'

'Downstairs, outside your flat.'

Kylie wasn't sure what to think. She held the phone away from her face while she gathered her thoughts. Was Jeremy trying to use Brian's name to get into her apartment, or did he really have some information? Earlier, he said that the Brian he was looking for wasn't the same Brian as Kylie was trying to find.

Could she trust Jeremy?

The answer to that one was an obvious no, but she needed to find out what Jeremy knew. If he was only trying to get inside her pants, then he would get a hefty kick in the groin for his troubles.

She could hear a noise coming from her phone.

'Kylie, Kylie, please answer and let me in.'

'Okay, but you had better be telling the truth or, so help me, I'll injure you for life.'

'Honest to God, I'm on Brian's side. I'm on your side,' he said.

'Come up the stairs, I'm on the fifth floor.'

Kylie opened the door to her apartment. She heard Jeremy coming up the stairs from a long way off. Obviously, he was not fit; she could hear him puffing away loudly.

She laughed when she saw the sweat coming off his brow as he turned the corner onto the last flight of stairs.

'It's no laughing matter. Why do you live right at the top, anyway?'

'To ward off idiots like you.'

'Not friendly,' Jeremy remonstrated.

'Sorry, come in and I'll pour you some wine.'

'That's better.'

Whilst Jeremy recovered his breath, Kylie poured a large glass of Merlot for each of them.

Jeremy sat on Kylie's favourite leather inclining armchair. Kylie stood in front of him, arms folded, in a menacing pose.

'You said that Brian was having problems.'

'Yes, I lied to you today when I said I was looking for a Brian Fuller. I'm actually looking for Brian Jenkins, but I didn't want Helen and Joe thinking we were looking for the same person.'

'Oh, I can see that. Helen's antennae would have been alive. She would have had so many questions about me and my men friends, she wouldn't have known where to start,' Kylie said.

Jeremy's face was now serious. He looked at Kylie curiously.

'That's not the reason.'

That stopped Kylie in her tracks.

'You realise what Helen and Joe do for a living, don't you?'

'Why no, actually. They're merely a friendly couple I met at the boat race a few years ago. Helen and Joe sort of took me in and take an interest in me. They're perfectly harmless.'

'Nice couple, yes. Harmless, no.'

This got Kylie's full attention.

'They're spies. MI5.'

'You're not serious?'

'Deadly.'

Kylie sat down abruptly, the wind taken out of her sails. She took a long sip of her Merlot and addressed Jeremy.

'How do you know?'

'They've helped me once or twice, tracing suspects for me. You understand I work at the Financial Securities Authority, FSA, right?'

'Right,' Kylie said, without giving away that she was completely unaware.

'What about Brian?'

'He came to see me the other day, at our offices, and said he had some evidence about his boss. He said it would prove that his organisation was laundering money.'

Kylie let go a long, low whistle.

'So where is he now?'

'That's just it. I said that I'd get back to him, but I couldn't do it at once. When I tried to contact him at his office, they said that he no

47

longer worked there. Now, this morning, I see on the news that one of the security staff at his office was killed, and that he is being blamed for the murder.'

Kylie interjected. 'When I got home last night after our so-called date (Jeremy laughed), I turned on CNN and they also said that he was wanted for murder. I tried a few times to call him on his mobile but there was no answer and the last time I left him a message.'

'Have you got his mobile number?'

Kylie stood up and retrieved Brian's business card, which she handed to Jeremy.

'If he's sensible, he won't be using this number again,' Jeremy muttered.

'How do we contact him then?'

'We don't. We wait for him to contact us.'

This worried Kylie. Whose side was Jeremy really on? If Brian had gone to him about money laundering, would Jeremy have shared this information with the police? And would they be interested enough to share some information with Jeremy?

CHAPTER FIVE

SUNDAY 6TH APRIL 2008
KAILUA-KONA, HAWAII (06.30 HONOLULU TIME)

Brian opened his eyes. He was still weary and felt that he had not had a restful sleep. His neck was stiff from sleeping in the chair. The pillow Miriam had provided to give his head support had fallen to the floor several hours ago. But the candlewick bedcover she wrapped around him was still in place. It was so tight; he struggled to free his arms to have a good stretch.

Just then, the door opened.

Brian tensed.

It was Miriam; she was carrying a tray of fruit and orange juice.

'Ah, you're awake,' she said.

'So it would seem,' Brian replied, scratching his head and trying to smooth his hair. 'What's the time?'

'Oh, it's still early yet, only six thirty. You should get some more rest.'

'No thanks, the armchair is not very comfortable. I could really do with a coffee.'

'I'll make you one. Why don't you take a shower if you're sure you don't want to go back to sleep?'

'That's a good idea.'

'Afterwards I'll tell you the news.'

Brian stopped in his tracks.

'Tell me now.'

'Well, it's not good news, but it will clarify your next move.'

'Go on.'

'After you had fallen asleep in the chair, I found it difficult to go to sleep. I kept thinking about the attempted robbery when we came back from the restaurant.'

Miriam paused.

'What about it?'

'You remember I said the police didn't think it was anyone local. Well, that got me wondering what they wanted. They might be looking for you.'

'But I had only recently arrived, how would they know where to find me?'

'I'm not sure, but I took the elevator back down to your room and had another look inside. I couldn't see anything out of place. However, as I closed the door, I pulled out a hair and slipped it in around the lock. If anybody opened the door during the night, the hair would fall on the floor.'

'And?'

'Well, I woke about six, went downstairs again and opened your door. Somebody had been inside and your room was a mess. They had turned it upside down. I stopped off at the kitchen. It was too early for room service, so I said I wanted fruit and juice to take to my room. This is what you saw when I came back into the room.'

'So somebody *is* looking for me,' Brian said.

Miriam nodded and put her arm around his shoulder for a gentle hug.

'What do I do now? I can't stay here any longer.'

'Right now, they don't know where you are. If they did, they would have disturbed us last night. So we have time,'

'How much can we trust the hotel staff?'

'They may have been nice to me over the years, but at the moment, I would not trust them as far as I could pitch them. That is not far at all. In my experience, you can't trust anyone,'

'I'll need somewhere to stay.'

'But first, we need to get you a cell phone. You need to talk to that girlfriend of yours.'

'She's not my girlfriend.' Brian insisted.

'Go take that shower. I'll make us some coffee and then we can figure out a plan over breakfast. We need to make you disappear.'

Brian nodded.

'I'm not hungry,' he said, as he walked stiffly towards the bathroom.

Brian sat on the toilet seat and put his head in his hands. He didn't move for a few minutes. Shortly, there was a knock on the door.

Are you all right in there?

'No,' Brian said, speaking through his hands, barely audible to Miriam.

'Come outside if you're finished in there. We need to make a plan.'

Brian opened the door. He looked frightened. All the colour had drained from his face.

'I feel sick,' he announced. 'I'm on the far side of the world and I'm on my own. Dangerous people are looking for me. I can't contact anyone for fear of being traced, and you say I need a plan.'

'Brian, you must assess your options.'

'Options? What options?'

'Do you stay here and let the dangerous people, as you put it, find you? Or do you take the initiative and return to the UK? Or go somewhere else where it will be easier to find out what's going on.'

'Well, I can't go back to the UK, because they'll be looking for me at the airports.'

'There are ways.'

'I can't stay here.'

'Agreed.'

'I have friends in Switzerland.'

'Possible.'

'So, now if I leave Hawaii, how do I get away without the police finding out?'

That's easy, I'll make a phone call to one of my old friends. I think you'll need a passport and a change of identity. Do you have any money?

'I own a Swiss bank account, which I use from time to time when I'm travelling. I used it to buy the airline ticket to Hawaii.'

'Good, it shouldn't appear suspicious if you use it again.'

'All of this might take a few days to organise, so we will need to relocate you to a safer spot. Leave that to me.'

Brian nodded.

'But you need to contact that girlfriend of yours.'

'She's not my girlfriend.'

'Whatever.'

'There is a place near here where you can get an untraceable phone,' Miriam said. 'Nobody will have its number, so they won't realise it's you when you use the phone. If you're careful how long you're on the phone, the call is untraceable. Also, I suggest getting another tablet, so you can send e-mails also without being found.'

Brian was in a daze. How lucky was it he had met this amazing woman on the plane?

Was it lucky? he asked himself.

He returned to the bathroom. As the reality of his situation became clear, he really needed to use the toilet.

Brian finally emerged from the bathroom. He felt a little better now. He'd had a shower and put his dirty clothes back on, because they were the only ones he had to wear.

'You seem more human,' Miriam announced. 'There's more colour in your cheeks. I was a little worried about you.'

'Thanks,' Brian responded, looking curiously at this strange woman. 'I was getting a little worried myself. I still am, in fact.'

'Right,' Miriam declared. 'I don't think fruit juice and coffee are enough. You need some solid food in your belly. We'll eat breakfast downstairs.'

'Is that wise?' Brian asked. 'You said you didn't trust the hotel staff.'

'True, but if they realised who you were, and that somebody was looking for you, they would sell that valuable information. You would not be standing here shaking.'

Miriam busied herself around the room, collecting her stuff. She visited the bathroom. Brian stood at the end of the bed. When she came out a few minutes later, wiping her face, he hadn't moved.

'Come now, Brian, it'll be all right. You don't need to talk to anybody. Go up to the buffet table, help yourself, sit down and eat.'

Brian nodded, unconvinced by what Miriam had said, and moved towards the door.

'Oh, yes, there is something you should do, just be normal.'

'How can I be normal?'

'Just be yourself, then.'

With that, Miriam pushed him towards the elevator. When the lift arrived, they took it down to the first floor, in front of the hotel foyer. Miriam took Brian's hand, much to the amusement of the desk clerk. She led him to the poolside veranda, where Brian could see an expansive buffet. He realised he was hungry.

The Maître D' led them to an empty table overlooking the beautifully shaped swimming pool, where Brian had his pre-dinner beer last night. At eight o'clock in the morning, the sun was already high in the sky and it was hot. Brian perspired in his totally unsuitable clothes.

Miriam noticed his condition and proclaimed, 'We really must get you some new clothes.'

A server appeared with a large white jug and poured coffee into their cups.

'Do you wish for any milk, *Senor*?' he enquired of Brian, who simply shook his head.

Miriam explained the breakfast set-up to Brian and got up to serve herself. There were three tables groaning with a variety of food. One had a choice of cold meats, smoked salmon, cheese, various breads, and salads. Another table offered an Asian selection of chicken and rice, fried noodles and steamed buns. Yet another included more typical American choices, such as pancakes with maple syrup, hash browns, scrambled eggs, bacon and pineapple.

Brian took a plate from the end of a table and filled it with a mixture of all three of the buffet tables. There was no discernible order to his selection, and this amused Miriam. He had taken a piece of Parma ham, smoked salmon, a steamed bun, two hash browns and a few rashers of bacon topped with a ring of pineapple.

'So, you are hungry after all?' Miriam asked.

While they were having breakfast, a tall man with slicked black hair, dressed in a shiny light beige suit, wandered amongst the tables, talking to guests. When he spotted Miriam, he smiled and made his way directly to her table.

Before he arrived, Miriam whispered to Brian, 'The man approaching is Miguel Jimenez, one of the family that owns the hotel. I've known Miguel since he was a young boy.'

'Ah, Mrs Miriam, so nice to see you again. We missed you.'

Miriam smiled in return. Brian sunk his head deeper in to his food.

'And who is this young man with you?'

'Hello Miguel, it's nice to be back at your lovely hotel.'

'Are you not on your own? Is this young man staying with you?'

'No, we met on the plane from Honolulu. He didn't have a room, so I brought him here. He checked in with me yesterday.'

'Ah, yes, Mr Jenkins from England. I hope you enjoy your stay in Hawaii.'

'Thank you,' Brian said.

'Miguel,' Miriam enquired, 'when we returned from dinner yesterday evening, police cars surrounded the hotel. Was there a problem?'

Miguel laughed. 'No, not any problem. Somebody came to the front desk and threatened my people. We pushed the alarm; there was a quick response from the police, but they didn't catch him.'

'That's strange,' Miriam replied. 'You don't keep any money there, do you? If he was local, he would know that.'

'True, but my men said he was not from here. He had a strange accent, like an Australian. Or he might have been English.'

Alarm bells rang as Brian lifted his head and looked into Miguel's dark brown eyes. Miguel returned his stare.

'And what of you, Mr Jenkins, what brings you to the Big Island and with no forward booking?'

'It was a spur-of-the-moment decision,' Brian said.

'Sorry, Mr Jenkins, I didn't quite hear you.'

'I said I just needed to get away. I didn't have a plan.'

'Hawaii is a long way to come from England without a plan. It's strange, but the police said the thief tried to look at the registration book when he threatened the desk clerk. They thought he might be looking for somebody.'

Brian's heart sank. Miriam reached out to touch his arm.

'Still, he couldn't have been looking for you. Even *you* didn't know where you were going. Have a pleasant stay.'

With that, Miguel turned away to talk to guests at another table.

Miriam looked over at Brian, whose eyes followed his interrogator.

'Right, Brian, eat up. We have a busy day ahead of us.'

***

As they left the breakfast area, Miriam persuaded Brian to go to his original room so he might see if his nocturnal visitor had taken any of his belongings.

'Come up to my room when you're done, but first, I need to make a phone call,' she said.

When Miriam passed the front desk, Miguel was on the phone.

'Yes, he is here,' the manager said. 'What do you want me to do?'

As Brian came out of his tiny room, on his way up to Miriam, Miguel called to him from behind the front desk.

'*Senor* Jenkins, may I have a word?'

Brian reluctantly ambled across the hall towards Miguel.

'*Senor*, have you decided on any plans?'

'What do you mean?' Brian asked.

'Well, are you planning to stay here for more nights, or do you wish to check out now?'

'I, er, don't know. I haven't decided yet.'

'Because if you were staying, I could give you another room. A much better room and it's next to your friend, Mrs Miriam.' Miguel emphasised the *Mrs*.

'That room is small,' Brian agreed, pointing to the door from which he had exited, 'and it looks as if somebody has turned it over. It certainly wasn't me.'

'I'm sorry, *Senor*.' Miguel looked concerned, 'I'll see if anybody knows who damaged your room. This new room will be ready after two o'clock.'

'How long can I have this room?'

'As long as you like, *Senor*,' Miguel said, with a broad smile, and Brian was certain that he saw a sparkle from a gold tooth.

Brian said he would confirm in the next few minutes and then entered the elevator on the way up to see Miriam. The door to her room was already open when he stepped out of the lift. He could hear her on the phone.

'Right, you're sure that you have all the items I need? Oh, come on in, Brian, I'm just finishing. No, I was talking to a friend. It'll take us a few minutes to reach you. I know where you are. Excellent.'

With that, Miriam finished the call and turned towards Brian.

'Are you ready? We need to get going.'

'Your friend Miguel offered me a new room if I want to stay.'

'Did he?' Miriam mused. 'That's interesting. What did you say?'

'I said I wasn't sure, but I can have it as long as I want. It'll be ready after lunch.'

'Would you be happy with that? You will need to stay on the Big Island for a couple of days.'

'Apparently, the room is right next to yours. It has just become empty.'

'I know the room. It's bigger than this. Bert and I used to stay in it. Strange, though, I didn't realise it was occupied. There was no noise coming from that room.'

'I don't know how much he'll charge, but it would be convenient being right next to your room.'

'That's settled, then. We'll tell Miguel when we go downstairs.'

Having confirmed that Brian would take the room offered, they exited the hotel towards the Kona Inn Shopping Village, where they ate the previous evening.

'This way, Brian,' Miriam directed. 'We're going to the Kona Farmer's and Crafts market. It's just down the road. A short walk, less than five minutes.'

As usual with Miriam, Brian did as he was told.

'This is a lovely little flea market, and it's right here on our doorstep. It's where the local farmers sell their produce and their handmade arts and crafts, souvenirs and Kona coffee. You'll love it.'

Brian thought he must be used to Miriam by now. If she said, 'you'll love it', he probably would.

'There's a man I've arranged to meet. He runs the stall and he'll provide the phones and tablet you need so you can contact your not-girlfriend.'

'How much will it cost?'

'Don't worry, it's all sorted. You won't need to make any payment.'

'That sounds very trustworthy.'

'It's not you he trusts, Brian. I've given him my word.'

As they exited down the slope from the hotel onto Ali'i Drive, Brian was becoming more aware of his surroundings. Across the road from the hotel, the Kona Inn Shopping Village sprawled out in front of him. There was the gate they entered through last night, on their way to the restaurant. He hadn't noticed the Hawaiian flags on either side of the gate with Union Jack flags to show that Hawaii had English heritage. Neither did he see the clothing shop by the gate and thought he should look in there to buy more appropriate clothes. The name of the outlet was "Iron Man", so maybe not the right one for him.

Miriam directed him left, along the street, towards an intersection. The shopping village continued on his right and seemed to go on forever. It was an enormous collection of single storey units, and even on a Sunday morning, there was a crowd of people. They had to wait at the intersection to cross the road. There was a line of cars, many of which were open-top vehicles; many were trucks, mostly pale coloured. It seemed to Brian the entire island of Hawaii was in this small area.

Once across the road, a green park came into view as the shopping village ended and he could hear the sea. Brian saw the waves lapping on the shore, creating white foam. If he was not so traumatised by recent events, he might enjoy this walk.

On the left-hand side was a large open-air car park, already full. He thought it looked like the entrance to a car boot sale. Next, he saw a collection of tents and outdoor stalls, selling many vegetables and fruit, most of which Brian was familiar with, some he wasn't.

Miriam guided Brian between the tents. He was glad she knew her way because he was lost in this maze. Soon, they reached the end of their journey. They had come upon a four-sided stall made up of shelving, baskets and tables piled on top of each other, covered in a variety of colourful fabrics. This stall contained an array of hand-crafted woodwork, small statuettes, jewellery, and other tourist junk.

Partly because of its position, Brian assumed, there were no shoppers inside the stall. Nobody could find it, he thought.

There was one man inside, the stall owner, who stood with his back to Miriam and Brian as they entered. He looked typically Hawaiian, six feet tall with a full head of shoulder-length black hair. A big man with a broad back wearing a multicoloured loose-fitting shirt together with shorts which would hold two people of Brian's size. He had no shoes on his feet. As a rugby player, Brian was impressed with his overall girth and more so when he turned round to expose the full expanse of his chest. Was it fat or pure muscle? Brian decided not to argue with him.

'Hello, Pika,' Miriam said formally. 'Do you have my goods?'

'All here, Missus, all loaded, ready for use.'

Pika went to the back of the stall, lifted what looked a heavy pallet with one hand. He reached into the underneath basket and withdrew three small mobile phones, a laptop, and a miniature camera.

'Who wants these?' he asked, looking at Brian.

Brian held out his hands to take the phones and laptop. Pika kept the camera.

'You can call anywhere in the world with these. They are fully paid-up phones with international SIM cards. They are untraceable by GPS or by origin. I already loaded the tablet with Tor, so you can send messages and nobody will realise where they originated.'

'Tor?' Brian asked.

'It's a piece of software, also known as "the Onion Router", used for sending e-mails anonymously through the internet.' Miriam said to Brian. 'You can access the Dark Web using Tor, but I wouldn't advise it and if you do, always put some dark tape over the camera.'

'Right now, I need to take your picture,' Pika said to Brian.

'Why?'

'You need a new passport,' Miriam said. 'Do you want a British or Swiss passport? Possibly both?'

'Why Swiss?'

'Miriam said you used to work at a bank in Switzerland.'

'It's an idea,' Miriam said. 'Particularly if you need extra anonymity.'

Everything was happening too fast for Brian. He shook his head, clearly exasperated. He was used to being in control, not being controlled.

'Look, I understand the problem I have. The fact that I need to contact people, but to hide my whereabouts at the same time. If I take a plane, I'll need to use another name. I need money, so I'll have to access my bank account in Zurich. I wish I'd never left the country. This is all too much to take in.'

'Sit down, Brian,' Miriam said, in a soft voice. 'Take a deep breath.'

Pika looked at Brian sympathetically but continued.

'Sorry, Brian, but we have to do this now. The passport can be ready for you by Tuesday afternoon. There is a flight from Kona to San Francisco on Wednesday morning. The tickets will be ready for you with the new passports, but Miriam says you have to act quickly or some nasty guys may find you.'

OK, so what do I do now?

'Sit still, while I take this photo, then we are done.'

CHAPTER SIX

SUNDAY 6TH APRIL 2008
KAILUA-KONA, HAWAII (12.00 HONOLULU TIME)
LONDON (23.00 GMT+1)

After their trip to the flea market, Miriam and Brian crossed the road to the beach. There was little wind, but the sea was lively with enormous waves crashing in regularly. Brian appreciated why the coast attracted surfers. The native Hawaiian sea birds, boobies, flew around, making raucous grunts.

'You should be able to get a good connection here; why don't you give your not-girlfriend a call?' Miriam said.

Brian turned on his old mobile phone and searched for the number on which Kylie rang him. He put it into one of his new phones and pressed the dial button.

***

In London, Kylie prepared to go to bed. Tired from the previous night at Helen's and the worry over Brian, she sat on the toilet and reflected on the events of the last few days. Then she heard her mobile phone ring.

Why does it always ring when I'm in the bathroom? she entreated.

Kylie finished her ablutions and jumped up from the seat.

'Where was that damned phone?'

It continued ringing, but she couldn't find where she had left it. The sound came from her galley kitchen. Eventually, she saw the phone

60

on the counter next to the sink, but as she reached it, the ringing stopped.

'Oh, that's so annoying. Who would ring at this time of night?'

Kylie looked on her phone for the number that had just rung. Not one she recognised. An overseas number, beginning with 00993. Kylie accessed her computer for the international dialling codes and saw that +993 was the code for Turkmenistan.

'Must be a scammer,' Kylie assumed.

***

Back in Kona, Miriam asked Brian what happened.

'I don't understand, the phone just rang and rang.'

'You didn't consider it right to leave a message? She would not have recognised the number you rang from, so she probably didn't answer it.'

Brian had forgotten that the SIM cards in the phones came from different places around the world. What Miriam said made sense. He picked another phone and redialled Kylie's number.

***

Kylie had slipped into bed, but she had placed the mobile phone on the bedside cabinet in case it rang again. No sooner had she put her head on the pillow than the phone rang.

She looked at the number. This time a dialling code she recognised, but early morning where the call emanated. Must be stock market news.

Kylie took the call. 'Hello?' she said. 'Moshy, moshy.'

'Kylie?' Brian asked, 'Kylie, is that you?'

'Is that you, Brian? What are you doing in Tokyo?'

'I'm not in Tokyo. Is that you?'

'Brian, you're ringing from a Tokyo number. Where are you?'

'I can't say. Why did you phone?'

'Jeremy and I wanted to know if you're all right. You're wanted for murder!'

'*What?* I realised I had a problem, but not murder!'

Kylie spoke in a frantic rush.

'I turned on the television and CNN said you were wanted for killing a security guard at your office.'

'I didn't kill anyone. Oh no!' Brian cried in anguish.

Miriam butted in, 'Brian, you'd better get off the phone now.'

'Who's that? Who are you with?' Kylie asked.

'That's Miriam, she's helping me. Her husband used to be with the CIA,' Brian said.

'Helping you with what?' Kylie asked.

'Who's Jeremy?' Brian intervened.

'He's your friend at the FSA. I met him when Helen and Joe tried to set me up with him on Saturday night. They work for MI5.'

'What's happening, Kylie? It's like I'm involved in a really weird situation. MI5! CIA! What next?'

Miriam grabbed the phone from Brian.

'He'll speak to you later.'

She turned off the phone.

***

Back in London, Kylie was totally confused. She got up from the bed, went into the kitchen, and poured herself a glass of water. She tried to assess the conversation she'd just had with Brian. None of it made sense. Why did she tell him that Helen and Joe worked for MI5? Did she say it because he had said that this woman, whatever her name was, had a husband who was with the CIA?

Kylie was annoyed with herself.

She paced around the kitchen, taking slurps from the glass of water. She was in a daze and needed to talk to somebody. Kylie phoned Jeremy. She still did not fully trust him, but he was the only person available right now.

Kylie pressed Jeremy's number and a sleepy voice replied.

'Jeremy? Are you awake?'

'Kylie, is that you?'

'Jeremy, I've spoken with Brian. He called me from Tokyo, but said he wasn't in Tokyo.'

Jeremy, now wide awake, said, 'Then where was he calling from?'

'I don't understand. He wouldn't—no, couldn't say.'

'How is he?'

'Brian knows he has a problem but says he didn't kill anyone. That shocked him.'

After a pause, Kylie added, 'He's with a woman, she sounded old and craggy. Her husband works for the CIA.'

'That doesn't sound good,' Jeremy said. 'Maybe this thing is bigger than we assumed.'

'I told him that Helen and Joe were MI5.'

'Oh, Kylie, you didn't. I only told you in secret.'

'Sorry.' Kylie felt embarrassed. 'The conversation was so wild. It caught me on the hop.'

'Kylie, have you had any other calls tonight?'

'Yes, one from Turkmenistan. It was a scammer.'

'I don't expect it was. Did you answer it?'

'No, I only answer calls from people or numbers that I can trust.'

'OK, leave it with me. I'll get back to you.'

'Who do you think it was?' Kylie persisted. 'what should I do?'

'Nothing for now, I'll talk to you tomorrow.'

With that, Jeremy hung up, leaving Kylie still restless. Sleep was the last thing on her mind, but she appreciated she would need all of her batteries fully charged for tomorrow.

***

In Hawaii, Miriam held a very tense Brian by his shoulders. He stared at her with eyes which recorded utter disbelief at the situation in which he found himself.

'What just happened, Brian?'

63

'Kylie said I was wanted for murder. That I had killed a security guard at my office. That's a lie. Trust me!'

'I have faith in you, Brian. But this increases your difficulties. You can't just contact the authorities with your allegations of money laundering. You must deal with this murder charge first.'

Brian was in a state of complete panic. He walked back and forth along the beach, away from Miriam, back to her, waving his arms about, with tears rolling down his cheeks.

'I wish I was back home,' he said. 'Why did I ever come to Hawaii?'

'To meet me.' Miriam spoke gently. 'I can help you, but I need you to calm yourself. There's a café over there. Why don't we just sit down, have a coffee and take a moment?'

Brian took a deep breath, shook his head, and nodded.

'You're right, you're right.'

They walked across the beach to the café. Miriam ordered Brian a double espresso and a latte for herself. They sat on the deck outside the café, which had a few tables, all of them unoccupied. Miriam and Brian could talk without being overheard. This made Brian feel much better.

They just sat quietly for a few minutes. Brian looked at the sea, so tranquil. His mind was still in turmoil but settling down slightly. Miriam sat looking at Brian, wondering how this poor boy ever got himself into this situation. Brian was totally unprepared for the events that would follow, but Miriam could help him, and she would.

Miriam recognised it would be impossible to tell him at this stage about how, or why, they had met. That it wasn't a complete accident, but she would have to feed him material at a pace he could handle. Too fast and she risked him blowing a fuse again, leading to a possible nervous breakdown. Too slow, though, and the people she was after might cover their tracks and avoid her scrutiny.

This murder was not something she had expected, but Miriam was correct about what she had said to Brian. He would have to deal with the murder first because she needed more intelligence.

Brian looked at her and saw her looking at him with concern written on her face. He smiled.

'Why are you here?' Brian asked calmly.

'I've already told you, Brian. Bert and I used to come here for our holidays. Since he died, I still come back.'

'But this is not holiday season. It's too early.'

Brian's brain was now back in its normal inquisitive mode.

'Was our meeting purely an accident?'

'Of course, how would I know you would be on that plane and that we would sit next to each other? But as I also said, Bert used to work for the CIA and I have experience in these matters. I can help you and I will.'

Miriam's reply appeared to settle Brian, but he still had a nagging doubt about this little old lady with the beaky nose. For the time being, he trusted her and so their relationship moved into a more collaborative mode.

'Now, tell me what your friend said, in detail.'

Brian repeated Kylie's conversation exactly, such were his memory skills.

'Who is Jeremy?'

'Jeremy Crichton-Smith; he works for the FSA. I met him when I was working for the asset management company in Switzerland. He was investigating somebody, also for money laundering.'

'How does he know Kylie?' Miriam asked, using Kylie's personal handle for the first time.

'I didn't realise he did. Kylie said that she was being set up by friends of hers. They're always doing that. She is a very attractive girl and her friend, Helen, really believes that every attractive girl should have a man.'

'Kylie said that Helen and Joe worked for MI5?'

'Yes, I didn't know that. She's never said that she had met anyone in that game.'

'How do you feel about that, Brian?'

'What do you mean?'

'Well, Kylie knowing someone who works for MI5.'

'I don't know. I suppose everybody has to have a job. You just don't meet many people in that secret service occupation, do you?'

'No, I suppose you don't.' Miriam agreed. 'How did Kylie react when you said that Bert used to be with the CIA?'

'No reaction, really, but that was when she blurted out that Helen and Joe were MI5.'

Miriam paused her gentle interrogation of Brian and brought her hand up to cup her chin in contemplation.

'What are you thinking?' Brian asked.

'Well, we need more clues about this murder you were supposed to have committed.'

'Which I didn't.'

'Which you didn't,' Miriam said. 'We need to find out what time this person was killed so we can fit your movements to this timeline. But who to trust in finding this material? Kylie is the most obvious one to trust, but she won't have access to the report without exposing your friendship. Jeremy, presumably, has worked with the police before and might make an innocent request. But how much can we trust him? You said before that he didn't come back to you straightaway when you told him about the money laundering.'

'Kylie could ask Helen and Joe to find out for her?' Brian suggested hesitantly.

'Oh no, I wouldn't want to involve MI5 at this stage. In any case, we don't understand in what capacity they work at MI5. That may be too much of a risk.'

'So, what should we do?'

Miriam pondered a little longer.

'I think you have to phone Kylie again and we have to trust Jeremy for the moment. You ask Kylie to contact Jeremy and see if he can ask the police for these details. The name of the security guard, which will show whether you knew him. The time the murder took place, so we can place your whereabouts. You said that you checked in for your flight from Heathrow at about four o'clock last Friday. There must be security cameras that identified you. If the flight had already taken off, so much the better.'

'Okay, when should I phone?'

'Right now.'

'But it'll be after midnight in London. Kylie will be asleep.'

'There's no time to lose. Do it now!'

***

Kylie was in bed, trying to sleep, but sleep wouldn't come. She was tossing and turning, bashing her pillow to help her find a comfortable position. But it was of no use.

Then the phone rang. She picked it up and looked at the dialling code. Kylie was familiar with this one, it was Australia.

'Yes,' she said, shouting at the phone.

'Kylie, it's me.'

'Brian, where are you now? Tell me you're not in Australia.'

'I'm not in Australia.'

'Brian, why are you doing this to me? What's happening? I'm worried that you're involved in something beyond your control.'

'So am I, Kylie. But listen, there is something you can do to help me and I need you to act quickly.'

'I will, but it's early in the morning here. What can I do?'

Brian then told her about the questions he and Miriam wanted answered, that she should do nothing herself but let Jeremy use his contacts. Kylie agreed, clicked the phone off, and dialled Jeremy.

Jeremy approved of the scheme but wasn't sure who to contact.

'Jeremy, it's Brian, and he has a problem. We have to help him,' she said.

'Okay, I'll see what I can do in the morning,' Jeremy replied.

Kylie put the phone down, annoyed at Jeremy's weak response. She couldn't trust him.

Next, she looked in her diary for Helen's telephone number. Kylie realised she shouldn't do this, but Brian needed help, and that was the most important fact. Helen would be sure to ask so many questions.

How did she meet him?

How important was he to her?

And how much did she like him?

But even with all of that hassle, Helen might find the information Brian wanted. But at what price?

Kylie could hear the phone ringing and then somebody answered, it was a man's voice.

'Joe, it's Kylie, can I speak to Helen?'

'I'm afraid not, my dear, she's fast asleep right now.'

'It's very important,' Kylie implored.

'Maybe I can help, and if it's as important as you say, I'll wake her. But I warn you, she doesn't like to be woken unnecessarily.'

'All right, Joe,' Kylie said. 'You heard about my friend Brian from the conversation in the pub the other day, and well... he's in difficulty.'

'Go on,' Joe responded, switching on his voice recorder.

'He's accused of murder but says that he didn't do it.'

'Ah, they all say that,' Joe said, chuckling to himself.

'Well, I believe him. He needs some advice, such as the name of the man killed, his job, and the time of death. This could help him prove his innocence.'

'And how do you think Helen can help?'

'Jeremy told me in a moment of weakness that you and Helen worked for MI5.'

'Oh, he did, did he? Naughty boy.'

'I thought, if that were true, you could use your contacts and find the information Brian wants.'

'I don't think so, Kylie, and you shouldn't listen to everything Jeremy says. He was probably trying to impress you.'

'Don't you work for MI5, then?'

'Look, Kylie, it's late and you are tired. I'll ask Helen to phone you tomorrow. I think she has someone else in mind she'd like you to meet. Ta-ta.'

With that, Joe replaced the phone. Kylie threw her phone across the room and stormed into the kitchen.

'I need a glass of Merlot,' she decided. 'no, make it a whisky, a large one!'

***

SUNDAY 6TH APRIL 2008
KAILUA-KONA, HAWAII (14.00 HONOLULU TIME)

'Right,' Miriam announced, 'there's nothing more we can achieve today. I suggest we go back to the hotel and relax. Your new room should be ready by now.'

'Must be something we can do,' Brian said. 'I can't relax.'

'Look, you contacted Kylie and she will try to find the material you need. But it's after midnight in London and it will be another eight hours at least, before she will contact you.'

'We just got your new phones and a new tablet,' Miriam said. 'Unless you want to send an e-mail on your tablet, I'd suggest you don't contact anyone for a while. After all, you've made three calls, one on each phone since we left the flea market and you're not supposed to use them regularly for fear of being traced.'

Brian nodded.

'And you won't get your new passports until Tuesday, probably in the afternoon. I can book you a flight for Wednesday morning, but I suggest leaving that until you are sure you don't need to stay on the Big Island any longer. You can always book a last-minute ticket.'

Reluctantly, Brian had to agree with everything that Miriam had said. But what else could he do? Brian was useless at waiting around doing nothing. He'd get bored, and that was when he made mistakes. Brian couldn't afford to make mistakes now.

CHAPTER SEVEN

MONDAY 7TH APRIL 2008
LONDON (06.00 LOCAL TIME)

After a restless night, Kylie finally fell asleep at four. She resolved to phone her office, saying she needed a sick day. Kylie set her alarm for seven, but she awoke just after six to the sound of her phone blasting out 'Nut Rocker' by Bee Bumble and the Stingers. It was one of her dad's favourite records of the 1960s. She downloaded it after she learned she might have it as a ringtone on her phone.

'Hello,' Kylie answered, sleepily, thinking Brian has no sense of the time in London.

'You rang?' the caller asked in a sharp voice.

At first, Kylie did not recognise Helen.

'Oh, it's you Helen; why are you phoning so early?'

'Shouldn't you be up by now, getting ready for work?'

'I'm not going in. I'm taking a sick day. That reminds me, I must phone the office and tell them.'

'Wait, Kylie. You phoned me, remember? In the early hours? You spoke to Joe.'

'Yes, it was a mistake. I shouldn't have phoned. Sorry.'

'Hang on, girl, you don't get off so easy. What did you want? Joe said you thought he and I worked for MI5.'

'Do you?'

'Don't be so ridiculous,' Helen said with more than a hint of sarcasm.

'Actually, Helen, what *do* you and Joe do for a living?' Kylie asked.

'Well, we're not spies.'

'Well, that's settled then.'

70

'Look, Kylie.' Helen spoke more softly now. 'Don't put the phone down. I want to help if I can.'

'No, it's all right; Jeremy said he would help.'

'So, we're back with Jeremy now, are we? I knew you'd come round.'

'Helen!' Kylie screamed her annoyance.

'OK, OK, I'm sorry. I should have realised your sensitivity on that subject. But if I can help, I will.'

'All right, Helen, but stop trying to set me up. I'm happy the way I am.'

'With Brian? A murderer?'

There's something wrong with a mobile phone. If a call makes you angry, all you can do is swipe it to end the call. What is the point of that? With older Bakelite phones, at least you could slam the device back on its handle. Kylie did the next best thing. She threw the phone across the room.

***

For the next three hours, Kylie paced her room impatiently, waiting for Jeremy to call. She had tried to call him several times, but he did not answer. Kylie notified her office of her absence that day. She walked to the local newsagents to find out if anyone carried the story (which they didn't) and drank countless cups of coffee.

Finally, her phone rang. It was Jeremy.

'Right, I've had some success. I remembered an old friend in the City Police, CID, but they weren't handling the case. I needed to be very careful not to give too much away. For the time being, I haven't mentioned you or your calls from Brian, because that might cause you problems. In due course, though, I might have to give them some more information.'

'Such as?'

'I haven't even told my contact that Brian came to me with his suspicions of money laundering. I only said he was a friend of mine and I couldn't believe he murdered anybody.'

'What happens next?'

'My man will try to find out the time of death and the name of the person killed. Also, there's someone I know who works on security at Heathrow. He worked a night shift yesterday, but I'll call him at his office later to enquire if they have Brian on CCTV.'

'That's excellent.'

'One other thing, Brian spoke of a colleague called Ron. I don't know his surname. Has Brian mentioned him?'

'No.'

'Can you try to contact Brian's office and speak to Ron? He must work on the same floor. If we can talk to him, we may find out what the word is from their end. But be very careful, we don't understand Ron's involvement in all of this.'

'When my CID man comes back to me, they'll make me an insider, which will mean I must be extra careful contacting you.'

'I understand,' Kylie said. 'Good luck.'

***

Kylie's view of Jeremy had changed. He impressed her with his achievements in contacting the City Police and it made her happy he offered to get in touch with Heathrow security. Added to that, his suggestion that she should contact Brian's office was positive. At last, she had something to do.

But how to go about it? Kylie needed a plan. She couldn't just walk into Brian's office and ask for Ron. There might be a problem, given that, technically, it was a murder scene and there might be police around. She didn't want the police or anybody else asking her troublesome questions.

However, if she phoned his office and asked to speak to Ron, maybe she would get lucky. But she needed a reason for speaking to him. She didn't really know what Ron did, his seniority level, or if he might speak to her at all. But supposing he did, she couldn't ask outright the time of death and why they suspected Brian. She needed a plan.

A light bulb suddenly shone in her head. Brian told her about the presentation he intended to make to a group of potential new and existing clients. His boss wanted him to introduce himself as the new chief strategist. The company for whom he worked, PMC Hedge fund, was attracting considerable interest as its performance outstripped its rivals. This occurred since Brian started to dictate the fund's strategy and helped establish a positive reputation within the industry. A number of financial journalists had taken note and would also be at this presentation.

***

One of the firm's operators answered Kylie's phone call.

'Hello, PMC Hedge fund.'

'Hi, can I speak to Ron, please?'

'And to which Ron would you like to speak?'

'How many Rons do you have?'

'Well, there's Ron Delamere in accounts or Ron Mathis in research.'

'Ron Mathis, please.'

'Who should I say is calling?'

'Miss Minogue, from *Hedge Fund Strategy* magazine.'

Kylie hated her nickname of Kylie Minogue, even though she was part Australian herself. Her name was Kylie Griggs, and she was proud of it, but in this case, she had a ready-made alias.

'Putting you though, Miss Minogue.'

'Hello, Ron Mathis.'

'Hi, it's Miss Minogue from *Hedge Fund Strategy* magazine. I had been due to attend the presentation, which is not now going to happen, but I wondered if we might have a chat about the fund.'

'I'm not really sure that would be a good idea, Miss Minogue. You appreciate we are up in the air at the moment.'

Just then, Patrick Covington walked by and overheard Ron's comment.

'Who are you talking to, Mathis?'

Ron acknowledged Covington's presence.

'Just a journo, sir,' he said. 'She wants an interview about the fund. She should've been at Brian's presentation.'

It annoyed Covington that this all happened when they were becoming well known and money started rolling in.

'Give her the interview, Mathis, we need all the help we can get. You've got Jenkins's notes, haven't you? Tell her nothing's changed and we expect to perform strongly.'

Ron returned to the conversation.

'Apparently, it's OK for you to come in and I'm pleased to talk to you. When would be convenient?'

'How about today?' Kylie asked. She didn't want to sound too eager. 'I want to get my copy in for the weekend.'

'I can see you at two o'clock,'

'That's great, I'll be there.'

Kylie put the phone down and wiped the sweat off her brow. She couldn't believe the call went so well. Nobody questioned her or her motive, and Ron's boss seemed keen to maintain the growth in its client base. She'd even made up the name of the magazine. How easy was that?

***

Kylie heard a clock chime two as she walked towards Brian's office near Leadenhall Street. Outside the Lloyd's building, somebody called her name.

'Hey, Kylie, what are you doing here? I thought you were off sick.'

Oh no, not George! Kylie winced, the gormless fellow whom Helen had tried to set her up with. Another failure.

'Yes, but I'm feeling better now,' she replied, hoping he would go away. 'How did you realise I wasn't well?'

'I phoned your office in the hope we might go out for dinner. You know, pick up where we left off.'

'We didn't leave off, George. We ended. Anyway, I have to rush; I'm late for a meeting.'

'Not going in to that hedge fund where they had the murder, are you? I heard they have a vacancy now,' he said, snorting in that priggish way of his.

Kylie cringed. She wished the world could swallow her up and let her disappear from his sight. She was afraid that now George saw her here, it would be all around the City. He'd tell his underwriting colleagues that one of his many ex-girlfriends worked at that infamous hedge fund. Why not? He already told them he'd had a passionate affair with her, the liar. She understood this because a girlfriend told her he had spread it around. How did Helen become acquainted with these people, and why?

If Kylie thought it was easy getting the appointment with Ron, now she understood not to be so complacent.

She entered the PMC building, shaking and holding on to the handrail as she walked up the steps to the reception. The woman behind the desk saw her and became concerned.

'Are you all right, miss?'

'Sorry, I've just had an unfortunate experience with a man outside your building. I'm OK now.'

'Do you want me to call a police officer? We still have a few in the building.'

'No, no, that's all right,' Kylie said, steadying herself. 'I'm here to see Ron Mathis.'

'Oh, yes. Miss Minogue. Would you like to step into the meeting room?' the receptionist said, pointing the way across the hall. 'I'll tell Mr Mathis you're here.'

Kylie opened the Perspex door and entered the room. She realised people could see her from all angles. Three of the walls were of clear glass, or Perspex, whilst the fourth wall appeared to be of grey brick. There was a grey plastic desk and three grey plastic chairs. Kylie noticed it gave a little as she placed her bodyweight on it, but it was reasonably comfortable. On the desk, a carafe of water sat with three glasses.

Interesting, she thought. *Am I meeting him alone or will somebody else join us?*

Kylie looked up to the ceiling, where she noticed a closed-circuit camera.

This might be more difficult than I expected.

Kylie opened her briefcase, took out a notepad, placed it on the desk, and awaited her visitors. Ron entered momentarily, accompanied by a young woman. They were both dressed smartly in suits, both had short hair styles and they both wore forced smiles.

'Hello, I'm Miss Minogue from *Hedge Fund Strategy* magazine.'

'Hi, I'm Ron Mathis and this is my colleague, Julie Simpson.'

Julie still smiled as Kylie began her speech, still wondering how she might get Ron alone to ask him her relevant questions.

Ron delivered the presentation Brian had prepared, which Kylie found impressive. Julie made notes whilst Kylie kept looking up towards the camera.

'I'm sorry,' she said, 'but is that recording us? I find it a little off-putting.'

'Yes, it is,' Ron acknowledged. 'You'll appreciate that we are security conscious, especially after recent events.'

'Of course,' Kylie said. 'Look, I'm sorry, but I need to use your facilities.'

'I'll show you where it is,' Julie said. She rose from her chair and opened the door for Kylie. Julie surprised her when she came in as well. Inside the ladies' toilets, Julie waited whilst Kylie entered one cubicle. It perplexed Kylie. This would not be easy, but she had a piece of paper and a biro in her pocket with which she wrote a note for Ron.

She took an enormous risk in presuming that Ron was on Brian's side and that he would talk to her with no surveillance present. How might she get the note to him, though? That would be another matter.

Back in the meeting room, Kylie asked a few more questions, surprising herself that they sounded so reasonable. The meeting ended and as they left the room, Ron went to shake Kylie's hand. As he did so, she secreted the piece of paper into her hand and transferred it to him as they shook hands, without Julie's knowledge. Not even the closed-circuit TV would have seen her actions. Now, all Kylie needed to do was wait to see if she had succeeded.

***

Outside, Kylie took a deep breath. She was glad it was over, but scared Ron would tell his security people, who would alert the police to her presence. If that happened, it might force her to say she knew Brian; that he had contacted her, and that Jeremy was also involved.

Kylie walked through Leadenhall Market, then took the back streets towards Fenchurch Street. On the way to her flat, she passed Tower Hill and crossed Tower Bridge. In the twenty minutes it took to reach her apartment, Kylie turned around several times to see if anybody had followed her.

Upstairs, Kylie kicked off her Lou-be-Lous and flopped onto her sofa. She booked a table at the La Pont de la Tour restaurant downstairs for that evening, hoping she wouldn't be eating alone.

Next, she phoned Jeremy, but only got his voicemail. She left a brief message asking him to call her.

***

At seven thirty, Kylie sat outside the restaurant, facing the embankment wall overlooking the River Thames. In front of her stood an empty glass of gin and tonic. A server came out to take her order.

'Not yet, James; I'm expecting somebody.'

'But you said that at seven o'clock, and yet you are still alone.'

'Have faith, and bring me another G&T, a large one.'

'Certainly.'

Kylie couldn't help but think James was right. Ron had not taken up her offer of a free meal for information.

She took a sip of her drink and looked to her left. There, striding purposefully towards her, waving his hand theatrically, came Ron Mathis. Kylie gave a subdued wave back to him, not wishing to appear too enthusiastic, but relieved he had appeared. Still dressed in his grey work suit, she noticed he had changed into a black shirt, open at the collar.

77

Ron really looked a sight. He was tall and the bottom of his trousers clearly had had an argument with his ankles, suggesting that the suit was not bespoke. His shoes were well-worn brown loafers, and he wore lime-green socks. His jacket flowed in the wind created by his long gait. He stepped through the gap in the hedge that separated the restaurant from the walkway along the embankment of the Thames. Kylie couldn't suppress a grin as he slid in an ungainly fashion into the seat opposite.

Even though it was a warm spring evening, the wicker seats still wore their sheepskin throws that the restaurant used for its customers during the winter. As Ron slid down, the throw moved with him, exposing the back of the chair. He did not appear comfortable.

Ron ordered a pint of Guinness. Kylie wasn't sure how to address the subject, as she didn't want to give much away. She still didn't know Ron's position regarding loyalty to his firm or his boss. She would find that out.

Kylie ordered from the à la carte menu. They started with six rock oysters; Ron was eager to try them. Then she ordered the steak frites, always a popular choice, and chose the larger but cheaper Bavette. Kylie also ordered a bottle of Côte de Beaune-Villages, one of the less expensive reds, but always top rated for quality. Ron was impressed. He had never dined at La Pont de la Tour, nor any other restaurant of similar quality.

Whilst they waited for their order to arrive, Kylie started her gentle interrogation.

'Ron, you'll gather from my message that I'm a friend of Brian. Not much of a friend, because I don't know where he is. However, I'm sure that he is not a murderer.' Kylie stopped at that point and waited for Ron to respond.

He took a sip from his Guinness, wiped the froth off his upper lip with his tongue.

'I agree with you, Miss Minogue. Sorry, can I stop calling you Miss Minogue? I feel I should be able to address you by your first name.'

'Of course, sorry, it's Jaimie.'

'Right, well, Jaimie, I've not known Brian that long, but I sat next to him for a few weeks and he seems very pleasant. Firm, in that he knows his mind and what he expects from his colleagues, but definitely not a murderer.'

'So, what can you tell me about the murder?'

'We've been told not to discuss this with anybody, but I can't hold it in any longer. I need to speak about it, and as you say, you are his friend.'

'Exactly.'

Ron took a deep breath. Kylie still didn't understand how honest he was or if he wanted to attend this meeting, on the chance he might gather some extra information. If the latter, then he was very good.

'The murdered man was one of our security guards and they found him at the bottom of the stairwell at the back of the building. His neck was broken.'

'Do you know his name?'

'Yes, Pablo Seguro.'

'That's an unusual name.'

'It's Mexican; all of our security team are from Mexico.'

'That's rare, isn't it?' she asked. 'I've never heard of Mexicans involved in security before, certainly not working in London.'

'I'm not sure about that.'

'Well, what time did the murder take place?'

'Late Thursday evening, around ten o'clock we were told.'

'Are you sure it was Thursday? Not Friday?'

'No, definitely Thursday. I remember seeing Brian on Friday morning and he seemed very nervous. He left early, saying he had to go to a meeting, but he never came back.'

Kylie's mouth became parched. Not good news.

'Did you tell the police that?'

'Well, yes, I had to, didn't I? It might be relevant and even if you and I don't think he killed that man, we might be wrong. You can never tell with some people.'

That comment took the wind out of Kylie's sails. She looked at Ron and he stared back at her, unblinking. Kylie wondered if Ron had not told her everything.

'I hear what you say, Ron, and I agree. You don't want to get into any trouble. Look, I'm not really in the mood to finish this meal or the wine. Go ahead, don't let me stop you. I'll settle the bill as I promised.'

Kylie stood up and walked inside the restaurant, leaving Ron on his own to enjoy himself. After she paid the bill and collected her coat, Jeremy joined Kylie by the door. He had been sitting inside, making sure there were no problems.

When Kylie saw Jeremy, she burst into tears. He put his arm around her and escorted Kylie out of the restaurant.

Back in Kylie's penthouse, Jeremy waited for Kylie to speak.

'That didn't go well.'

'What happened?'

'He said that the murder took place late on Thursday evening.'

'When Brian was in the office. So, I don't need to contact my guy at Heathrow.'

'No, but what do we do now?'

'I'll have to own up about the money laundering issue,' Jeremy admitted. 'I may find out more then. I wish we could speak to Brian. Maybe he can provide some more information.'

'I think I remember one number he called me on. I'll try it and see if I can contact him.'

Kylie remembered the Melbourne number. She recognised the Melbourne dialling code because she had relatives who lived there. She dialled, it rang and somebody answered in a noncommittal voice.

'Hello?'

CHAPTER EIGHT

After a late breakfast, Brian and Miriam stayed by the pool. The sun was shining, and it was another wonderful day in paradise. Except Brian didn't see this as paradise, more like a living hell.

'OK, Brian, today is a day for relaxation. What shall we do?' Miriam asked, eager for Brian to release the tension from his body. She recognised he could not continue like this. The strain would put even more pressure on him. Pressure he was not used to handling.

After thinking a while, Brian said, 'We can go to the Kona Village Shopping Centre to buy me some clothes.'

'That's an excellent idea, let's go.'

Upstairs, the maid was cleaning and tidying Brian's room. She recognised him as he entered.

'Your phone rang. I answered it, but there was nobody there.'

'What's that, Brian?' Miriam asked from her room. 'What did she say?'

'She said my phone rang, and she answered it.'

'Who was there?'

'Nobody.'

Miriam came into Brian's room and spoke to the maid.

'Why did you answer the phone?'

'I don't know. It might have been important. I could take a message. Please don't tell,' the maid begged with a frightened look on her face.

'Which phone?' Brian asked.

'That one, on the chair.'

'That's not where I left it last night,' Brian said.

'OK, Brian,' Miriam said, then turning to the maid, she added, 'I ought to report you for this, but I will let it go just this once. Don't do it again.'

The maid, now terrified, nodded and ran out of the room, crying.

'See who called,' Miriam said.

'It was Kylie. I wonder what she wanted? I'd better return her call?'

***

Kylie's phone rang. She answered it.

'You rang,' Brian said.

'Oh, it *was* the right number. It worried me when somebody else answered the phone.'

'Yes, that was the maid. She shouldn't have answered it. I was down by the swimming pool.'

'So, you are having a relaxing time, wherever you are.'

'It's not what you think, Kylie. Anyway, what did you want?'

'I've got Jeremy with me, can I put it on speaker?'

'Sure. Go ahead.'

'I had dinner with Ron Mathis tonight and he said the murder took place on Thursday night, not Friday, and the name of the man killed was Pablo Segura.'

'One of the security guards. Yes, I knew him, but I didn't see him that night. What time on Thursday night was he killed?'

'Ron didn't say.'

'If you can get the time and then check with reception, it's manned twenty-four hours a day. They will tell you what time I left and the time I retrieved my mobile phone.'

'Hi Brian, Jeremy here; it's a pleasure to talk to you.'

'And you,' Brian said.

'Do you have to check in your mobile phones at reception?'

'And laptops; it's part of Covington's security protocol. He's paranoid about us stealing propriety information.'

'Like downloading onto a USB stick?' Jeremy laughed.

'Something like that.'

'It's going to be difficult getting that info,' Kylie remarked. 'I can't go in again after pretending to be a reporter from a Hedge Fund magazine.'

'And after Kylie's dinner engagement with Ron Mathis tonight, I'm not sure how much help he will be, or even if he is on your side,' Jeremy interjected.

'You had dinner with Ron, Kylie?' Brian asked. 'Where d'you go? The local greasy spoon? He doesn't know much else.'

'No, we went to the Pont de la Tour. I don't think he's eaten much of the food on the menu before nor drunk any top-class Burgundy.'

'You fed him well. Look, Ron's OK. He doesn't get on with Covington, who regards him as his personal doormat.'

'So, should I try him again?'

'Yes, why don't you wait for him before he arrives for work. He usually gets in by seven. Oh, and Kylie, how were the markets today?'

'The FTSE was down again, under pressure from the Dow.'

'Looks like we were right about the weakening background. I only hope the traders are continuing to short the market'

'I can mention it to Ron tomorrow if you like.

'That would be good, but be careful, he might start asking questions about talking to me.'

'I'll be cautious.'

'OK, Miriam is telling me to end this call. I'll ring again tomorrow.'

'Where from?' Kylie asked.

***

'How did the maid find the phone?' Miriam asked Brian after he had finished the call with Kylie and Jeremy.

'She said it was on the chair, over there,' he said.

'Didn't you put it in the safe with the others?'

'I thought I had, but I can't remember.'

Miriam checked the room safe and confirmed it was locked. She also said that the other phones were there, as well as the tablet.

'You must have misplaced it,' Miriam said. 'You ought to be more careful.'

Even though Brian felt he was slipping deeper into the mire, his spirits had revived after talking with Kylie. She sounded as lovely as ever. Jeremy also sounded solid.

Brian was more relaxed than Miriam had seen him for a few days.

'Let's go shopping,' he said.

***

After an invigorating day visiting various shops and bars, they returned to the hotel. It was six o'clock, and the sun was setting. Miriam and Brian were laughing as they walked up the steps towards the swimming pool, carrying shopping bags.

Miguel Jimenez stood in the foyer and watched them arrive.

'It's marvellous to hear laughter,' he said. 'You're looking much brighter than at breakfast, *Senor*.'

'I've been shopping and bought the most ridiculous gear,' Brian replied. 'Miriam made me.'

'Oh no, I didn't,' Miriam retorted. 'I just made suggestions. Show him your new shirt, Brian.'

Brian opened one bag and took out a bright yellow short-sleeved shirt with a floral pattern.

'Very nice, *Senor*,' Miguel acknowledged. 'Typically Hawaiian.'

'It's from Tommy Bahama,' Miriam stated. 'They're having a pre-season sale.'

'And I've got shorts, sneakers and a lovely light cotton jumper in lime green.'

'Everybody will see you coming, *Senor* Jenkins. Can I get you a beer?'

'Why not?' Brian conceded. 'It'll be a change from the Mai Tais that Miriam's been feeding me?'

'Ah, Kona Village Mai Tais, no doubt, the best Mai Tais in the world.'

'Aha, I told you so!' Miriam giggled.

Miguel clicked his fingers, and a server brought a beer over to Brian.

'And for you, Mrs Miriam?'

'Oh, nothing for me, thank you. I've already drunk too much today.'

'And where will you be eating tonight?' Miguel asked.

'I haven't considered it, but we might eat here. Brian, are you OK with that?'

'If you think I'll love it, Miriam, then we'll eat here.'

'I'll reserve a table for you. Shall we say eight o'clock?'

Miriam nodded.

'Oh, *Senor* Jenkins, how is your new room? To your liking, I hope?'

'Absolutely excellent, *Senor* Jimenez,' Brian said. 'I have more than enough room to swing a cat.'

With that, Brian took his beer and his shopping to the lift, leaving Miguel with a quizzical look on his face following Brian's Anglo-Saxon remark. After exiting the elevator, Brian and Miriam walked past her room. Brian used the key card to open the door to his room. The difference in size to Miriam's was amazing, let alone the vast increase compared to his earlier room.

Brian threw his shopping on the floor. Miriam walked around the room, making sure the safe was locked securely and that there was nothing wrong. Brian placed his beer on the bedside table and flopped backwards onto his super comfortable bed. He went to sleep at once. Miriam tip toed to the communicating door and walked into her room. She left Brian to rest quietly. It would be best for him as he had not had a relaxed sleep for three days and he'd need all of his strength.

***

After a very pleasant dinner, during which Brian had a few more beers, Miriam suggested they go for a walk to the beach.

'Are you sure that's a good idea?' Brian asked. 'I'm feeling light-headed after those drinks and it's dark.'

'Don't worry, I'll take care of you. I want to show you the beach and sea in the moonlight.'

'You're not trying to have your way with me again, Mrs Miriam, are you?' Brian laughed.

One server overheard Brian and rushed to report back to his colleague on the front desk, having proved their suspicions.

At the beach, Brian saw the view and said, 'It really is lovely. You were so right to bring me here.'

However, Miriam was in serious mode.

'Brian, sit over here. We need to talk and I didn't want anyone at the hotel to hear us.'

'Okay.' Brian asked, 'What do you want from me?'

'I want to know what you know.'

'What do you mean?' Brian asked. 'I told you why I was here.'

'Yes, I have confidence in you. After we prove to the police that you didn't murder that guy, you must tell them about your money laundering information. But before you do that, I want more information from you.'

'Such as?' Brian was clear-headed now.

'Such as, what evidence is on the USB stick and do you have the names of the clients involved?'

'Why is that important to you, Miriam? Just who are you and whose side are you on?'

'Brian, you must trust me now. I am on your side and that is the side of the good guys. But I have not told you my entire story, and it's time to learn the truth.'

'What is the truth, Miriam? Why should I trust you? I wondered whether it was an accident that we sat together on that plane. Are you following me?'

'Whoa, so many questions. Okay, in reverse order, I did not follow you. Yes, it was an accident we sat together on the plane, but in a freakish way, it may be fate that brought us together.'

'What do you mean?' Brian asked.

'I told you about my husband, Bert, who worked for the CIA until he died. He didn't just die; he was shot on assignment in South America.'

'What kind of assignment?'

'That's classified, but I can tell you that when I said I worked with him on various cases; I was in charge.'

Brian's jaw opened in a big, round 'O'.

'Did you send him to the job where he was killed? And is that why you're here?'

'That's all classified. But the information you have may be of help to me. At least, if it's not, then I can dismiss it and get on with my investigation.'

'So, you are working on the case right now?'

Miriam said nothing.

'Do you have the USB stick with you? Of course, you must have, it wasn't in the safe when I checked. You wouldn't leave it the room, I presume?'

'It's at the hotel. It's hidden,' Brian replied.

'Oh, Brian,' Miriam remonstrated. 'You silly boy. That's your lifeline, your security. If that falls into the wrong hands, you're lost.'

Miriam and Brian rushed back to the hotel. When they were close by, Miriam suggested to Brian he slow down. They didn't want anybody to get suspicious of their actions.

They walked casually into the hotel. There was no sign of Miguel Jimenez. The diners had finished eating, but the bar remained crowded and noisy.

Back in Brian's room, he walked over to a corner, lifted a piece of the carpet, and retrieved the USB stick.

Miriam breathed a huge sigh of relief.

'I'm getting quite adept at hiding objects in weird places.'

'Right,' Miriam said, showing with her fingers that he should keep quiet. 'I'm going to my room now.'

She waved for Brian to follow her, 'Sweet dreams, Brian, I'll see you for breakfast.'

With that, Brian followed her through the communicating door. Inside her room, she held out her hand for the USB stick.

'We should view it in my room, on my new laptop.'

'You may be in a new room, but I'm not sure how secure it is. It could be bugged. I've checked my room already, and it's safe. Now let's see what's on here.'

Miriam opened her tablet and inserted the USB stick. Suddenly, the screen opened a spreadsheet containing many entries showing numbers under the debit and credit columns, with dates and client codes relating to these entries. Clearly, it was familiar territory for an accountant, but initially, the details looked overwhelming. After a few minutes, Miriam had reached a similar conclusion to Brian that money laundering was taking place.

'Do you recognise who these clients are?' Miriam asked.

'No, these aren't client codes we use in our normal system.'

'There may be names here that I recognise, but I need to verify them.' Miriam said. 'Can I download the information on to my tablet?'

'I'd rather you didn't,' Brian said. 'You told me earlier that it's my security, after all.'

'Yes, but can you leave this with me and I'll go through the data for you? I've done this before.'

Brian knew he had to place his trust in Miriam and returned to his room to get a full night's sleep.

CHAPTER NINE

Matt Booker and his two companions reached their destination in Istanbul after a ten-hour drive across Turkey over two days. They settled into the third-floor *safe* apartment in Divanyolu Street, close to the old town.

Because they arrived in Istanbul later than expected, going straight into their separate rooms for much-needed rest, Booker suggested they wait until after breakfast to begin Santos's interrogation.

However, in the morning. Booker became frustrated that Santos was still asleep in his room across the hall, and Johnson was nowhere in sight. They only had this flat for a short while and had much work to do. There was plenty of information to collect from Santos, and this lack of action caused Booker to become agitated.

He heard footsteps coming up the stairs. Heavy footsteps on wooden planks and then along uncarpeted floorboards. A key turned in the lock, Booker tensed and then relaxed as the sight of his colleague filled the doorway.

Sam Johnson smiled as he saw Booker standing sideways, making himself look small in case the wrong person entered. Ready to pounce like a tiger.

'You're looking edgy there, boss. Don't worry, it's only me. I've just been out to find us breakfast,' Johnson said in his Southern drawl. 'I saw a McDonald's down the road, so I got Big Macs, fries and proper coffee. Have you had that Turkish coffee? It's all grit and shit, makes me wanna vomit.'

'How can you eat a Big Mac at this time of day, Johnson? You're a slob. How d'you get to work for the company in the first place?'

Sam Johnson ignored him. Oh, he knew of Matt Booker as one of the CIA's top agents, but they needed him more than he needed them. His language abilities were the best to come out of UCLA, and added to the technical skills he gained at MIT, no other agent could compare. Booker accepted this, and reluctantly, he had to admit to Johnson's ability.

But why did he have to eat like a pig? Why couldn't he eat healthy food? And how would he do under pressure from the enemy? They would shoot him to pieces, unable to miss a guy of his size.

Johnson put the food on the table, took the lid off one of the coffee cups and took a slurp.

'Where is our guy, anyway? Not still sleeping?'

'Still sleeping,' Booker confirmed. 'He can sleep, like you have the capacity...'

'To eat?' Johnson finished the sentence. 'Go on, say it, you know you want to.'

Stunned at Johnson's response, Booker just stood there and found it impossible to suppress a laugh.

'That's better, now we're becoming friendlier.' Johnson smiled. 'Why don't you wake our man and I'll get prepared.'

A few minutes later, Santos emerged into the kitchen, yawning, as he straightened his hair with his left hand and scratched under his armpit with his right hand. Dressed in his string undervest and blue boxer shorts, Santos was not a pretty sight, but he complied with his protectors. He knew that, had it not been for the CIA, he would be dead by now. All he had to do was give these gringos the information they wanted and they would give him a new life, safe from his enemies. He'd had a good run, put many people in power, made lots of money, but that life was now over and he didn't feel ready to die.

But what had Johnson bought? Santos looked aghast at the tray containing the Big Macs and fries.

'What is this?' he said. 'You bring me across the world to a land of undisputed gastronomy and try to feed me American crap? I am not eating this!'

Booker stood behind Santos, grinning. Johnson, meanwhile, didn't understand Santos's attitude.

'If you want me to work with you, I demand only the finest food. The cuisine of the Ottoman Empire. I want meze, goat's cheese, pastries, Turkish bread, eggs, tomatoes and honey. I want Turkish tea. It's too early for coffee, especially this American muck.'

The Americans looked at each other quizzically. Who knew that the *great hacker*, a South American, understood so much about global cooking? Booker realised why he was glad they brought him to Istanbul. True, he had no known contacts in Turkey, but Booker concluded he must have been to this country before, possibly many times. He realised Santos was not just a tech wiz, but he was fully aware of the history of Turkish cuisine and hence, the country.

Santos practised hacking his way through the political spectrum in South America, and the CIA recognised they needed this skill. So, there was no question. They had to give Santos what he wanted.

This time, Booker left the apartment in search of food and walked in the opposite direction to the route Johnson took. After a short stroll beyond the Sultanahmet tram stop, he found a suitable restaurant that sold takeaways. With a little help from the owner, he picked up a breakfast feast that he hoped would satisfy Santos's appetite.

***

Walking back to the apartment, Booker reflected that the journey to Istanbul had been uneventful, apart from leaving Bogotá, but even that was minimal. He regretted that sniper fire had cost the life of Juan Luis Santos's friend Mateo and left holes in the undercarriage. But it did not impact on the flight worthiness of the plane. Once airborne, the guerrillas had insufficient fire power to delay their departure.

They had arrived at Incirlik Air Base, near Adana in south-western Turkey earlier than expected, benefiting from a following wind. And that was where he met Johnson.

Sam Johnson had been here before.

'The Turks built the base after the Second World War and named it from the fig tree grove, which used to be there,' he said to Booker. 'Its strategic location proved important during the Cold War period, and more recently, following the 9/11 attacks and the Gulf Wars.'

At first, Santos feared his captors and asked why they had removed him from his cell in Bogotá.

'We had to make sure your enemies didn't kill you,' Booker said.

'But why?' Santos asked. 'What do you get out of it?'

'Better relations with Colombia; a healthier involvement in South American politics, and maybe, increased information on your hacking ability.'

'So that's it, you want me to go to prison for crimes I did not commit. I have done nothing illegal,' Santos said.

'We don't want you in prison,' Booker confirmed. 'We want to protect you and learn from you. Work with us and we can give you a good life, where nobody from your old life will find you.'

***

When they arrived at Incirlik, Matt Booker was keen to reach Istanbul, but he knew it would include an overnight stop in Ankara. As he walked across the hangar, he saw a man dressed in jeans and tee shirt eating a large iced bun.

Booker addressed the man with caution.

'I'm supposed to pick up someone here to go with me and my friend to Ankara.'

'That'll be me, boss. Sam Johnson at your service,' the man said with his mouth full of bun.

'Are you CIA?' Booker asked, not believing that this individual could be an agent.

'Sure am, boss. I've been with the company for over five years.'

'Right, I am Agent Booker and we are escorting Mr Santos to Istanbul,' he established, then muttered, 'Just who are they hiring these days?'

Santos laughed to himself.

'It's a long drive and I would like to get going. Where's the car?'

'Over here, boss. A lovely 1990 grey Toyota pickup with only 115,000 miles on the clock. Comfortable and very anonymous.'

'Let's get going. I'll ride in the back with Mr Santos.'

'Yes boss.'

'And stop calling me boss!'

'Okay boss.'

They set off towards Tarsus, west of Adana. From there, they took the E90 highway towards Ankara. The journey to Ankara lasted five hours.

***

Matt Booker had been a CIA agent for over twenty years, recruited straight out of Harvard. He prided himself on his appearance and always dressed in a dark suit. At just over six feet tall, with dark hair, in a military style crewcut, Booker was exceptionally fit. He worked out on most days and still fitted the 32-inch waist trousers he wore when he joined the company.

He was a stickler for appearance, but the rough-and-ready style of the southerner, Johnson, did not cut it for him.

***

Santos slept for most of the flight from Bogotá. It amazed Booker that he was able to lean back against his head rest and drift off once the car started moving. Booker needed to be alert and constantly looked around for any signs of danger.

In Tarsus, they turned off towards the E90, but a police roadblock halted their progress. A Turkish police officer walked up to the car and Johnson wound down the window. A conversation ensued, which Booker didn't understand and through which Santos slept. Then they were on their way again, as Johnson pulled out of the halted traffic, through the road block and onto the highway.

'What just happened?' Booker asked.

'Apparently, young troublemakers had robbed a shop in town. I explained we were on our way to Ankara on urgent political business and they accepted my word.'

'You speak Turkish?'

'Yes boss, majored in European languages at UCLA.'

That information not only impressed Booker, but helped explain Johnson's relaxed attire, being a student at an LA campus.

As they continued, Booker became more comfortable with the journey. Johnson, an excellent driver, kept to the speed limits, not wishing to draw any attention to themselves. The scenery was relatively boring, mainly hard pan desert and bush. Small towns came and went, the land rose and fell whilst the weather was unspectacularly sunny. Just the way he liked it.

Then Johnson slowed down as he approached a road sign Booker didn't recognise.

'What's up, Johnson?'

'We're approaching a gas station, boss. We need to fill up and I could do with a pee. It's just after seven and I'm feeling hungry.'

'I don't want anything and I don't need to go. Sonny boy here is fast away, so let's keep going.'

'That's all very well, boss, but the car is thirsty.'

Reluctantly, Booker agreed to Johnson's appeal, still wishing he wouldn't always refer to him as *boss*.

***

Laden with a brown bag filled with food that should be more suitable for Santos, Booker returned to their room. Satisfied that Johnson had already set up the recording equipment, he knew he was ready for the first interview.

Santos emerged from the bathroom, and Booker saw he had tidied up his appearance.

This man is taking the process seriously, he thought.

Meanwhile, Johnson leaned back on his chair, with his feet inclined, whilst he delved into the red bag of skinny fries.

'Hi boss, we were about to start but he said he couldn't talk until his mouth had savoured fresh Turkish tea.'

Santos took out a small cardboard mug of Turkish apple tea, which Booker had placed on the table. He looked at Booker and smiled.

'I shall be ready for my discussion soon.'

***

The interview began slowly. Johnson and Santos conversed in Spanish. Johnson's tone was civil and Santos's responses monosyllabic, but they appeared to be making progress. Booker's command of Spanish wasn't great, but he understood Johnson asking Santos about his younger life, where he grew up, about his friends.

His eyebrows raised when he thought he heard the word *Medellín*. This would put Santos amongst the illegal drug community.

Booker stood by the side of the window so he could look without being seen. He scrutinised the flow of people passing by, whilst watching for something unusual. He didn't know what, but knew he would when it happened. This was a suitable location for a safe house, even though too many people thronged the streets.

Istanbul is a busy city, particularly near the Sultanahmet district. The apartment was only a short distance from the gardens surrounding the Blue Mosque, where the faithful prayed five times each day. Many tourists also visited the area to enjoy the beautiful sights of the vibrant old town. There are always crowds of people visiting the Top Kapi Palace and the Hagia Sophia. Though no stranger to Istanbul, Matt Booker was never a tourist here.

After two hours, Santos stood up and stretched. The questioning had become more intense over time, but he did not complain. It was what he expected.

At this stage, Santos left to go to the toilet. Johnson crossed the room to the fridge, opened a bottle of water and drank it down in one go.

'How's it going?' Booker asked.

'Oh, it's only the beginning. I'm getting a picture of his background, his childhood and his friends. That guy, Mateo, who we saw in Bogotá, seems to have been his best friend until they were fifteen.'

'What happened then?'

'They grew up in the town where Escobar ran the drug cartel.'

'Yes, I heard him say Medellín.'

'That's right. Mateo didn't like what was going on with the drugs, so he ran away. But Santos appears to have been a mathematical genius and was interested in computers. Escobar liked that and fostered his skills.'

'Very interesting.'

'By his mid-twenties, Santos had learnt how to infiltrate other people's computers.'

'Do you mean hacking?'

'Well, yes, before personal computers originated, they were large and cumbersome, limited to businesses and universities. After personal computers, the main frames became virtually extinct. This made it possible for individuals to own computers and demand for hackers grew and grew.' Johnson continued.

'Escobar asked Santos to hack FARC's computers to gather information on their operations and finances, which he did and at which he proved adept.'

'But I was not the only person in the cartel doing that,' Santos said as he re-joined Booker and Johnson. 'Others, far more skilled than I, and more dedicated to Escobar, were much more involved. I couldn't wait to leave the influence of the cartel.'

'Why?' Booker asked.

'My friend, Mateo, warned me that the Americans were closing in on Escobar and they were getting help from FARC, so my life could be in danger.'

'But Mateo had escaped? Yet you were still in contact with him?' Johnson asked.

'Yes, we had a secret arrangement that allowed us to stay in touch.'

'What was Mateo doing?' Booker asked.

'He worked for the government, involved in the fight against the FARC rebels. He also liaised with *Los Pepes* in their fight against Escobar.'

'But I thought *Los Pepes* wanted you dead?'

'They did, but Mateo didn't tell them the truth about me. He kept me safe.'

'So, you really owed him a lot,' Booker acknowledged.

'Yes,' Santos said.

'He also introduced you to *Senor* Alvarez, a political strategist who lived in the United States, and who used you to hack elections.'

'That is correct.'

***

The interview continued, concentrating on the methods that Santos used.

'When you started, social media was nowhere near as sophisticated as now,' Johnson stated. 'How did you approach your work?'

Booker listened on intently, insisting now that they spoke English.

'Messages had little encryption, very simple to break. It was easy to source information from e-mails. Even cell phones were in their infancy and defences minimal. It involved us taking e-mail addresses from computer databases and spamming disinformation on various accounts.'

Later on, Santos explained, the advance of 3G, allowing user-to-user encryption, made it slightly harder. But newer services, such as Twitter and Facebook, became popular, meaning he had much more scope to delve into his subjects' personal lives.

One day, Mateo referred Santos to a *Senor* Alvarez, who helped to decide election results, mainly by spreading rumours and offering bribes, but he realised that more sophisticated tools were available.

'Mateo pointed him in my direction,' Santos said. 'He wanted me to find out this politician's diary over the next few weeks. It was very easy; I entered the politician's outer office, took out my laptop and downloaded his schedule whilst I sat there. Also, that gave me access to his policy speeches.'

'I impressed Alvarez, and he hired me straightaway,' Santos said. 'He gave me work, and for ten years, he paid me well.'

'How many elections are we talking about?' Booker enquired.

'Many elections, not just national elections, but also local ones. South American politics was very dirty. This has carried on for many years, even though there have been reforms. Rigged elections happen, even now, in many places.'

'With which countries were you associated?'

'Argentina, Guatemala, Nicaragua, Honduras, El Salvador and Costa Rica. Many others.'

Both Johnson and Booker whistled in unison at the number of countries involved.

Santos laughed.

'Have you always been effective at putting people into power?' Johnson asked.

'Yes.'

'Can you put anybody into power?' Booker asked, a note of incredulity in his voice.

'Yes.'

'But not in the US, surely.'

'If you give me a third-rate television game show host, I can make him President of the United States.'

Johnson and Booker looked at each other and laughed nervously at this thought.

'It'll never happen,' they agreed.

CHAPTER TEN

'C'mon, wake up, sleepyhead.'

Miriam walked into Brian's room without knocking. She decided that, although he may still be sleep deficient, this was long enough. She was aware there was much to do today. So much to tell Brian, and she knew the place to tell him.

'What is the time?' he moaned, lifting his head from the pillow.

'It's after eight and time we were on the move. I've already had coffee. Do you want me to make you a cup?'

He nodded as Miriam walked over to the automatic coffee making machine in his room. Soon, the water was boiling, and she made him a cup of instant coffee. Kona coffee, of course, made from freeze-dried, roasted Kona coffee beans.

The caffeine flooding his brain, after only one sip, brought Brian fully awake in an instant.

'Wow,' he exclaimed, 'you look as if you are ready for something.'

Brian wasn't the only one who shopped yesterday. Miriam wore her new red and white candy-striped shorts and her new loose-fitting peach blouse over a red camisole. On her feet, she wore elegant coral-coloured sneakers.

She did a twirl.

'You approve?' She smiled.

He nodded enthusiastically.

'Seriously, Miriam, is there time for this? What if Kylie rings?'

'Then you can answer it. Why don't you put on your new shorts and that lovely shirt? Afterwards, come down to the lobby. I'll go to pick up the car.'

After finishing his coffee and dressing according to Miriam's instructions, Brian rode the elevator down to the lobby, where Miguel greeted him.

'Good morning, *Senor* Jenkins,' he said. 'You look splendid in your new Hawaiian clothes.'

'And it's more suitable in this Hawaiian temperature,' Brian responded, as Miriam was coming up the steps.

'Ah, I see you're ready. Shall we go?'

'And where are we off to today, Mrs Miriam?' Miguel asked.

'I thought I'd show Brian the sights for which the Big Island is famous, such as the Volcanoes.'

'Ah yes, the volcanoes. You might say they made the Big Island what it is today.' He laughed.

Miriam laughed along with Miguel, but Brian did not quite get the joke.

The drive to Volcano National Park took them to the other side of the island along the Hawaiian Belt Road. Miriam turned left out of the hotel, driving south out of Kona, past Captain Cook, where the great explorer lost his life to the local natives. She drove further south to Ocean View, which marks the southern tip of the Big Island. Then the road turned north east through Pahala and on to Volcano National Park. She turned off the road and soon, Brian was at the home of the world's most active volcano.

'We can get food at the Rim Café. You must be starving? I am.'

Brian agreed that he was. He felt sure Miriam was up to something, but he couldn't figure out what. She had said nothing about his USB stick, or the information it contained. He wasn't even sure she had it with her.

Just as he had this thought, Miriam spoke.

'I suppose you must wonder why I've not said anything about your evidence?'

'It had crossed my mind,' Brian said.

'Last night, I said the evidence is clear, but I was thinking about how I might discuss it with you. You need to be very careful. You must not lose it. Your security is vital, but this might be the most dangerous article in your possession. If it falls into the wrong hands, well, you would not like the consequences.'

That didn't make him feel any better.

Miriam found a parking space right outside the café. They walked in and she directed Brian to an empty table on the far side, while she went to buy the food. There were few people in the café, which usually filled up around lunchtime, so they might talk freely.

Miriam sat down and placed the tray of coffee, cakes, and biscuits on the table.

'So, it is incriminating?' Brian asked.

'Very,' she said. 'There's positive proof of money laundering. I've worked on money laundering scams over the years, and I recognise it when I see it. And it's right here.'

Miriam continued.

'There are colossal sums involved. OK, last night, when I had a brief look, I saw the flow of money going in and out. There are bank details, showing where monies came from and other accounts showing where they were sent. I could see transactions were made, mainly buying and selling bonds with only a few days between the various dealings in an effort to hide the information relating to the ultimate destinations for these funds.'

'But will you be able to trace them?' Brian asked.

'Over time,' Miriam said. 'We have experts who can do this.'

'Next, we come to the client codes. Are you sure they don't relate to your normal client account systems?'

'Definitely not.' Brian agreed.

'Our experts can also go through these if you will allow the CIA to become involved.'

'Okay,' Brian held up his hands, trying to stop Miriam from talking for a second.

He took a deep breath and continued.

'In my mind, I had assumed that if I took the information to my friend Jeremy, he might see the evidence and arrest somebody.

Probably, my boss, Patrick Covington. But it's getting far too complicated.'

'I understand what you're saying.' Miriam said.

'I assumed it just involved British criminals, but are you saying it might also involve the US?'

'I don't know, Brian, and that's the truth. Even if it is a purely domestic issue, the CIA can still help and liaise with the authorities in the UK.'

Brian's mind was whirring, and he was not sure what to do. This was way bigger than he originally supposed. Could he trust Miriam? Did she want to take the matter out of his hands, for her own purposes, or to take the weight off him?

'Was there any other data you found?' Brian asked.

'Well, yes,' Miriam paused, 'and I wasn't sure that I wanted to tell you, but it's only fair you should be aware of everything.'

Brian could feel his heart on the verge of exploding.

What next? he wondered.

'On delving deeper, there were various names shown on the accounts and I could link a few of these with the client codes.'

'You must have been up all night,' Brian said.

Miriam smiled. 'You don't know the half of it. After a while, I could see one name linked to several accounts.'

'What name is that?'

'Well, that's a problem. It didn't seem like a name at all. Not anything I've seen before.'

'What is it?'

'A. Hintout.' Miriam answered.

'It's not a name I recognise,' Brian confirmed.

'Nor I, but then it came to me. It must be an anagram.'

'Are you good at anagrams? I wouldn't have seen that.'

'As it happens, I am exceptional at anagrams. I love crosswords and we often use them in code breaking at the CIA.'

'So, what is it an anagram of?'

'Tonatiuh,' Miriam said.

'Tonatiuh?' Brian queried. 'What does it mean?'

'Tonatiuh is an Aztec Sun God, meaning the fifth sun. A. Hintout is an anagram of Tonatiuh.'

'OK, is that significant?' he asked.

'Well, it could be. What I am about to tell you is extremely classified. I should not tell you this under normal circumstances.'

'But these are not normal circumstances, and you will tell me. Yes?'

'Yes,' Miriam said.

She continued.

'The case in which I am primarily involved at the moment involves drug cartels around the world. One person we are investigating is a senior figure in government. This is a drug cartel, far bigger than anything that happened in Colombia. The father started the cartel but has died and we understand one of his sons now rules the cartel. He is the fifth son of his father. This son is also part of the government; he exerts a tremendous amount of power.'

'Why is this significant to me?'

'The world's largest drug cartel is run from Mexico and this man, the fifth son, is a senior politician in the Mexican Government.'

'What's his name?' Brian asked.

'Jimenez.'

'Jimenez?' Brian repeated, 'but that is the name of—'

'Yes, and that is why you should be aware why this information is so dangerous to you. I'm so sorry. I should never have brought you to this hotel, but I'm very glad I met you on that plane.'

Brian was silent after receiving this revelation. He needed to get away from Miriam. He needed to rationalise everything that she had just said.

'OK, I need to take a walk to digest this information. I need to clear my head.'

***

Brian left Miriam and crossed the road from the Rim Café to the Visitor Centre. Here, he wandered around the exhibits looking at, but not seeing, the wealth of information about volcanoes on Hawaii. All the while, his mind was buzzing with Miriam's comments.

Was he lucky to find her? he asked himself.

'Yes, he replied to his own question. *Because without her I would never have found out so much. But was it too much?'*

'No. He realised now what he had started, albeit accidentally. *But I have to follow it through to the end. Am I in a position to trust Miriam?* This was a question he was almost afraid to ask.

Nearly, because she was being fair to me. Is this acceptable? he questioned himself again. *And acceptable, or not, would I do it again?* Brian recognised the answer to this question was a resounding 'yes.'

He walked out of the Visitor Centre and wandered round to the other side of the café, where he could view the actual rim of Kilauea. He could see plumes of smoke rising from the fissures, while all around the opening there was evidence of earlier eruptions, the black lava spread around the massive caldera.

Miriam joined Brian and linked her arm into his.

'Are you all right?' she asked.

'I think so,' he hesitated, whilst continuing to view the smoking eruption straight ahead, 'but it was a lot to take in all at once.'

'Sorry,' she said. 'I've tried to break the news to you as gently as I could. You must be aware that the information you downloaded is real and has consequences.'

'I agree and thank you for treating me gently.'

Then there was silence between them until Miriam squeezed Brian's arm.

'Come on,' she said. 'We need to get your new passports.'

***

Back at the Kona Farmer's and Crafts market, their man was standing outside the parking lot, which was empty. The flea market looked devoid of visitors, stalls were closed and only a few people wandered around.

104

'Hello, Pika,' Miriam said. 'Is everything all right? Where is everybody?'

'Oh, the market is closed on Tuesday. It only opens from Wednesday to Sunday.'

'Sorry, have you been waiting long? I've been showing Brian the volcano.'

'It was spectacular,' Brian added.

It was obvious Pika was not interested in small talk and didn't want to stay any longer than necessary. He directed them across the road and walked over to the deserted beach.

'It doesn't matter, but the papers are here and I want to give them to you.'

'Of course,' Miriam said.

'The phones worked well,' Brian said, 'but do you have any more SIMs? I've used all three once already.'

Pika looked shocked at this news, as the SIMs were supposed to enhance anonymity. However, he reached into his pocket and produced three more.

'That will be an extra $300.'

'I'll make sure you get your money,' Miriam confirmed.

'What, $300 for three SIMs. How much is all this costing?' Brian asked.

Pika gave Miriam the passports. A nervous twitch of his eyebrows showed he was not relaxed. She had a quick peek inside and seemed satisfied. Then she took her phone, dialled a number, and spoke.

'It's done, looks OK, but we need another $300 for a few more SIMs.'

Miriam waited patiently for a reply.

'OK?' She spoke quietly. 'I can confirm that's OK?'

Then Miriam turned to Pika.

'The money is in your account.'

Pika smiled, thanked Miriam, turned, and walked away briskly.

'He seemed keen to be on his way,' Brian observed.

'So would you if you realised this area has police patrolling regularly and checking the CCTV cameras.'

'Sorry, didn't realise.'

'No, you didn't, but then you are not used to living on the dark side.' Miriam spoke harshly. 'And I would've been appreciative if you'd asked me about the extra SIMs.'

'Sorry,' Brian repeated.

'Here are the passports. They look excellent.'

Brian took the passports from Miriam. He was less interested in the photos, more in his new identities. Even so, he wasn't prepared for the first name he saw. Was this a coincidence?

'I knew somebody called Brian Roberts once. It'll be strange to use that name. This other one, Bernd Muller? Do I seem Germanic?'

'Well, you don't have to use it if you don't want to,' she laughed, 'but if you're going to Switzerland, it might be useful.'

'Oh, so I'm going to Switzerland, am I?'

***

They drove back to the hotel, parked the car, and returned to their rooms.

On the way, Miriam said she would check the flights out of Kona tomorrow.

'We need to plan your departure carefully, so we don't give rise to the smallest amount of suspicion.'

'I agree,' Brian confirmed.

'It's useful that Miguel already appreciates that you have no plans, so your abrupt departure can be a spur-of-the-moment decision and he should think it normal. You will need to pay your room charge when you leave, but you said you had a Swiss credit card. If I paid for you, as I've done everything else, he would really suspect some collusion between us.'

'I understand you've paid for everything,' Brian retorted, 'but I'm willing to pay my fair share. Just tell me the cost.'

'That's not what I meant. Don't worry, it's all being billed to the company,' Miriam said. 'We are supposed not to have known each other before we met on the plane.'

'We didn't.'

106

'Yes, but if it looks like the situation is not what he believed it to be, then he will get suspicious. Believe me, people like Miguel Jimenez consider everything from all angles to protect their back.'

'OK, so you'll check the airlines. And buy my ticket? Under what name?' Brian asked. 'Will you drive me to the airport or shall I get a taxi?'

'I'll drive.' Miriam said. 'That's it, Brian, think it through, just like you need to protect your own back.'

'This is the way my mind works when I'm doing my job. Every eventuality has to be factored in before I can reach a conclusion.'

'That's my boy!' Miriam exclaimed, beaming. 'We can talk more over dinner.'

'If this is to be my last night on the Big Island, can we go back to that restaurant where we went on our first night?' Brian asked.

'The Kona Inn?' she asked. 'why of course, my favourite restaurant in the whole world!'

'And they do the best Mai Tais.'

'You're right,' Miriam said. 'I'll catch you at six and we can watch the sun go down. Right now, though, I must make some calls.'

***

It was just before six o'clock, Brian sat on a stool by the bar, overlooking the pool. He was drinking Dos Equis beer and reading the financial pages in USA Today. He was feeling good as the markets had plummeted again and his fund should have benefited accordingly. Hopefully, Kylie was able to get his message to Ron.

Miriam arrived, and the servers continued to fawn over her.

'Thank you, boys, but Brian and I are off to dinner at the beach. Are you ready?'

'Yes, ma'am,' he said, tipping his bottle towards her.

As they walked through the gates of the Kona Inn Shopping Village, Brian reflected on the events of the past few days.

'If I knew then what I know now, I'd have got straight back on the next plane out of here.'

But even as that thought entered his head, he saw it would have been the wrong decision. It was best that he met Miriam, even if it was not as fortuitous as she made it seem. Because she had the experience in these matters and the contacts to help him, he felt he had the right backing to resolve the situation.

The odd couple returned to the venue of their first night together, she with her arm linked into his. One six foot plus, the other barely five feet and with more than thirty years difference in their ages.

As they approached the Kona Inn, Gregor was out of the restaurant entrance in a flash.

'Mrs Miriam, you have returned. It is so lovely to see you!' Gregor gleamed. 'And you have brought your young man again. We were so worried.'

'Yes, Gregor, we're back. Nothing happened, our usual seats, please.'

'Yes, of course, of course. I'll get Charlie to serve you.'

'And ask him to bring two Kona Village Mai Tais,' Brian said.

Miriam laughed as her legs gave a little skip.

The sunset was amazing, with the great red orb sinking into the ocean. The meal was delicious, the tuna so fresh and chilli spiced, and the Mai Tais seemed to have an extra kick. Brian loved this place and understood he would return one day, but now it was time to get serious.

Miriam told Brian her suggestions for his departure. He listened and had a few questions, but it was quite straightforward. He had no problems.

Then he looked at his watch. It was after ten o'clock, which made it after nine in the morning in London. Why hadn't he heard from Kylie?

'Why don't you ring her?' Miriam said. 'She may not have wanted to phone you or forgotten your number or something.'

Brian nodded and dialled Kylie's mobile. It rang. Nobody answered.

'That's disturbing,' he said. 'She's not answering her call.'

'Mmm, that's not good,' Miriam said.

'Hang on, Jeremy's number is on my old phone.' Brian said.

'Do you still have that? Has it been used since we've been here?'

'Yes, it's in the safe, and no, I haven't used it.'

'The moment you turn it on, your location becomes visible.' Miriam warned.

'What do you suggest?' Brian asked. 'I need to know if anything has happened to Kylie.'

'It's a risk, but if you just turn it on, take the number, switch it off and ditch the phone straightaway, you might get away with it,' Miriam said, fearing the worst.

***

Back at the hotel, Brian took his old phone out of the safe and tried to turn it on, but the battery had run out and the phone was dead. He found his phone charger and tried to resuscitate the phone.

Miriam shook her head, knowing the situation was worsening.

Brian saw there was a three per cent charge on his phone, which was enough to turn on the memory and allowed him to find Jeremy's mobile number. As soon as Brian did this, he turned the phone off and took out the charger. Miriam held out her hand for Brian to give her the phone.

He took out another phone from the safe and dialled Jeremy's number. It rang a few times before being answered.

'Hello?'

'Jeremy?'

'Brian, is that you? Where are you phoning from?' Jeremy said.

'That doesn't matter. Where is Kylie? I tried phoning her, but there's no answer. Have you seen her, or spoken to her today?'

'No, I haven't. I'm worried, Brian. She was going to talk to Ron this morning before he got in for work. I was going to follow her, but something came up and I couldn't.'

'That's not good,' Brian said.

'Sorry, mate. I'll try again to see if I can find anything. Can I phone you on this number?'

He turned away and whispered to Miriam.

'Can I tell him to phone me on this number?'

'No.'

'Sorry, Jeremy, that's not possible. I'll get back to you later.'

With that, he ended the call.

'Give me that phone as well, Brian,' Miriam said. 'You really have to be aware of who you can trust now. And you are not sure you can trust Jeremy. Neither is Kylie.'

'That makes sense, but I don't like it.'

'You have taken an enormous risk in turning on your old phone and if you give them the number of this phone, that increases the risk. I'll get rid of both phones.'

'Just as well I have more SIMs.'

Miriam gave a grunt, as if she only grudgingly approved.

CHAPTER ELEVEN

Kylie had a restless night, filled with dark thoughts about Brian, Ron, and Jeremy. How might she do her best to help Brian? Could she trust Jeremy? Was Ron truly on their side, as Brian suggested?

She would find out soon, but the time for action had approached faster than she wanted.

With great anxiety, she walked across her living room and opened the French doors of her apartment. She stepped over the threshold and onto her balcony, where the dampness of the previous night seeped between her toes.

The River Thames seemed so still, almost like glass in its appearance. As the morning mist lifted, barges drifted along the river, carrying their loads to appropriate destinations for the tasks ahead.

Kylie pulled her dressing gown tighter, concerned with her own responsibilities, and realised she should be on her way. Brian said that Ron regularly arrived at work before seven, but what if he arrived early today? She must not be late.

***

Kylie reached the offices of PMC Hedge fund a minute after six thirty. The City of London is never quiet, even at this time of day, especially with the Lloyd's market nearby. People already began moving into position and traffic was brisk, with taxis dropping customers off to begin their day. This was always a busy spot with Liverpool Street

Station around the corner and the main commuting tube stations of Bank and Moorgate nearby.

Leadenhall Market was no longer the bustling covered market of its heyday, when it sold meat, game and poultry. Historically the original centre of Roman London, it was now home to butchers, cheesemongers and florists, together with boutique shops selling jewellery, cards and alcohol. At this hour, the market had not yet opened, with only a couple of coffee shops trading.

Kylie stood on the corner of the market and PMC Hedge fund's offices. The cool morning air made her feel she needed to move in order to keep warm. Not knowing from which direction Ron would arrive, she walked on the spot, trying to keep the blood flowing in her legs.

Then she saw him, to the right of her, crossing Leadenhall Street from St. Mary Axe.

Ron spotted her from twenty yards away. He looked around but recognised he couldn't avoid her. Kylie walked towards him and they turned in to the market.

'What are you doing here?' he asked. 'I told you everything yesterday.'

'Not quite,' Kylie said. 'I've a couple more questions.'

'You'll get me into trouble.'

'Ron, please listen to me. I need to understand what time Brian left the office and picked up his mobile phone that night.'

'I can't do that.'

'Yes, you can. There's a register kept on the reception.'

'How do you know about that?'

'I just do, OK? Help me, Ron. Help Brian if you're a friend of his.'

'Well, I can't do it straight away. I must look at how the markets are starting. With Brian no longer here, I'm now in charge of the morning meeting and responsible for dictating strategy.'

'Yes, and Brian says to tell you that with the markets falling the traders should continue shorting the funds.'

'You've spoken to him then?'

'Well, yes, very briefly. Please, Ron. Do your best.'

'I'll try, ten-thirty, that's my coffee break.'

'I'll be in the coffee shop around the corner. Thanks, Ron,' Kylie said, and planted a kiss on Ron's cheek.

***

What to do for the next three hours? Kylie's office was nearby. She decided that work was less important, with Brian's future at stake, so she went into the office to talk to the head of her department and request a leave of absence for the next few days.

Kylie was a senior analyst in the research department of Hunter, Dawson & Co., an old and respected firm of London stockbrokers. At the start of the new tax year, the financial markets were quieter. Her assistant would look after business while she took some time off. However, she wanted to see if her manager agreed.

When Kylie arrived at her desk, many of her colleagues asked her how she was, after taking a sick day yesterday. A day off was a rarity for Kylie. If she took more holiday, it would set them wondering if a serious problem existed.

It did.

She walked over to the door of her boss's office. The wording on the door read, *James Carlton, Head of Research.* Kylie knocked on the door, opened it, and popped her head into his office.

'Hi Jim, have you got a moment?' she asked

Jim Carlton beckoned Kylie to enter.

'How can I help?' he asked.

'Jim, I need a few days off. I'm not sure how many. I have a friend who needs my help.'

'Sounds serious,' Jim replied.

'It is.'

Jim didn't need any time to consider this question. Kylie was a trusted colleague.

'Okay, take as much time as you need, but keep in touch. If I can be of any help, I'll do what I can.'

'By the way, somebody called yesterday, asking for a Miss Minogue,' Jim said.

'Oh, yes?' Kylie asked, blushing. 'How did you realise it was for me?'

'Well, we are all acquainted with your nickname, which I appreciate you hate. But he described you and it couldn't have been anyone else.'

'Who was it? What did you say?'

'He said his name was Covington, in charge of a hedge fund, into which you were enquiring. Are you acquainted with him?'

'I know of him, but I didn't realise he had my work number.'

'I didn't ask him about that, but why did you enquire about this hedge fund?'

'It's a long story.'

'So, you're not looking for a new role elsewhere?'

'Good lord, no,' Kylie laughed. 'I'm very contented here.'

'Does it concern your friend?'

'Yes, but it's best if I don't discuss it any further.' Kylie said, reassured at his manner.

Kylie left the office, thankful and not expecting as positive a response as she received.

Before she left, she spoke to her assistant, Hector, about a few outstanding matters. She also gave him her home telephone number to call if anybody needed to get hold of her over the next few days.

From her watch, she saw it was almost ten thirty. She had to run.

***

Kylie stood in the queue at the coffee shop, just behind Ron, who hadn't noticed her arrival.

'Black instant,' Ron requested.

'Make that two,' Kylie said.

Ron turned around, saw Kylie, and smiled as he bought two coffees.

'Would you like a bun?' he asked, Kylie nodded. 'And two Chelsea buns, please.'

They moved to an alcove at the back of the coffee shop, where they would see everybody coming in, but where they were not visible.

Ron bit into his bun.

'Lucky, I guess, the receptionist needed to go to the loo, and I said I'd mind reception while she disappeared. She should've called a secretary to mind the shop, but she left me in charge. She would get into serious trouble if Covington found out.'

'So, while she went to the toilet, you looked at the register?'

'Yes, I flicked the pages back to last Thursday, and you're right, Brian left the building after picking up his phone at nine fifty-eight.'

'And you said they found the security guard dead around ten o'clock?'

'Before or after ten o'clock?'

'I'm not sure, it might have been before ten.'

'So, that still doesn't clear Brian.'

'No, but from where the stairwell is situated, it takes over ten minutes to get to reception, and that doesn't include the time it would take Brian to go back to his desk, if that's what he did. The stairwell is right at the back of the building, and it's near where the Security offices are located.'

'That's interesting.' Kylie said.

Ron was becoming more animated and really helpful. However, Kylie stopped him in his tracks.

'Ron, stop, who has just come in?' she asked.

They both looked towards the café entrance as Patrick Covington arrived in the coffee shop, closely followed by Jeremy Crichton-Smith.

'That's my boss, Covington. He'll kill me if he sees me here with you. Are you aware of who's with him?'

'I know him,' Kylie said through gritted teeth. 'That's Jeremy Crichton-Smith, and I thought he was a friend of Brian.'

'I'm not sure of his name, but I have seen him in Covington's office a few times recently.'

'We have to get out of here,' Kylie said, 'but how?'

'That door over there leads into an alley. We can get into the market that way.'

Trying to be as quiet as possible, Ron and Kylie moved towards the back door, with Ron leading the way. As they exited, Patrick Covington lifted his head and caught sight of Kylie.

He frowned.

'I know that girl,' he hissed.

Jeremy turned round and looked towards Kylie. A sick sensation entered his stomach.

Covington was up and out of the door in a flash. Ron was faster than Kylie and had dashed ahead into the office building, so that Covington never saw him. As she turned the corner into Gracechurch Street, though, Covington grabbed Kylie by the wrist.

'Let go of me, you bastard!' she screamed, hoping that somebody, anybody, would come to her rescue.

'Were you spying on me, you hussy?' Covington leaned over and roared into her face.

'And what if I was?' she replied, looking around and seeing the street remarkably empty. 'What are you going to do about it?'

Covington realised it was not the time, nor the place, to go any further. He let go of her wrist and brushed down the front of his suit.

'Just be careful, young lady. You might land yourself in deep trouble.'

Patrick Covington turned round and strode back towards his office, as if nothing had happened, leaving Kylie visibly shaken and shivering with fright.

What should she do? Go to the police? She had no witnesses, so it would be his word against hers and it would be very difficult. Each would accuse the other, and she would not make any progress in Brian's situation. Covington would close up immediately and make sure she had no access to Ron or other members of his staff. No, that would do no good at all.

Then she remembered Jeremy. Of course, by the time she returned to the coffee shop, he had disappeared. But Kylie realised he had seen her, and it would be impossible for him to contact her again. Not if he valued his life, that is.

Kylie felt a mixture of loneliness and anger as she walked back to her penthouse, through the crowds of people now filling the streets of

London's financial centre. Where were they when she needed them? At least, with Jeremy allegedly a friend, she had somebody to talk to, but now she recognised he was not on her side. Had he ever been? Ron had been useful and had provided as much information as he was able, but what more could she ask of him? And Brian? Where was he?

Kylie trembled as she opened the door to her apartment, and feeling like a wretch, she burst into tears, sobbing uncontrollably. She sat on her sofa and buried her head in her hands between her knees. She didn't move for what seemed like hours.

She needed a friend, someone to talk to, someone like Brian. Where was he? Why was he so far away? She could just pick up the phone and dial his number?

Why didn't she?

Kylie had no way of knowing the time wherever Brian was right now, but she didn't care. Kylie picked up her phone and dialled the Melbourne number. It rang. It rang, and it rang.

Nobody answered. Now angry and frustrated, Kylie launched her phone across the room. It bounced off the carpet and into one of her favourite Chinese vases, taking a chip out of the neck.

Kylie shrieked out loud, and then buried her head between her knees again.

A ring on her door phone broke Kylie from her sorrows. She half ran to see who might be at the door, fearing it might be Jeremy. Looking into the security camera, she saw a man turned away from her, looking distinguished in a dark overcoat and bowler hat.

'Yes?' Kylie shouted. 'Who are you? What do you want?'

The man turned round and looked straight into the camera.

'Somebody told me you might need a friend.'

'Oh, Joe, yes please. Do come on up. I'll put some coffee on.'

Joe was just the man to help Kylie emerge from this mess. The number of times he had come to her aid, primarily to put off unwelcome male friends, was countless, but he was always good to talk to, especially if she had a problem.

Kylie had forgotten that the last time she spoke to Joe, late a couple of nights ago, he had been more evasive than helpful. But that didn't count as he was here now, when she needed a friendly ear, and that was more important.

Kylie opened the door; Joe entered and removed his bowler hat. Kylie helped remove his Brook Taverner black cashmere overcoat, which she hung on her coat stand. She stood back and admired his outfit, complete with blue check tweed waistcoat.

'My oh my, Joe,' Kylie said. 'I've never seen you looking so smart.'

'Well, it is a work day and you've never seen me in my work clothes before. I tend not to wear them in the pub.'

'So, this is how you dress for work?'

'It depends. If I'm just going to be in the office, I'll dress more casually, but if I have to meet people, then it calls for more formal attire, such as this,' Joe said, sweeping his hands down his body to emphasise his outfit.

'So, you're meeting people today, then?' Kylie asked.

'Yes, but when Jeremy told me you might need somebody to talk to, I rushed over. And here I am.'

It deflated Kylie when she heard Jeremy's name.

'So, that arsehole Jeremy told you, did he? Well, I'm sorry Joe, it's lovely to see you, but goodbye.'

'Now, now,' Joe said, speaking tenderly. 'Jeremy said you might get the wrong impression, and it looks like he was right.'

'So, I've got the wrong impression, have I?' Kylie asked in a scathing tone. 'The fucking idiot I thought was on my side, on Brian's side, talking with the man, the crook who is trying to get Brian. Where did I get that wrong, Joe?'

'Calm down, Kylie. Listen to me. Jeremy is helping Helen and me.'

'Where is Helen, by the way?' Kylie asked.

'She realises you don't have any romantic feelings for Jeremy.'

'She's got that right,' Kylie, now in a temper, said.

'So, she thought it best she was not here for this little talk.'

'Joe, what is going on?'

'Right, from the beginning, Jeremy was correct when he said that Helen and I work for MI5, but he shouldn't have told you.'

'So, you *are* spies?'

'Well, yes and no. We're not spies in the James Bond sense of the word. Helen and I don't get sent overseas on missions, except on very rare occasions. We collect people.'

'What do you mean?'

Our role within the organisation is to meet people, across a wide range of backgrounds, and build up our knowledge of capabilities which might come in useful one day.

'Useful to whom?'

'Why, the British Government, of course. We meet people, find out about them, talk to them and introduce them to other people to build up an interactive network of contacts.'

'Is that what you did to me? Collected me?'

'You might see it that way.'

'It sounds sick.'

'No, it isn't, it helps everyone with whom we come into contact. For instance, take Helen. She believes that everybody should have a solid relationship and so, from all the people we meet, she tries to link people together. You may not agree with her choices, but she truly believes that you will be happier with another person, with whom you can share your innermost secrets.'

'But that doesn't consider those people, like me, who are happiest on their own.'

'Are you happiest on your own, Kylie?'

'Of course. I like my independence.'

'But when I rang your entrance phone, I said a somebody told me you needed a friend, and you agreed.'

'That's not the point. At that precise moment, I was frail and wanted someone to whom I could talk.'

'Well, here I am. Let's talk.'

Kylie sat in silence for a few moments. She poured Joe his coffee and took a sip from her cup, all the while pondering what she should say next.

'All right, tell me why Jeremy was talking to Covington.'

'Sorry, Kylie, I can't breach Jeremy's confidentiality in that situation. You must understand.'

'I don't, but can you tell me if it had anything to do with Brian?'

'I can't because Brian is not on my radar. Why don't you start by telling me about him?'

Kylie became more and more frustrated with Joe's evasiveness. Just like the other night, when he wouldn't confirm that he and Helen were spies, or collectors. Or, whatever.

'The truth is, I can't decide where he is. He calls me from Melbourne, then it's Tokyo or even Turkmenistan.'

'I understand.'

'You do? I wish I did. Can you explain?'

'Yes, he is in none of those places.'

'What do you mean?'

'He is using phones with different SIM cards to make his calls untraceable. He doesn't want you to know where he is calling from.'

'Why not?'

'Presumably, he needs to keep hidden, even from you. Does he have a problem?'

'Well, yes, he's accused of murdering someone at Covington's office.'

'There you are.'

'But he didn't do it, and he asked me and Jeremy to find out some information that would help him prove he's not a murderer.'

'So, maybe that's why Jeremy was talking to this man. Covington, you say?'

'Yes, but that wasn't why he talked to Covington. I spoke to one of Covington's employees who gave me some information and when I turned back to talk to Jeremy, he had fled.'

'I understand.'

'Do you, Joe? Do you actually understand and don't want to tell me? What was Jeremy doing there?'

'Let's get back to Brian. Did he give you any clues where he might be calling from?'

'Well, he said that he was by a swimming pool.'

'Maybe a hotel, then. Apparently, somewhere warm.'

'Ah, I remember! He said he was with a woman named Maureen or something, whose husband was with the CIA.'

'Did you speak to this woman?'

'No, but I heard her when she grabbed the phone from Brian one time.'

'What did she sound like?'

'A very gravelly voice. I wouldn't want to argue with her.'

'Would it have been Miriam?'

'Yes, that's it.'

'Brian's in Hawaii,' Joe said.

Kylie's jaw dropped and her eyes almost shot out of her head.

'How can you tell that?'

'The woman you described is Miriam Snape; she works for the CIA, mostly in Hawaii. A few years ago, somewhere in South America, rebels shot her husband. She hunts drug barons for a living, and yes, I wouldn't argue with her even though she is only five feet tall.'

Joe is not being evasive now, Kylie thought

'Right,' Joe said. 'I must go. Thanks for the coffee.'

'But you still haven't told me anything about Jeremy.'

'Not much I can say, old love, but I can tell you the discussion you witnessed had nothing to do with your friend Brian.'

CHAPTER TWELVE

Matt Booker woke at seven o'clock, which was late for him. He needed the sleep, and the fact that yesterday's proceedings had gone so well settled his nerves. However, this good feeling shattered when he walked into the communal room and noticed Santos's open bedroom door. Looking inside, Booker saw Santos's empty bed.

Booker hammered on Johnson's bedroom door.

'Wake up, you idiot. He's gone.'

'What do you mean?' Johnson asked, still dressed in his night shorts and half asleep.

'What part of gone don't you understand?'

'Oh my God, he's not there!' Johnson stated. 'Where is he?'

The two CIA agents rushed haphazardly around the apartment just in case they hadn't seen him. But he was nowhere to be seen.

Booker sat at the kitchen table, head in hands, where the recording equipment remained ready to go from yesterday. Johnson wandered aimlessly.

'Well, boss, what do we do now?'

'You eat this wonderful breakfast that I have brought you.'

Booker looked up, astonished at hearing Santos's voice.

'Where have you been?' he almost shouted at Santos.

'Getting you this breakfast, to repay you for your kindness and for taking me to this amazing city. I have always loved being in Istanbul. So vibrant.'

'You've been to Istanbul before?' Booker asked.

'Many times. It is true, you said I had no contacts in Istanbul, but I didn't need to work all the time. And where do I go to escape my work? To a city where I have no contacts. Istanbul, where East meets West.'

'So, you are glad to be here?' Johnson asked.

'Of course, didn't I just say that?'

'OK,' Booker said. 'Where did you get the breakfast and how did you pay for it?'

'I went on to the street, looked to the right and saw the McDonald's. So, I turned in the opposite direction and walked in the glorious sunshine until I reached a café. Inside, I asked if an American came in yesterday and bought a takeout breakfast.'

'Takeaway,' Booker corrected.

'OK, takeaway,' Santos said. 'When I found the right place, I ordered what you now see in front of you.'

'And how did you pay?' Booker asked again.

'I didn't have any money, so I said you would pay later.'

'Why did they agree to that?'

'You were the only American that has been to that café, so they were satisfied you would be back to pay. They said you looked honest.'

'That's a nice epitaph, boss,' Johnson said.

'OK, I'm hungry. Well done for your initiative, Juan Luis.'

'I'll be back in a second,' Johnson said. 'I need my McCafé.'

Booker and Santos laughed and tucked into the feast that Santos had bought.

***

The plan of the day would take Santos through all the elections he had hacked to see what particular techniques he used. Initially, Booker sat in on these conversations, but as they became repetitive, he left them alone. Although, from time to time, he overheard the conversation proceeding.

Johnson started by asking Santos about his first experience, when Escobar told him to hack FARC. Santos did not want to do this because he knew Mateo worked for FARC, but Escobar was very persuasive.

123

Later on, Santos related his experience of impressing Alvarez, which led to him being used in small elections, which interested Alvarez. As his success grew, Alvarez used Santos in larger elections until he worked on the Paraguayan Presidential election. This saw the Colorado party elected following their military coup the previous year, in which they ousted the former dictator.

'That was easy. The people wanted the Colorados to win, and we didn't have to do much to enable them. But we learnt valuable lessons for future elections. You could say that Paraguay became our blueprint.'

Santos described further elections in countries such as Ecuador, Chile, Argentina, and Venezuela.

To every question that Johnson asked him, Santos would respond, 'same', 'same', 'same'.

Then, they reached the Argentine election, with no clear winner between the two contenders.

'We exerted pressure and one stood down, leaving the road clear for our favoured candidate. One of the misguided beliefs of rigged elections is that there has to be a large majority. That is completely false. If I am doing my job correctly, then the closer the result, the more likely the election has been affected, if my man wins.'

Santos illustrated this by talking about the Guatemalan general election.

'And it is especially true with a low voter turnout. In Guatemala, the turnout was below forty per cent. Why? Because my influences made voters feel insecure. Although, I did nothing to harm them.'

These comments challenged the beliefs of Booker and Johnson.

The discussions continued into the late afternoon.

'Wow, *Senor* Santos, you have been busy over the years. I can see how you became very rich, particularly if Alvarez paid you on your success,' Johnson remarked.

'Well, that about wraps it up for the day. Juan Luis, we can talk about your new life tomorrow.'

Juan Luis Santos looked confused.

'You have only asked me about elections where *Senor* Alvarez employed me. Don't you want to talk about the most recent election that I was involved in and which had nothing to do with *Senor* Alvarez?'

Johnson and Booker looked equally confused.

'Sure,' Booker replied. 'We do, don't we, Sam?'

'Absolutely, but I thought you only worked for Alvarez, apart from your early days with Escobar.'

'Didn't you say you received your employment from Alvarez, not direct?' Booker asked.

'That is correct, apart from my last job, and that is the reason I remained under house arrest in Bogotá, not because I had acted against Colombia. I love my country and I am sorry I won't be going back there. The men I worked against wanted to kill me. Mateo understood this and arranged with the mayor of Bogotá to put me under house arrest so they couldn't get to me. But it looks like they succeeded and the man who came to visit me and was paid to kill me, was a puppet for these men.'

Booker and Johnson now sat totally engrossed in Santos's story. They focused on every word, like the sharpness of crystal smashing on a concrete floor.

'Okay,' Johnson recommenced. 'Which country did this involve?'

'Mexico.'

'The last election that brought in the current president?' Johnson asked.

'The recent one?' Booker wanted verification.

'That is correct. This president was not the problem, the previous president was,' Santos confirmed.

'He had already served two terms,' Booker agreed, 'and under Mexico's constitution, could not serve again. He wanted his party to win to maintain his influence?'

'Yes, but the new president was not the ex-president's man.'

'Who was?' Booker asked.

'Jimenez.'

That resulted in a loud intake of breath from Booker, who knew of the Jimenez family.

'Let's go back a few steps,' Booker suggested. 'Who offered you the contract?'

'A friend of Jimenez. He came to see me in Bogotá and told me he acted on the advice of Jimenez and the former president.'

'Did he mention the new president?' Johnson asked.

'No, he said the new president should know nothing of this and that I should liaise through a member of the Jimenez family.'

'Are you familiar with the Jimenez family, boss? They are one of the world's richest families. The CIA has suspected for years that they are involved in drug running and money laundering, but they cannot prove anything.'

'Also, they own a chain of worldwide hotels and operate banks in many of the leading tax havens, such as the Cayman Islands and Switzerland,' Booker confirmed.

'Which is why we can't get them for drug running,' Johnson established.

'It surprised me they made direct contact and not through Alvarez. *Senor* Jimenez said they had heard of all the excellent work I had done.'

'Henrique Jimenez is the Minister for Culture,' Booker told them, 'but he keeps his nose clean on the surface.'

'Who runs the family businesses?' Johnson asked.

'That will be Francisco. He's a piece of shit.' Booker clearly had nothing good to say of him.

'So, the Jimenez family used you to rig the election. How did that work?' Johnson asked.

'Many tactics,' Santos said. 'It was my biggest job. Before the election, I sent so many e-mails to influence people to vote one way. I scanned web sites to find evidence of illegal finances relating to the opposition. I adjusted certain official web sites that controlled who would be selected to count the votes. These people should be chosen at random, but I made sure we chose the right people.'

Booker and Johnson could not believe what they were hearing.

'On election day,' Santos said, 'the office became less technically minded, and I sensed they had side-lined me. They arranged for votes to be trashed or annulled. They used their people to go through the poorer communities and threaten to cut off benefits unless that community delivered a certain percentage of votes. There were so many devices used. More than any other election in which I was involved.'

'Talk about dirty tricks,' Booker sneered, 'and you say you did nothing illegal?'

'They happened, but I didn't do it.'

Booker let that last comment pass. He had other work to attend to now.

Four o'clock in the afternoon in Istanbul meant the time was eight o'clock in the morning at the CIA's headquarters in Langley, Virginia. Booker went to his bedroom in the apartment and put in a call to his boss.

Thirty minutes later, he emerged from his room. Both Johnson and Santos were sitting in silence. They understood that something important had occurred with Santos's last confession.

Santos realised he couldn't take back his comments and regretted that he had become so confident in talking to these agents that he had boasted about his work.

Johnson sat there, stunned.

'Okay, Juan Luis Santos,' Booker began, 'our relationship has changed. Initially, we asked for help on how to rig elections, for which you were very generous and we thank you. We promised to set you up in a new life, with a new identity where nobody would know you. And we will, all in good time.'

Santos looked up from his seat to Booker who stood in front of and appeared to tower above him. He wore a look of bewilderment on his face.

Booker turned to Johnson.

'Turn the tape machine on,' he instructed.

'Now, following your revelations about the Jimenez family, you have given us an avenue which could lead to the USA bringing down that family and their illegal operations,' Booker informed him.

'To this end, we require you to be a witness in a trial that we will bring against the Jimenez family at a later stage. Now, if you agree, we will provide witness protection for you as long as it takes,' Booker said.

'If you don't agree, then the situation changes, dramatically.' Booker's voice was ice cold.

'We have your words on tape, and we will use them. But this information carries more weight if it comes from you directly at the trial. If you do not agree, you are free to go, to leave this apartment, but we will not protect you. Moreover, if we can use any of your words to indict you personally, we will. Trust me, *Senor* Santos, you need to work with us, not against us.'

A shiver ran through Santos's body.

Johnson was impressed by his boss and smiled.

***

WEDNESDAY 9TH APRIL 2008
KONA-KAHLUA, HAWAII (04.00 LOCAL TIME)

Miriam awoke to the ringing of her cell phone.

The call came from CIA Headquarters, Langley. It was from a manager of another section. Miriam didn't speak, she just listened, paying full attention to the voice on the other end. What she heard applied to recent events with Brian. Miriam did not respond, but she needed to work out a plan of action, which would involve him.

Miriam recognised now that Brian should leave the Big Island as soon as possible. If she thought he wasn't out of danger when they spoke yesterday, he was even less secure today. She wanted to protect him as a mother would, but there were risks.

There were also risks to herself. If the news of what she had just heard became more widely known, even she would not be secure on the Big Island. She would have to leave, but for both of them to leave at the same time would provoke unwanted interest and that would be hazardous.

The next twenty-four hours would be difficult and she might need help. It was time to make some calls.

First, she phoned Pika. He was already awake from the screaming of his newborn child, now being cared for by his wife. He understood what Miriam required.

Next, she spoke to a colleague in Orlando, who was surprised at the latest turn of events. The colleague said she would do whatever was necessary.

Finally, Miriam dialled the secure line to Langley to bring her own manager up to date. She discussed the various events of which she and Brian had spoken over the past few days. He agreed with her suggested plan of action.

Against Brian's wishes, Miriam installed the information from the USB stick on her tablet.

Now to talk to Brian.

CHAPTER THIRTEEN

WEDNESDAY 9TH APRIL 2008
KAILUA-KONA (06.00 LOCAL TIME)

Brian arrived in the lobby just after six in the morning. Only two servers were outside preparing tables for breakfast. It was another sunshine day in paradise, and by ten o'clock, the swimming pool would be full.

The desk clerk raised his head from his computer screen as Brian approached.

'Can I help you, *Senor*? You're up early this morning.'

'Yes, I want to settle my bill.'

'*La cuenta, Senor?* You're leaving us?'

'*Si*, I mean yes, I'm leaving. I've had a wonderful time here, but now I must go.'

'Okay, *Senor*. I'll tell *Senor* Jimenez. I'm sure he'll want to say goodbye.'

'There's no need. I don't wish to disturb him; he must have more important jobs to do. I'm just going back to my room to pack my bag and I'll be on my way.'

Brian turned around and heard the click-click footsteps of somebody striding along the marble floored corridor. It was Miguel Jimenez.

Just my luck, Brian thought. *I wanted to make a swift and clean departure, with no fuss.*

'Ah, *Senor* Jenkins,' Miguel called from twenty yards away. 'Are you leaving before breakfast? There is no rush to catch your plane. Hawaii is an extremely relaxed country.'

Brian stumbled over his words.

'Well, I need to see what flights are available and I need to buy a ticket. You know what it's like, so many things to do at airports.'

'But not at Kona, *Senor*. It's just a small airport with a tiny gift shop and only one lounge.'

'That's all very well, but I'm not a confident flyer and I don't like to rush.'

'So,' Miguel said with a smirk on his face, '*Senor* Jenkins, who plans nothing, but comes to Hawaii, the furthest country from England… Then he leaves on a whim at six o'clock in the morning, before any shops are open?'

'I haven't got time for this, Miguel. I just want to leave and pay my bill, my *cuenta*. Is that OK with you?'

Miguel could see that Brian was losing his temper.

'Of course, of course. I apologise. You pack your bag and we will have the account ready for you.'

'Thank you,' Brian said firmly.

As Brian was about to enter the elevator, Miguel called to him.

'Is Mrs Miriam going to take you to the airport?'

'No, she's still asleep.'

'Then I will call a taxi for you.'

'Thank you, but no thank you. I'll walk to the taxi queue and take a taxi myself.'

'But it is too early, *Senor*; there may not be any taxis waiting in line,' the desk clerk said.

'Then I'll walk to the airport,' Brian said, determined to get away.

***

Upstairs in his room, Miriam entered through the communicating door.

'How did that go?' she asked.

'As planned. It surprised them I was leaving so early, but they expected you to drive me to the airport.'

'That's good; I'll make a phone call.'

As Brian put his clothes together, with his new tablet in his backpack, Miriam came over to him and put her arm around his waist.

'Brian, I'm sorry for the mess you're in and I wish I could help more.'

'What do you mean? You've been fantastic! I don't know what I'd have done without you. The mess I'm in is not your fault, but at least I've found the right person in the right place, which makes me feel so much better.'

'You appreciate it's far from over and there may be worse days to come before you can lift your burden?'

'I understand.'

'But I'll be watching out for you from afar.'

'Don't be silly and promise something you can't control. I realise I'm on my own now, but I understand, and hopefully, my friends in London can help me.'

'One thing I will promise is that, when it's over, I'll see you in London and you can show me the sights.'

'Miriam, that's a date.'

Brian was becoming emotional now, which surprised him. He hadn't considered when he met this little red-headed crow of a woman on the plane that they'd become so close. Even if the meeting wasn't as accidental as it appeared, he didn't care. He hadn't a clue how he would have coped had she not been there.

Miriam left Brian's room to make her phone call. Meanwhile, he retrieved the tablet from his backpack.

This is one method of communication I haven't used yet' he thought.

Brian hadn't discussed sending an e-mail with Miriam and he wasn't sure she would approve, but he wanted to let Kylie know he was all right. He hadn't been able to contact her, as arranged, after her second meeting with Ron, and this worried both him and Jeremy. He remembered Kylie's e-mail address and sent her a simple message. It was seven o'clock in Kona, which made it six o'clock in the evening in London. Perfect timing.

I'm travelling, can't phone, hope you're OK, please reply, Brian.

***

Brian settled his account with the desk clerk, paying with the credit card from his Swiss bank. He asked if he could say goodbye to Miguel Jimenez, but the desk clerk said he was on the phone.

Good, Brian thought as he smiled to himself. *It's working.*

With a confident step, he walked past the breakfast tables, now prepared and ready for the residents. The swimming pool was pristine, with the still water reflecting the clear blue sky as it waited for its first bather of the morning. Brian saw the gates of the Kona Inn Shopping Village opening and the Kailua-Kona Sanitary Department workers were making the streets clean for the tourists in the area.

Brian strolled down the ramp from the hotel and turned to the right, carefully avoiding the dog poo on the sidewalk. Miguel was correct when he said it was too early for taxis to form a line. But the taxi that Brian was expecting was already waiting for him. He opened the passenger door and sat directly behind the driver. They spoke no words as the taxi turned one hundred and eighty degrees to head for the airport.

Along the route, the taxi pulled into a Safeway Supermarket where Brian got out to go to the toilet. When he returned, Brian got back into the taxi, which pulled out into a line of traffic heading along the Ane Keohokālole Highway. Before the taxi reached Kona International Airport, it made a minor diversion.

'Are we being followed?'

'We are now.'

The taxi headed towards the I-19 highway, past the Kaloko-Honokohau National Historical Park, before turning left onto Keahole Airport Road. It drove into the public area, parked, and its passenger got out.

The car that had followed the taxi parked nearby. The driver stopped the car and ran over to the taxi's passenger. He recognised his target from the clothes he was wearing, shorts, a bright yellow shirt and lime- green jersey, especially the lime-green jersey.

The assailant grabbed his victim by the shoulder. The Hawaiian features of his prey completely surprised him, especially the girth of his waist. The punch to the face that swiftly followed knocked him senseless.

Brian, now dressed in his European attire, rushed over as Pika pulled the dazed thug to his feet.

'Do you recognise him?' Pika asked.

'Why, that's the ruffian who burgled my flat in London. How did he get here and who is he working for?' Brian asked.

'Miguel Jimenez must be behind this,' Pika said, 'but if this sonofabitch doesn't report back soon, Miriam may have a problem.'

'We'd better get back to help her,' Brian said.

'No, you've got to take a plane. You leave, I'll help.'

'What will you do with him?'

'I'll take him to my brother, Keoki. He won't get away in a hurry.'

***

Brian walked from the public parking lot through the shuttle pick up area to the Hawaiian Airlines office. The first part of Miriam's plan had worked well. Persuading Pika to dress in the same outfit that Brian had bought was a brilliant idea. It completely fooled the thug who had targeted Brian's flat in Ealing.

Now, Brian had to decide which flight he wanted to take out of the Big Island. Miriam had bought two tickets for him, one going to Los Angeles and the other for San Francisco. He decided on the latter, bought in the name of Bernd Muller, so he had to cancel the ticket in the name of Brian Roberts.

Miguel was correct that the airport was empty at this time of day, but it gave Brian time to think, to make sure of his part in the plan.

However, he was still concerned about Miriam and he wanted to be sure she was all right. That said, he felt comforted that Pika would look after her.

They found a mobile phone on the thug's person, which stupidly was not password protected, so they could see his call log. As Brian expected, there were calls from Covington and Jimenez, so there was no doubt there was a connection. Pika took the phone and said he would give it to Miriam.

***

Back at the hotel, Miriam had breakfast by the swimming pool. Miguel wandered over to her, smiling, his white teeth gleaming.

'So, your friend has left?'

'Apparently. I must have been asleep when he went.'

'He did not say goodbye?'

'Not in so many words. He left a message under my door, saying it was time for him to leave.'

'A strange man, *Senor* Jenkins; I hope he doesn't get into any trouble.'

'What do you mean, Miguel?'

'He comes and goes, with no plans. He is unsure of himself and that type of person often gets himself into difficult situations.'

Miriam pondered Miguel's comments just as her cell phone rang.

'Excuse me, Miguel, there is a call I need to take in my room.'

***

After dealing with Hawaiian Airlines, Brian wandered over to the Laniakea Café while he waited for the announcement of his flight to San Francisco. It was due to leave in an hour, at quarter past eleven, and would arrive in Honolulu by midday. From there, it was a wait for two hours before switching to a plane bound for San Francisco, arriving around nine in the evening local time.

He had some time before the flight left, so he picked up a copy of *USA Today* and scanned the financial pages. There were rumours that the Federal Reserve would lower interest rates. They had already added $50bn by auctioning more government bonds and continuing to buy back high-risk bank debt. The newspaper questioned the financial security of even the biggest investment banks. Also, there was a small

135

paragraph speculating that Royal Bank of Scotland (RBS) planned to issue new shares as well as selling some of its insurance companies, to raise further capital. This convinced Brian that a massive period of volatile trading in global markets was imminent. He hoped the traders at the hedge fund were on top of this.

While digesting this news, Brian thought about staying at the Mark Hopkins hotel, a hotel he had frequented many times, but they also recognised him under his former name. Now, he was Bernd Muller and he should get into the role. Brian decided he would stay at the Courtyard by Marriott hotel, which had a shuttle service to and from the airport. He had stayed there once before. It was a large hotel, large enough for Brian to be anonymous, but comfortable enough for the night.

***

Miriam returned downstairs, fully packed and ready to leave the hotel. This surprised the desk clerk, who called for Miguel to come to the lobby.

'Why are you leaving so suddenly?' Miguel asked.

'That phone call was about my sister-in-law, Bert's sister. She is very ill and not expected to live. I must go to her.'

'Of course, but what has happened? Is there anything we can do?'

'No, I've packed everything. I've just paid my cheque and I really must go. This is awful, I must go. Sorry Miguel, I'll see you again. You can be sure of that.'

With that, Miriam went down to the garage with one server carrying her heavy suitcase. She screeched the tyres as she drove fast out of the hotel and headed for the airport.

Miguel watched her go, with concern and confusion etched on his face.

If I'm lucky, I can get onto the same flight as Brian, Miriam thought.

Brian finished his teriyaki chicken sandwich and drank his cup of Kona coffee. This was probably the last cup of Kona coffee he would drink and he meant to enjoy its taste, so rich and black, full of fruit and spicey aroma.

Brian put his newspaper back in the rack, looked at his watch and realised the flight should depart soon. He stood up to exit the café, but as he did so, he saw the ridiculous sight of a large suitcase coming towards him on a trolley. Brian couldn't see if anyone was pushing the trolley, but there was only one person he knew who was smaller than their suitcase.

'Miriam!' he yelled.

She peered around the luggage at the moment she lost control and the suitcase veered towards Brian on a downward slope.

'Brian,' she shouted, 'help me! Catch the suitcase.'

Seconds later, with the trolley under control and the baggage secure, Brian hugged Miriam like a long-lost friend.

'What are you doing here?' he asked.

'No time to talk now, they're calling the flight. We're sitting next to each other, Herr Muller.'

Brian, confused as ever with Miriam, shook his head.

Why not? he thought. *We came here together, so why not leave together?*

***

Back at the hotel, a very annoyed Miguel Jimenez made an international call.

'Your man was useless, he got away. What do you want to do now?'

Miguel listened and frowned.

'No, I don't know where he is going, probably to Honolulu. From there maybe he'll go to San Francisco or LA, but then, who knows?'

Miguel's ear hurt as the person he was talking to raised his voice.

'No, I don't have the resources. You shouldn't have let him get away.'

Further shouting ensued.

'This is not getting us anywhere. My guess is he's trying to get back to London. Do you want me to find out who's got your boy?'

More shouting.

'I'm glad you're not protecting me if that's your attitude. Look, I've got to go. I have other problems. Your man, Jenkins, has teamed up with a woman guest who works for the CIA. She has left as well.'

A stunned silence came from the other end of the telephone line as Miguel replaced the receiver.

No sooner had he put the phone down than it rang again. Miguel assumed it was Covington calling back.

'Yes, what do you want now?'

'Is that the way to address your father?'

'No, no, sorry Papa.' Miguel hesitated. 'How are you? To what do I owe the pleasure?'

'I'm coming to see you, my son. I'll arrive on Friday.'

'Will Mama be with you?'

'No, this is strictly a business trip. I'll leave on Sunday.'

'I'll have your room ready for you. Is there anything I need to prepare?'

'I want to discuss our investments in London. I am aware of recent difficulties.'

Miguel could feel bubbles of sweat forming on his brow.

'I'm sure there is nothing to concern you, Papa. I have been in touch with *Senor* Covington and he is dealing with the matter.'

'Dealing? *Dealing!?*' Miguel's father's tone became more sinister and his voice more rasping. 'Haven't they caught the murderer?'

'Murder, Papa? I didn't realise someone was killed. Who was it?'

'It was young Pablo Segura, the youngest son of my old friend Antonio.'

'Oh yes, I knew him.'

'What has Covington been dealing with that does not worry you?'

'Nothing for you to concern yourself with, Papa,' Miguel said, sweating profusely now and hoping he might convince his father, but he knew it would be no good.

'What is it! And I will not ask again.'

'Covington said there was a security breach in his office and some files were stolen, but it has nothing to do with us. I'm sure.'

'Why did he involve you in this situation?'

'The man who stole the files stayed in the hotel, but he has left now.'

'What do you mean he stayed at the hotel?'

'He came here with the CIA woman. She comes here regularly; I think it was purely accidental.'

'Did he know of any connection between us and that Irishman?' Henrique spat out the last word.

'I'm sure he didn't.'

'Did she make the link?'

'No, I'm certain of that.'

'Did you retrieve the files?'

'No, I understood we had them this morning, but there was a mix up and now Covington's man has gone missing.'

'This is a disaster. I'll arrive on Friday. Contact The Professor and tell him I want to see him urgently.'

This is not good, Miguel thought.

***

Whilst the aeroplane made its way to Honolulu, Miriam and Brian brought each other up to date with the events of the morning.

'I was planning to leave tomorrow,' she said, 'but Pika's call after he left you made me realise the need for urgency. I told Miguel Bert's sister-in-law was terminally ill, and I had to go to her bedside.'

'Oh dear, is that true?'

'No, you idiot, she died four years ago,' Miriam said with a laugh. 'But when he finds out we've got your burglar and have evidence of a collusion between him and Covington, my life would not be safe at the hotel.'

'What are your plans in Honolulu? My flight to San Francisco leaves two hours after we land,' Brian said.

'I'm going to LA and I'll catch a plane to DC from there,' Miriam replied.

Miriam turned her head away from Brian for a few seconds and then returned to look at him with that serious face she sometimes used. Brian recognised the expression.

'There is something else I have to tell you. It's sensitive, but it's something of which you should be aware.'

Brian gulped. His face crinkled in fear as he awaited the news.

'I had a call from Langley at four o'clock this morning.'

'Go on,' Brian said, not wanting to hear.

'Apparently, one of our agents interrogated someone who hacked the last Mexican elections. This brought Henrique Jimenez into the Mexican Government. He is also the father of Francisco Jimenez, who we suspect is the ringleader of the drug cartel. Francisco is Miguel's brother.'

'So, my USB stick provides the money-laundering information whilst the thug's phone gives the link between Jimenez and Covington. You have the Jimenez family's involvement in the rigged Mexican elections, but you do not have any information to confirm their involvement in drug running?'

'We're working on it, but the pieces are coming together.'

CHAPTER FOURTEEN

Patrick Covington sat in his office; he was still fuming from the events of yesterday. That woman, Jaimie Minogue, or whatever her name was, spying on him. Who did she think she was? Claiming to be from *Hedge Fund* magazine? It didn't exist.

That fool Mathis didn't suspect a thing, but Julie Simpson was smarter. She suspected the woman right from the start. She recognised her from the stockbroking firm where she used to work. Julie didn't recognise the name, but she could provide the firm's telephone number.

Now, he found out her name was Kylie Griggs, but what was she after?

As these thoughts were rampaging through his brain, there was a knock at Covington's door. It was the police officer handling the murder enquiry. Covington waved him in.

'G'morning, sir. I just wanted to inform you we're wrapping up here. We'll be out of your hair very shortly.'

'You've finished your investigation, have you? Do you intend to charge that man Jenkins?'

'Well, no. We can't find any evidence of Jenkins's involvement in mister Seguro's death. The man's unfortunate demise looks accidental, so we're not bringing any charges.'

'It was Jenkins, I told you,' Covington screamed. 'Why would he escape the country otherwise?'

'Well, we can't find any evidence that he has left the country unless you can prove to us otherwise. Can you offer any further information to that extent, sir?'

'Well, no,' Covington said, not wishing to disclose his relationship with Miguel Jimenez, 'but I'm positive he has.'

'In any case, there were no signs of a struggle, no fingerprints nor any DNA evidence to suggest he was there when mister Seguro fell. The only other DNA we found belonged to your chief of security, Emilio Jimenez. It looks like an accidental death to me. He just fell. It happens.'

'Look Sergeant,'

'Detective Sergeant,' the police officer corrected.

'Detective sergeant,' Covington said, emphasising the first word. 'I can assure you that I'll be in touch with your superiors if that is your conclusion.'

'Very well, sir, I'll tell them.'

With that, the detective sergeant left Covington's office and exited the building.

Patrick Covington picked up his phone and dialled his security chief.

'Emilio, come to my office, please.'

Covington observed his staff. Business seemed to progress as normal, traders were on their phones but they looked frantic. He looked at the big screen on the wall and saw the markets were plummeting. Just as Jenkins warned. After a few minutes, his chief of security knocked on his door.

'Ah, Emilio, come in.'

'Is there a problem?' Emilio asked.

'Possibly,' Covington said. 'The police said they were closing the case. They are calling it accidental death.'

'Maybe. That is possible, isn't it?'

'Emilio, the only other person in the building at the time, apart from you, was Jenkins and we are sure he has left the country. What am I supposed to believe, a coincidence?'

'What do you want me to do?'

'Do you have any evidence that the police might have missed, which points to Jenkins?'

'No, sir.'

'In fact, the only DNA evidence the police have is yours. Did you kill him, Emilio? What would you do if I asked the police to investigate your actions?'

'I'd say you were making a mistake, sir, and that is something you don't want to do.'

Emilio stared straight at Covington, who felt uncomfortable.

'Let the police call it accidental,' Emilio said, 'then there is no further investigation.'

'What about Jenkins? How much information did he download?'

'I know he downloaded some data, but not the full extent.'

'How could it happen; it should not have been possible?'

'I agree, but we must assume that the info he has is enough to implicate this firm and you.'

'Well, we know where he's staying, my man followed him and confirmed he is at your brother's hotel. I'll put a phone call in later to have him taken.'

'That might be difficult. I understand he befriended a woman who works for the CIA.'

'What!' Covington exploded. 'That's news to me. How long have you known?'

Emilio shook his head.

'Let me contact your man; it's about time he earned his free holiday.'

'That's a good idea,' Covington said. 'Now what's the situation at the bank?'

'I contacted them and said we had a potential breach. They closed the primary account and no further monies will come in along that route. Of course, it upsets our cash flow and could become a problem if any of your clients want to remove their money. But that shouldn't happen, especially with the recent fund performance.'

'I'm not sure. At his last morning meeting, Jenkins warned of the market peaking, and looking at what's happening now, he was right. He recommended the traders to liquidate ten per cent on any upside. Some clients might get wind of this and decide to remove the full amount.'

'You'd better hope they don't.'

'So, I should open a fresh account.'

Emilio nodded.

'That means I have to go to the bank and open it in person. Can you handle things here?'

'Not really, your staff here only recognise me as the head of security. Who is the next person in charge?'

'There's that clown, Mathis. He's an idiot, but an honest idiot, I think.'

'I'll keep him under surveillance, and I'll talk to Torres, the head of accounts. We need to let him understand the position. You'll only be away for twenty-four hours. Nothing should go wrong in that time.'

Covington had a nasty feeling about this, but he agreed with his chief of security, who was committed to the operation.

***

Jeremy was having afternoon tea in Helen Thompson's Kensington flat. Joe was out as he had an appointment at MI5 HQ, but Helen was aware of Jeremy's meeting with Patrick Covington yesterday.

'Are you sure that Kylie saw you talking to him?' she asked.

'Oh, she saw me, all right. Covington made such a noise that everyone in the coffee shop would have known and it would've been impossible for her not to see me.'

'What happened then?'

'Kylie left by the rear door and Covington charged out of the front door. He caught her by the wrist as she was running away. She screamed, but I couldn't help her, it would've blown my cover.'

'What happened to the other bloke Kylie was with?'

'Mathis was quick, he was ahead of Kylie and ran into the building before Covington got to her. I don't think he even saw him.'

'Did Covington hurt Kylie?'

'No, he threatened her, and she screamed for help, but there was nobody around. Covington realised the difficulty of the situation and let her go. But I couldn't be sure. I was off before she could see me.'

'Okay, it doesn't look as if there's any damage done. Joe had a word with Kylie, to calm her down, but he says you're the last person she wants to talk to right now.'

'I thought that would be the case,' Jeremy said, 'so should I proceed along the lines of the conversation I had with Covington?'

'That would be good. We need to infiltrate his organisation. Did he accept the story you gave him?'

'He was reasonably interested, but he needed to make sure of any new person's credentials before he hired a replacement. Do you have anyone in mind?'

'Possibly, but in the meantime, why don't you begin by setting up a meeting between Covington and this new candidate for some time next week?'

Jeremy dialled Covington's number. Unexpectedly, a female voice answered.

'PMC Hedge fund, Patrick Covington's extension, how may I help you?'

'May I speak to Patrick please?'

'I'm sorry, he's left for the day.'

'Will he be available tomorrow?'

'Unlikely. He's flown to Switzerland and is not returning until tomorrow afternoon. I don't expect him back in the office until Friday. Can I book an appointment for you?'

'No, but can you tell him that Jeremy phoned and ask him to get back to me when it's convenient?'

'Yes, when I talk to him later today, I'll give him your message.'

'Thanks.' Jeremy disconnected the call and turned to Helen.

'That's interesting.'

'Isn't it?' she said. 'I need to make a phone call. We must keep up to date on that situation. In the meantime, you might try to get back into Kylie's good books.'

'Do you think so?'

'If Joe is as good as I believe he is, she might have calmed down a little.'

'Worth a go,' Jeremy said.

'Worth a go,' Helen repeated.

***

By late afternoon, Patrick Covington was on a British Airways flight out of London City airport to Zurich. On the way, he could not help but reflect on recent events.

Things were not going well. By breaching his security protocols, Brian Jenkins had created havoc in his organisation, and possibly in his benefactor's, as well. One of his security guards was murdered, even if the police called it an accident, which he knew was wrong. And this woman, this Kylie Griggs, had assumed a false name so she could ask his staff questions about his organisation. Now, he had no choice but to go to Zurich and open a new bank account, which would become a big problem if left unattended.

When this became known to the Mexicans, he would have a great deal of explaining to do. And they were not likely to be on his side.

***

Jeremy took a taxi from Helen's place to the south side of Tower Bridge. From there he walked the back streets to Kylie's flat. He was extremely apprehensive about this meeting, but he had to get it done.

Kylie was a natural inquisitor, and he was a poor witness. When she got her teeth into something, Kylie didn't let the matter drop until she had received a satisfactory answer. That's what made her a first-class analyst, he thought, probing all the time and not letting go.

Jeremy recognised his weakness in the face of such interrogation, but he had to be strong. Kylie could not know his side of the story, even if Helen and Joe considered it the right time.

He also realised that he had to have this meeting with Kylie in person. If Jeremy had called her, Kylie would have cut him off in an instant, such was the anger she had for him now. Still, she'd had nearly twenty-four hours to mull it over, and he hoped Joe was as good as Helen said he was in calming her down.

Jeremy rang the call button of her flat. A light went on as the camera registered the caller. He stood back so she could see he was alone.

'Go away!' Her voice rang out in a shrill pitch.

She's still angry then? Jeremy thought. *Maybe Joe wasn't as good as Helen believed.*

'Kylie, I must talk to you.'

'Go away, I said. I have nothing to say to you.'

'Kylie, this is ridiculous. I know you saw me talking to Covington, but it's not what you think.'

'I understand that. You're helping Joe in something.'

'He said that?' Jeremy said, sounding hopeful. 'Kylie, what Joe and I are involved in has nothing to do with Brian.' Well, that was a lie, a white lie, but a lie, nonetheless.

'Jeremy, I'm confused. I'm not sure if I can trust you unless you are honest with me,'

'Let me come up. I can tell you more, but it's complicated.'

Kylie released the door, and Jeremy bounded up the stairs to Kylie's flat. At least he did for the first few flights, but by the time he reached her penthouse, he was stumbling up the steps, out of breath, coughing and red-faced. She saw him and laughed.

'Don't take this as an invitation, but you must get fitter if you're to come here again. I'll make the coffee.'

'Tell me why you were meeting with Covington?'

'No, first tell me about your meeting with Ron.'

Kylie was excited to tell Jeremy her news, and she didn't hold back.

'He said that Brian couldn't have killed this guy as it would take him too long to get from the stairwell to the front door on his way out.'

'That's good.'

'Oh, and Joe revealed Brian wasn't in Australia, he was in Hawaii.'

'Wow, how did he realise that?'

'Well, he didn't know exactly, but he recognised this woman Brian is with, and her raspy voice. He said she normally works out of Hawaii, and Brian said he was by a swimming pool, which meant it was warm.'

147

'OK, that's good intel. Unfortunately, I still can't say exactly why I was talking to Covington, but I can tell you I'm working with Joe on a case at the moment. It's purely coincidental that it involves Covington. But I understand he is on his way to Switzerland and will be back on Friday.'

'Why's he going to Switzerland?'

'Don't know.'

'Is it anything to do with Brian, or with Joe's case?'

'Don't know.'

***

Although Zurich Airport is the largest in Switzerland, it is relatively small in international terms. After an uneventful two-hour flight from London City, the plane landed at Terminal B. Covington could see why the terminal was due for upgrading. It was tired and would benefit from the proposed underground link to the main terminal.

Outside, Covington took a taxi for the twenty minute drive to his hotel, the Park Hyatt on Beethoven Strasse. He had made this journey many times, and no longer took any notice of the scenery, but when he looked up, he recognised the taxi was crossing Bahnhoff Strasse, with its large monolithic buildings, home to several department stores. The city was busy; people thronged the streets, still shopping into the evening.

After checking in, he asked the desk clerk to book him a table in the hotel restaurant. The meal was satisfying although he couldn't recall what he ate as his mind remained focussed on other matters. However, he enjoyed a pleasurable evening in the Onyx Bar, drinking several glasses of his favourite Glenfarclas single malt Scotch whisky, whilst talking with an attractive American lady as he fantasised about other possibilities.

At ten o'clock, Covington entered his room, slightly inebriated, when there was a call on his mobile phone. He cursed at it, especially when he saw it was Miguel Jimenez, the Latin buffoon, calling him.

'Miguel, why are you calling? I'm in Switzerland and it's late.'

Clearly, Miguel Jimenez was not happy.

'What do you suggest? Where is he going?'

To Covington, Miguel's response was totally impractical.

'You're the man on the spot. What can *I* do?' Covington's face turned a vibrant shade of cerise as he swore into the phone. 'This is a bloody mess. Don't you have anyone who can deal with this?'

When Miguel told him what happened to the thug he sent to keep tabs on Brian, Covington's anger level increased further.

'I don't give a damn about the idiot. He's had a free holiday in Hawaii. If he can't look after himself, it's not my fault.'

Then Miguel informed Covington that a woman from the CIA was helping Brian and that they had both left the hotel. Emilio had mentioned this previously, but he had paid little attention to it at the time. Obviously, Miguel considered it important. This news stunned Covington into silence.

The phone went dead.

Covington paced around his hotel room, not knowing what to do. He phoned Emilio in London, still simmering.

'Emilio, I've just spoken with your brother. He's not happy. Did you tell him about Seguro?'

'No, why?' Emilio asked.

'Well, somebody mentioned it. If not you, then who?'

Covington was shouting into the phone. Emilio was used to his rages and remained cool, which he knew would rile him even more.

'I don't know. If this gets back to my father, there will be trouble.'

'We need to find Jenkins,' Covington insisted, 'but Miguel says he left with this woman and disappeared. And the bloody idiot I sent out to Hawaii to track Jenkins has also gone missing.'

'That's not good news.' Emilio said.

'No, it isn't,' Covington said, raising his voice. 'What are you going to do about it?'

'Me?' Emilio replied, raising his voice slightly. '*You* sent him in the first place. I said he wasn't trustworthy.'

'Well, what are we going to do now?'

'I'll have a word with Miguel and see if he can help.'

'I just did, and he was no fucking use. Miguel thought Jenkins might go back to London.'

'Or he could go to Switzerland. You're going to the bank tomorrow. That's where you got him from. Why don't you ask them if they have had any contact with him?'

'That's the first sensible thing I've heard all day,' Covington conceded grumpily. 'I'll get back to you tomorrow.'

CHAPTER FIFTEEN

Patrick Covington ate breakfast in his hotel, accompanied by his lawyer. His head was a little fuzzy from the previous night, after disagreeable conversations with both Miguel and Emilio Jimenez, even though he had enjoyed a delightful evening in the bar.

Covington completed the normal greetings with his lawyer, Franz Josef Haas, and was about to explain the need for another bank account. Then, the American woman, with whom he'd shared the previous evening, arrived for breakfast.

Embarrassed, Covington was about to ignore her when she spotted him with his head lowered towards the tablecloth.

'Why, Patrick,' she said in her Southern drawl. 'How are you this morning?'

'Fine,' he said. 'Really fine.'

'I must say we drank a bit too much whisky last night, didn't we?'

'No,' Covington replied, 'not really. I enjoyed the conversation and your company.'

'Me too. The time seemed to go by so fast.'

'I agree,' Covington said hesitantly, still seated and not knowing quite how to finish the conversation.

'Patrick, aren't you going to introduce me to your breakfast companion?'

'Sorry, yes. Emily, this is Franz Josef Hass, my lawyer. We have a meeting at ten o'clock. Franz Josef, this is Emily… sorry I've forgotten your surname.'

Then, turning to the lawyer, Covington continued. 'We spent last night drinking Glenfarclas, putting the world to rights.'

'Yes, we did, didn't we?' Emily said. 'Pleased to meet you, Franz Josef, I'm Emily Winterburn.'

Franz Josef stood up as he greeted Emily.

'Pleased to meet you, Miss Winterburn. And why have you come to Zurich?'

'Oh, it's Mrs Winterburn, Franz Josef. My husband is arriving in Zurich tomorrow. We're spending the weekend here before going back to the USA.'

'So, today, you are Miss Winterburn?' Haas said, now standing and enjoying his joke. Covington was looking at her, eyes gleaming.

'Why, I suppose I am,' she said, laughing.

'And what do you intend to do on your own today, Miss Winterburn?' Haas asked.

'Well, I planned to go shopping this morning. There's no opportunity to look at European fashions back home.'

'I could be free after my meeting to show you the city,' Patrick said, butting in, to Haas's annoyance.

'I'm free for lunch,' Emily said, 'and, for the rest of the day, I'll be all yours.'

'That's settled, then. I'll see you in the bar at one o'clock.'

'We may never leave,' Emily laughed, 'but I thought you were going back to London today?'

'I've decided to stay on for another day.'

Franz Josef Haas looked askance as Covington took Emily's hand and kissed it.

'It was so nice to meet you, Miss Winterburn,' Haas said, upset at missing out on this charming lady's company. 'Enjoy your day with Patrick.'

'Oh, I will,' Emily said with a giggle. 'Now to soak up last night's whisky. See you later, Patrick.'

Covington waved his hand whilst Haas acknowledged Emily, trying not to appear jealous.

'Patrick, in the short time I've been your lawyer, nothing has come between you and business before. Where are you going now?'

'I'm going to delay my flight for twenty-four hours.'

***

Patrick Covington and Franz Josef Haas were by the offices of the International Bank of Ireland and South America (I.B.I.S.A), located a five-minute walk from the hotel, across the Schanzengraben moat that feeds off the lake.

Covington knew the Swiss reputation for punctuality, and they entered the building at precisely ten o'clock. Inside the sparse lobby, the two men took the elevator to the second floor, where Herr Fischer's secretary, Frau Schmidt, greeted them and led them to his office.

Shortly after their arrival, Herr Fischer entered the room. He was a rotund, jolly fellow, in his sixties, with thin white hair and a red nose. He greeted both of his guests warmly and bade them sit down.

'Herr Covington, it is a while since we have met, how are you?'

'Fine, thank you, Herr Fischer. You look well. May I introduce my lawyer, Herr Haas?'

'You were not Herr Covington's lawyer when the account was set up originally, as I recall.'

'No, as you may have been aware, my previous lawyer retired. This is the first time that Herr Haas has represented me in Switzerland, but he is up to date with the situation.'

'Ah yes,' Herr Fischer said. 'I am familiar with Herr Haas's work. I believe you have only been practising in Switzerland for the past two years, Herr Hass?'

'That's correct,' Haas replied.

'Yes,' Herr Fischer continued. 'I knew your professor when he was teaching at the university in Mexico City. His death was unfortunate.'

'Yes, he was caught up in the riots following the elections. Many people felt they were falsified.'

'Your tutor amongst them,' Herr Fischer said.

'That's as may be,' Haas replied.

Changing the subject, which he felt was becoming argumentative, Covington explained the need to open another account. He said they should transfer the money held in the first account into the secondary account.

153

Herr Fischer frowned.

Covington explained in simpler terms.

'You receive money from around the world, which goes into the first account, yes?'

Herr Fischer nodded.

'Money which goes to the first account will transfer to the secondary account instead of to our account in the Cayman Islands. Money from the secondary account will transfer to the Cayman Islands instead. Yes?'

Herr Fischer nodded, but he was not happy.

'There could be a problem,' he said.

'Why, Herr Fischer?' Covington said. 'I don't see any problem. We have had a security breach in London, which renders the primary account unsafe to use for sending money, although it remains perfectly safe to receive deposits from our sources around the world. It complicates the arrangements with our various depositors to make changes.'

'That means you transfer money from the primary account to the secondary account in Switzerland, so that this money does not leave the country.' The lawyer interrupted.

'And you can send sufficient funds to London to meet our operating costs, whilst sending the surplus to the account in the Cayman Islands,' Covington continued. 'Where is the problem?'

Fischer explained.

'As you know, our banking laws have been the envy of several countries for many years. The pressure is on us to become more...' Fischer hesitated, 'more open.'

'Surely that won't happen,' Covington said.

'But it might,' Fischer argued. 'The government is considering a change to the way our banks keep their clients' interests anonymous.'

'I've not heard of this,' Haas interrupted.

'No, it's not public knowledge. But I am involved in a committee looking into this prospect. We are asked to reveal the underlying ownership of every one of our numbered accounts.'

'That would be horrendous!' Covington said.

'For you maybe, but not for everybody, and certainly not for the global intelligence community. It could be difficult for Switzerland's economy, which benefits from monies held in secret.'

'Why is this happening now?' Haas asked.

'Amongst other considerations, there is increasing pressure from the US Inland Revenue Service,' Fischer stated.

The IRS?' Haas asked. 'But that has been going on for years. They have always been concerned with their citizens holding money outside of the country. Why now?'

'The Americans are also being pushed by the Israelis,' Fischer said.

'What do you mean?' Covington asked.

'In Israel and the USA, there have been questions asked about deposits made by the Nazis and how much that might contribute to the wealth of Switzerland. Now, the pressure is on us to release this information and return property to their rightful owners.'

'Is this going to happen? What will become of the numbered accounts that do not relate to the Nazis?' Covington asked.

'That is the problem. We think there is a solution where the banks involved will disclose only those accounts which might interest the Americans and those set up by the Nazis, but do we disclose all the underlying owners?'

'Well?' Haas pressed, 'are you going to bow to the Americans wishes?

'That is another problem. The Americans are also dealing with international terrorism and they believe it is being paid for by illegal funds held in Switzerland under numbered accounts. We can bring in new laws, which prohibit anonymity on new accounts, whilst keeping the status quo on existing accounts, not relating to the Americans or Nazis.'

'That sounds suitable for us,' Covington said.

'Yes, but when is the cut-off point?' Fischer asked.

'What do you mean?' Covington asked.

'I expect this new law to come into force soon, and it could mean that your new account gets trapped by the date at which it comes into existence.'

'So, we should open it immediately?' Haas suggested.

'Yes, but even today, that might not be sufficient. If this becomes known, there could be a rush of account openings. There is a suggestion that the new law should include all accounts opened from 1st January this year.'

'Retrospectively? That's impossible,' Haas said.

'Not necessarily,' Fischer confirmed.

Covington's mind was racing with the enormity of the situation. He felt trapped. Jenkins had the account information that Covington was trying so hard to keep hidden, but if he opened the new account, there might not be protection if the authorities moved, as Fischer suggested.

Eventually, after further discussion regarding the pros and cons of possible law changes, Fischer agreed to Covington's demands, particularly when he mentioned how well Herr Fischer's bank is remunerated for its minimal services.

Frau Schmidt drew up the papers, which Fischer and Covington signed with Haas acting as a witness. Covington was about to stand up when Haas touched Covington's arm.

'Wasn't there another question you wanted to ask of Herr Fischer?'

'What?' Covington seemed confused. 'Oh yes, that young man you recommended, Brian Jenkins, have you heard from him lately?' he tried asking nonchalantly.

'Jenkins, you say?' Now it was Fischer's turn to be confused. 'I don't know that name.'

'You must do. It was only six months ago. I said I was looking for a market strategist to help me grow the Hedge fund.'

'Oh, yes, I remember, but I don't think his name was Jenkins,' Fischer said with some hesitation. 'A friend who runs an asset management business recommended him. I'll find out his name. I'm sure it wasn't Jenkins.'

Covington did not know what to say.

Haas took the lead as he guided Covington out of Herr Fischer's office.

'Thank you for your help, Herr Fischer,' he said as he waved over his shoulder.

Outside, Covington still was not capable of speech. It was as if he had lost trust in everything happening to him.

***

Covington and Haas sauntered back to the hotel. They could see the University of Zurich Botanical Garden as they strolled alongside the Schanzengraben. The mighty trees, now displaying their fresh leaves for the new season, cast their shadow over the canal.

'Tell me more about this Brian Jenkins,' Haas asked, 'was he the reason for the security breach?'

Covington nodded solemnly and recounted his story.

'So, he never gave you any reason not to trust him?' Haas asked.

'None, whatsoever. He was very good at his job and soon the fund was outperforming every other. It was as if he had a gift. He knew how the markets would perform before they did.'

'I've heard that your hedge fund does not behave like most, it relies on old fashioned long-term investment principles.'

'That was the beauty of his investment style, and it was successful. In recent years, there has been exceptional growth in the number of hedge funds and the amount of money they control. This advantage has allowed them to manipulate a stock's share price through short-ladder attacks, whereby buyers and sellers drive prices lower, while supply and demand are pushing a stock's price up. Hedge funds short the stock using an insane amount of leverage.'

'This is where inside information is relevant?'

'Yes.'

'So, there is no fundamental reason for selling the stock in question?'

'Not always, and it must be said that many hedge funds employ legitimate strategies, acting as arbitrageurs, for instance to provide a moderating influence on markets. However, this can give rise to a conflict whereby some hedge funds increase their buying activity in selected stocks and produce a demand imbalance. If other investors have insufficient time to correct this imbalance it can provide the greatest impact on prices. But no, our fund was not the same.'

'If these manipulatory practices were successful, why then did you decide to go back to fundamentals?' Haas asked.

'Successful, yes, but also risky. I had an arrangement with the Mexicans that they would send money from around the world to Zurich, where they would not be questioned. The aim was to set up a business which would accept this money and which could be reimbursed to them from a legitimate operation.'

'Hence, the hedge fund.'

'Indeed,' Covington confirmed. 'We set up the hedge fund in Ireland, where there was freedom to do what we wanted. The Irish government was only interested in building up the Treasury, following its split from sterling back in the day. At the time, there were a variety of scams in operation, mainly involving the property market. It was like the lawlessness that existed in the days of the Wild West. When the Irish pound joined the Euro in 2002, the financial market exploded, but it was still far smaller than the London financial market.'

'Did the Mexicans get greedy?'

'You could say that,' Covington confirmed. 'Even though the London market was bigger, hedge funds were not regulated, and the Mexicans thought that if we opened in London, we would attract British investors. Also, they saw an opening, whereby for every dollar they sent us, we could return a dollar fifty, and it would all be clean.'

'Ah, a Ponzi scheme, but that would depend on you attracting more investors.'

'And that would also require the fund's value to be increasing.'

'Hmm, definitely risky.'

'As it happens, not very. After the crash following 9/11, markets recovered strongly, assisted by low interest rates. Banks lent money on property, on shares, on everything. They even generated further profits by taking these risks onto their own book. They say fear and greed drive the markets; well now greed is dominating by a long way, but fear follows closely behind.'

'I know that the number of hedge funds has exploded in recent years and the amount of money they invest is gigantic,' Haas agreed. 'It's no wonder they have such influence.'

'Yes, but Jenkins believes it will end shortly,' Covington said. 'He said that personal debt levels have risen so high they are unsustainable. He believes there will be a turning point, but he does not know when this will happen.'

'That could be a problem if his prediction is correct,' Haas said.

'He has an excellent track record, and that is why this security breach could not have happened at a worse time,' Covington declared.

***

Back at the hotel, Emily Winterburn sat at the bar with a large gin and tonic. She looked at her watch. It was twenty past one.

'Hmmph,' she grunted. 'Mr Covington is late.'

Covington left Haas outside the hotel and walked into the Onyx Bar for his appointment with the beautiful American lady. He was fully aware of his poor timing.

'Is this what they mean by Swiss punctuality?' she asked as he strode into the bar.

'My business meeting ran over, and I am not Swiss,' Covington said curtly.

'I'm only joking,' Emily said. 'I have my friend with me.' She pointed to her G&T.

Covington smiled wanly.

'Oh, I'm sorry, Patrick. Has it been a tough morning?'

'The meeting wasn't too bad, but the information I was hoping for turned out to be disappointing.'

'Well, let's have a drink. You can show me the city and tonight we'll have a lovely dinner. Remember, until midnight, I'm Miss Winterburn.'

This made Covington smile.

While the boy's away, he thought *it's time to play.*

Covington showed Emily the city of Zurich during the afternoon. They walked arm in arm through the old town, with its narrow streets rising steeply as they moved away from the lake. After a brief stop for a hot chocolate drink, Patrick and Emily walked back to the lake where they took a cruise. She admired the views of the Alps, and even Patrick relaxed a little. Along the shore, they saw many people enjoying themselves in the parks or just walking beside the lake. The weather was glorious, sunshine and a soft breeze, but they could still see the snow on the Alps at relatively low levels.

Emily related how she'd strolled along the pedestrianised Bahnhoff Strasse, looking at the shops, salivating over the assortment of cakes and chocolate in Confiserie Sprungli. However, she could tell that Covington's mind had drifted, and he wasn't really listening to her. Emily poked him playfully in the ribs.

'What is it, Patrick?' she asked. 'Are you still thinking about your meeting?'

'Yes, no, sorry. You have my full attention,' he said. 'Where would you like to go for dinner?'

'Well, that's very difficult. I don't know Zurich very well.'

'How about a restaurant on the lake?'

'That would be lovely. I presume there is more than one; which would you recommend?'

'Seerose, without doubt. It has a wonderful position; the food is excellent and we can have a pre-dinner drink on the veranda if it's not too cold for you.'

'You've sold it to me, Patrick. It sounds delightful.'

When their cruiser docked, Covington helped Emily off the boat and held her by the waist, with their faces almost touching.

'Your perfume is enchanting,' he whispered.

'Why Patrick, thank you, but aren't you being a little forward?'

'I thought today you were Miss Winterburn?' he said, making a move to kiss her.

Emily responded by moving her face to the side, clearly not in a similar mood.

'Now, Patrick, don't spoil what has been a beautiful afternoon.'

'I thought. You implied…' he said, stumbling over his words.

'You may have misinterpreted my intentions,' she said.

Patrick quickly redressed the situation as they walked back to the hotel.

'I'm sorry, Emily. I apologise for behaving incorrectly. You're right, this has been a lovely afternoon. I've been enjoying myself so much, your beauty carried me away.'

'Well, I forgive you,' she replied.

'I'll book a table for eight thirty and pick you up at eight. What room are you in?'

'401.'

'Oh, you're in a suite? How lovely.'

'It's nice and not too high. Skyscraper hotels annoy me.'

'I'll collect you at eight.'

'Or I could meet you downstairs in the lobby.'

'It's no trouble.'

***

Back in his room, Covington phoned Emilio.

'Where are you?' Emilio asked.

'Still in Zurich. I'll be staying overnight.'

'You said you'd be back this afternoon.'

'I decided to take some time for myself. Why, has anything happened?'

'No, nothing in the office, but apparently, the markets are plummeting. Some traders are calling it Torrid Thursday, so your man Jenkins appears to have called it correctly. Let's hope the fund holds up and we don't get investors pulling their money out.'

'Talking of Jenkins, the banker told me that wasn't his actual name.'

'What? And you didn't think to tell me?' Emilio was enraged.

'I'm telling you now,' Covington said, not liking Emilio's attitude.

'Then what is his proper name?'

'I don't know. The banker said he would find out from the person who recommended him, but I have heard nothing yet.'

'Don't you think you should get back to him? You need to find out his real name as soon as possible. If we let the police know, then they might accept that he left the country and they might re-open the murder enquiry.'

'Why is this so important to you, Emilio?' Covington asked. 'I thought you were all for letting the case drop?'

'I was, I am, but my father now knows about the security breach, apart from young Seguro being killed. He was great friends with Seguro's grandfather.'

'How did he find out about that?'

'Miguel might have mentioned it and the fact that Jenkins stayed at his hotel. He is very unhappy and when my father is like that, you don't want to be near him. So, you need to find Jenkins.'

'We need to find him, Emilio. Don't forget you are also involved.'

Emilio fell quiet.

'I'll give the banker a call tomorrow, but tonight I am dining with a very attractive lady and I am determined that nothing will spoil this evening.'

Covington rang off and looked at the time. There was just long enough for a shower and to preen himself.

***

At precisely eight o'clock, Patrick Covington was outside room 401. He knocked on the door and heard an immediate response from inside.

'Come in, the door's open. I'm just finishing dressing.'

When he walked in, Covington's eyes widened as he saw Emily wearing a black knee-length pencil skirt, over what he assumed were black tights, but hoped were stockings, and black stilettoes. Above the waist, she was wearing only a black brassiere, but she was holding out two blouses, one plain dark blue and the other a sparkly maroon shade. Around her neck, she wore pearls.

'Which one do you think I should wear, Patrick?' she asked.

The sight dumbfounded Covington.

'You look beautiful as you are,' he said.

162

Emily laughed.

'Come on, Patrick, which one? It could make a difference to how your evening goes,' she teased.

Patrick pointed to the dark blue blouse.

'Ah, the midnight blue, it's my favourite, but I feel sexier in the burgundy blouse.'

'Well, wear the burgundy one, then.' Patrick was confused.

'No, it's too late, I'll wear the midnight blue and that will be when I return to being Mrs Winterburn. Too bad; you could have had your wicked way with me if you'd chosen burgundy.'

Covington frowned. This woman was infuriating, but she was alluring, and maybe he could still prove himself charming to her this evening.

***

There was a chill in the air as they took the taxi to Seerose. Walking up the short pier to the restaurant overlooking the lake, Emily huddled in close to Covington. She felt chilled, even though she was wearing her fur wrap to keep her warm. Covington smiled to himself.

It is going to be a good evening, he thought.

It was too cool for pre-dinner drinks on the balcony, so they went straight to their table and ordered. Covington was in favour of this because they might return to the hotel earlier than expected. Well before midnight, he hoped.

Covington charmed Emily with amusing stories about his boyhood and his travel experiences. He tried to amaze her by relating tales of the people he knew and how his business life had been extremely successful. They ate well and drank well. Emily's ability to consume alcohol impressed Covington, and he ordered a second bottle of the Chateau Lynch-Bages Pauillac 2005, the most expensive wine in the restaurant.

Covington was exuberant, Emily said hardly a word all evening. On the way back to the hotel, Emily again snuggled up to Covington. He smiled confidently.

At the hotel, they rode the elevator to the fourth floor. Covington held Emily with her back toward him, his arms around her waist. Outside the door to her room, Covington again attempted to kiss her, but again she avoided his embrace.

'I said you had made the wrong choice.'

Emily opened the door and stumbled inside, closely followed by Covington, who wasn't taking no for an answer this time, when there came a voice calling from the bedroom.

'Is that you, darling? Have you had a nice evening?'

Covington froze on the spot.

'It's my husband,' Emily whispered frantically. 'He must have arrived early.'

Covington could not get out of Emily's room quick enough. He ran down the stairs, and as he entered his own room, the phone was ringing. He picked it up.

'Mr Covington,' an Irish American voice spat at him. 'You are a despicable man, getting my wife drunk and trying to have your way with her.'

Covington slammed the phone down. Then his mobile phone started ringing. He answered it.

'And if I catch you in the morning, you had better beware.'

Covington's fingers trembled as he tried to end the call. Visibly shaking and sweating profusely, Covington didn't know what to do, but he knew he must leave the hotel for the safety of London. Still quaking, he checked the flights out of Zurich. There was a flight to London, leaving at six thirty.

Twenty minutes later, Covington had packed and was standing in front of the night clerk, trying to appear as calm as possible.

'Yes sir?'

'I wish to check out.'

'Now?'

'Yes, now. I have a plane to catch.'

'But the first plane does not leave for several hours.'

'I need to go, now.'

***

Back in room 401, Emily and her husband were laughing uncontrollably.

'Joe, you were brilliant. You really put the shit up him.'

'Yes, did you like my accent? It was my version of Robert Shaw in that film, *The Sting*. Good, wasn't it?'

'The best.'

'But you had to suffer his bombastic behaviour all evening.'

'It wasn't too bad. He ordered some beautiful wine. Pity I couldn't drink it all. He was so far gone, he didn't notice I poured most of it in the plant pot by our table. So, what happens now?'

'He'll be on the first flight to London. Someone will track him back in the UK. Meanwhile, there's somebody I must meet, arriving in Zurich tomorrow.'

'You mean today, don't you? It's after midnight.'

Emily collected her clothes and packed to leave. At the door, she turned around.

'Best of luck. Give my love to Helen.'

'Will do, and on behalf of the British government, it's a pleasure being assisted by SND.'

'You're very welcome. Enjoy the room, I'll return to my humble quarters.'

Joe laughed.

Would that all foreign agents were as beautiful as Emily, he thought.

CHAPTER SIXTEEN

By the time Brian's flight took off in San Francisco, Miriam's plane had already landed at Dulles Airport in Washington DC. She had left Honolulu for Los Angeles the day before, and from there, took the red eye to Washington.

Miriam arrived at CIA Headquarters, fully refreshed, just before eight in the morning. She was in her office sipping a black coffee when Matt Booker knocked on her door.

'Hi Miriam, you got back OK?'

'Yes, thank you. I've only this second arrived. This is my first cup of coffee.'

'You're looking good for somebody who's just got off the red-eye. We flew in yesterday evening.'

'That was quick. I didn't expect you until tomorrow.'

'Well, the flights slotted in and there was no point staying any longer, even though Santos loved his Turkish food. I don't know how he'll get on in the US, he hates McDonald's.'

'It was fantastic luck you found out about his relationship with the Mexicans.'

'Yeah, we didn't suspect a thing until he offered it up. We were only interested in his hacking skills.'

'What now? Does he get a safe house with protection?'

'Yes, but we're not sure where and we don't want to let him loose with any IT equipment so he can go hacking again.'

'But you can't keep him cooped up for long.'

'That's the problem. What's on your radar?' Booker asked.

'I'd like to speak with Santos to see if he has any more information on their network. There was a murder in London, the grandson of one of old man Jimenez's best friends, which they tried to blame on Brian.'

Miriam continued.

'Also, we have the details from the hedge fund's computer.'

'Good.'

'Yes, my contact doesn't realise I copied it.'

'I see.'

'However, we don't have any definite proof the Jimenez family is supplying drugs. Nothing which will stand up in a court of law, only circumstantial. I need to contact the feds.'

'Okay,' Booker said with some hesitation. 'Have you contacted the Brits yet?'

'No, but we must do so, soon.'

'Best of luck.'

***

After Miriam fixed a meeting with an old friend at FBI headquarters, her phone rang. It was Pika. He sounded frantic.

'Hi Pika, what's up?'

'I've just had a call from my brother about the idiot you left with us. They're taking him to hospital.'

'Slow down Pika, what's wrong with him.'

'My brother awoke in the middle of the night, by this loud shouting and screaming. He'd tied the guy to the bed to stop him from escaping whilst they decided what to do with him. I was going over this morning, and we were going to dump him at the hotel.'

'Go on,' Miriam said.

'When my brother got to him, he was convulsing, vomiting, and he soaked the bed with his sweat.'

'Drugs,' Miriam said.

'That's what I said. My brother didn't want to get involved because of the questions he'd face, but what do you do? Do you let him die?'

'No, of course not.'

'I agree. I said I'd take the rap, but he had to go to hospital, so I called 911. The ambulance is on its way now.'

'Okay, Pika, calm down. You've done the right thing. When the cops ask you, give them my number. I'm talking to the Feds this afternoon and I'll make sure you're not bothered any further.'

'Okay,' Pika said, sounding relieved.

After she got off the phone, Miriam heaved an enormous sigh.

That's another conversation I need to have with Frank, she thought.

Then her brow furrowed, and she smiled.

But where did he get the drugs? Miguel wouldn't have supplied them, would he? Could we be that lucky?

***

In London, Jeremy was at his desk at the FSA. He was contemplating popping out for a coffee and a muffin. There was a new female server at the nearby Nero Café, who seemed worth getting to know. As he was putting on his jacket to leave the building, his secretary arrived.

'There's a police officer here for you, Jeremy.'

'Oh,' Jeremy said, looking confused. 'What does he want?'

'He only said it was personal. I've put him in room three on the first floor.'

'Thanks, Melanie. I'd better see what he wants.'

'Not been speeding again, have you?'

Jeremy laughed.

'Not that I'm aware.'

'Do you want any coffee?' Melanie asked.

'I don't think so. I'm sure it won't take long.'

Jeremy took the lift from his fourth-floor office at North Colonnade on Canary Wharf to the meeting rooms on the first floor, where he met Detective Sergeant Mortimer.

'Don't get up,' Jeremy said as he entered the room.

The police officer did not smile as he spoke.

'Jeremy Crichton-Smith?' he enquired.

168

'Yes, and to whom do I have the pleasure of talking?'

'Detective Sergeant Mortimer of the City of London Police. I have some questions.'

'Of course,' Jeremy said, wondering if his friend on the City Police force had mentioned him. 'Fire away.'

'Well, it's probably irrelevant to your work here, sir, but I have been investigating something and I just want to tie up a few loose ends. Dot the i's and cross the tees, so to speak.'

'Do you need to get permission?'

'It's only background information.'

'Go on,' Jeremy was a little unsure of how this might develop.

'I've been looking into a situation, it's probably nothing and I don't want to take up your time unnecessarily.'

Jeremy was becoming agitated.

'It concerns a young Mexican person who died recently.'

Jeremy's brow furrowed, and there were the beginnings of perspiration forming.

'The investigation showed there was no sign of a struggle, nor anything untoward which might suggest murder. Officially, it's an accidental death, but there's something that doesn't seem right. I need to satisfy myself I am not missing anything obvious.'

'How can I help, Sergeant?'

'Detective Sergeant.'

'Sorry, Detective Sergeant.'

'Are you familiar with the PMC Hedge fund organisation?'

'As a matter of fact, I am,' Jeremy said.

'I thought so. A colleague said he understood you monitored several hedge funds in the City.'

'Correct,' Jeremy said, feeling more comfortable that his connection with the City Police was now in the open.

'It's run by Patrick Covington.'

'Yes, also correct.'

'I know. Now, it might not be under your remit, but were you aware all of his security people are Mexicans?'

'I had heard,' Jeremy said, 'but it's not something that would concern me.'

'No, I thought not, but they would all need to have the proper papers. Too many people come into the UK on a short-term visa, essentially tourists, and then take part time employment. They are untraceable.'

'I understand.'

'Now, Emilio Jimenez, the chief of security, is interesting. His father is a member of the Mexican government, and Emilio is wealthy in his own right. Why would somebody like that want to be head of security?'

'I don't know,' Jeremy said. 'Possibly it's a role he enjoys.'

'Perhaps, or maybe he was there to look after his father's assets. Do you know about any relationship between Emilio's father and the hedge fund?'

'Not offhand, but if you provide a warrant, I can look in the files.'

'Not required at the moment, but I might take you up on that at a later stage.'

It disturbed Jeremy how this interview was developing and how it might affect him.

'Now, Emilio had a job offer from Patrick Covington; he has the correct visa and work permit. However, the young man who died, Pablo Segura, was another story. We checked with the Home Office and they can find no papers relating to a Pablo Segura. We don't even understand when or how he entered the UK. It looks as if he fell under the net.'

'I see,' Jeremy said, not seeing at all.

'I believe the domicile of the head company, PMC Holdings, is in Eire, but it banks in Switzerland. Is that correct?' DS Mortimer asked, switching subjects, which slightly confused Jeremy.

'Yes, they opened a UK subsidiary in 2002 and moved to London. They wanted to take advantage of the EU financial markets integration, which gave them increased accessibility to UK investors.'

'And that meant it came under the responsibility of the FSA?'

'Yes, but as you are no doubt aware, we don't regulate hedge funds in the UK. They take advantage of laws which allow them to operate in a tax-efficient environment.'

'They can get away with things UK domiciled companies can't.'

'Not specifically, we at the FSA still have a role in monitoring their operations to make sure market risk remains at an acceptable level.'

'But if they want to, say, do something a little dodgy, apologies for the lack of techno speak, they aren't obliged to disclose it to you.'

'Correct.'

'Do you monitor their investment strategies?'

'Yes, we look at their strategies, to see if they focus on arbitrage, relative value, distressed assets or long-term investment.'

'Interesting. What sort of strategy would you say the PMC fund operates?'

'Oh, long-term investment.'

'Do you know their investment strategist?'

Jeremy realised the conversation was now focusing on his relationship with Brian.

'Yes, his name is Brian Jenkins.'

'When did you last see Brian Jenkins?'

'He came to see me a week ago.'

'In a professional capacity?'

'He came in for a chat, nothing specific,' Jeremy lied.

'Have you heard from him since?'

Jeremy hesitated.

'I spoke to him on the phone a few days ago.'

'Where was he when he called you?'

'No, not a clue.' At least that was true, Jeremy thought.

'Could he be abroad, somewhere not in the UK?'

'I couldn't say, Detective Sergeant.'

'Couldn't or wouldn't?'

'That's not fair. I've answered all of your questions and you have given me no sign of where this conversation is going. If you think I've done anything wrong or I'm deliberately misleading you, please say so.'

'Calm down, Mister Crichton-Smith, let's keep this cordial, shall we?' DS Mortimer suggested, then continued. 'somebody told me Brian Jenkins has left the country, but I can find no evidence of that. Any reason?'

'I'm afraid not. Perhaps he was phoning from somewhere in the UK.'

'You could be right, but can you see now why there are these loose ends? What was Pablo Segura doing in the UK and where was Brian Jenkins? One person who shouldn't be here was here and one person who should have been here but wasn't.'

'Why are you asking about Brian Jenkins? What's he done?'

'Nothing, as far as I can see. He's just a loose end.'

***

At Newark, Brian boarded the overnight flight bound for Zurich. The Business Class cabin was almost empty, so he settled down for some shuteye, even refusing the offer of Champagne. He didn't notice the dark-haired woman seated a few rows away from him.

***

Miriam took a cab to the FBI headquarters in DC for her appointment with Frank McCarthy, a senior agent with whom she worked from time to time. Even though the CIA did not involve themselves in domestic operations, there were situations which made it impossible to ignore the company's position.

This was particularly true when she and Bert were in Hawaii. This was their base when checking on foreign nationals who were up to no good. But she almost always let the FBI know she was there in case she needed their help. It was an arrangement which worked well most of the time.

Now she had to tell Frank about the Jimenez family. This latest news from Pika about the English thug being on drugs provided an added dimension, which the local police should investigate.

***

In London, Kylie returned home from the office, frustrated there was nothing she could do to move forward on Brian's circumstances. Although, technically, she had taken leave for a few days, she went in to her office to deal with any accumulated post, and to talk to someone, anyone.

As expected, there was considerable gossip regarding the state of global equity markets. The FTSE 100 index had fallen by over ten per cent in the past week alone. It was something she and Brian discussed before these recent events occurred.

Kylie couldn't think of talking to Jeremy right now, but she was contemplating talking to Joe. Then she remembered Joe said he had to go to a meeting somewhere abroad. If she phoned Helen, it would only end up with Helen suggesting another ghastly date.

So, Kylie did what she normally did in these circumstances. She opened a bottle of red wine.

As she went to her wine store in the kitchen, she noticed her laptop sitting all alone on the coffee table.

'Hello, my lovely lappy toppy,' she said, addressing the laptop. 'What are you doing sitting there? Have I neglected you? Were you lonely?'

She turned the laptop on to see if anybody had sent her a message. There was one new message, but it was not what she expected. The e-mail address from the sender was unfamiliar, and her Google suggested it might be a spam message.

Across the screen, there was a broad orange strip.

Can you trust it? Google said.

There was no title to the message, but she opened it anyway.

The message read: *I'm travelling, can't phone, hope you're OK, please reply, Brian.*

This knocked Kylie off her feet. She almost fell onto the sofa. She felt dizzy as she thought about the message.

He's travelling, but where? Leaving Hawaii? Perhaps he thinks he can return to London. Kylie was hopeful. *I need to reply, but what should I say?*

173

If boredom drove her to wine previously, a mixture of hope and confusion took over. An enormous glass of Merlot was what she wanted right now.

***

Twenty minutes later, Kylie's mind was still buzzing after reading Brian's message. She had composed several replies in her mind, aided by the wine, but remained as confused as when she first read the e-mail.

Kylie thought of phoning Helen, even though she understood how the conversation would end. She'd prefer to talk to Joe, who she likened to a favourite uncle, but he had been noncommittal previously and would probably remain so this time.

Really, Jeremy was the only person she could talk to, even though she still distrusted him. Kylie dialled the number.

'Hello, Kylie, what's up?'

To Kylie, Jeremy sounded more hesitant than usual.

'I need to talk to somebody. Something has happened and I don't know what to do,' Kylie said.

'Me too,' Jeremy replied.

'I'll meet you in the Pont. Come as quick as you can.'

'I'll be there in twenty minutes.'

***

Jeremy was as good as his word and found Kylie in the bar. As they exchanged stories, it became clear there had been significant developments.

'What did the detective want?' Kylie asked.

'He's not sure the accident was a coincidence, and he's not ruling out murder,' Jeremy said.

'Does he believe Brian killed him?'

'I don't think so, but it is inconvenient that nobody knows Brian's whereabouts.'

'But he was in Hawaii, so the detective was correct if he assumed Brian had left the country,' Kylie confirmed, 'but now we don't know where he is going.'

'There's still one thing I don't understand,' Jeremy said.

'What's that?'

'If the detective told Covington the police couldn't trace Brian leaving the country, why was that? The CCTV should have picked him up at the airport; why didn't it?'

'Maybe they didn't look at the CCTV,' Kylie suggested. 'If they checked the departure records and didn't find a Brian Jenkins, why would they search for him on video evidence?'

'You've got a point, Kylie.'

The conversation halted. Jeremy took a sip of his beer, whilst Kylie just looked blank. Eventually, she spoke.

'I have to send Brian a reply to his message. What do I say?'

'Tell him something cryptic, such as the weather remains foggy and is taking a while to clear up.'

'That sounds creepy,' Kylie said.

'Possibly, but hopefully he'll consider it makes sense not to come back to London at the moment.'

CHAPTER SEVENTEEN

As Miriam got out of the elevator and walked to her office at CIA HQ, she saw Matt Booker running towards her. He was running fast, which surprised her. What was so important?

'Miriam, Miriam, I've been trying to reach you. Where have you been?'

'Did you forget I was meeting with Frank McCarthy? What's the hurry? Where's the fire?'

'They're moving Santos to Seattle. He's leaving this evening.'

'What?' Miriam said, gasping with disbelief. 'Whose idea, was it? Don't they realise he's a prized asset and we need more information out of him?'

'I don't know. Obviously, they've found a safe house, but I thought we'd have a few more days to talk to him. Sorry about this Miriam, I told the department expressly he was not to be moved until you had talked to him.'

'Can you get me a meeting before they take him away? I really need to talk to Mister Santos. Where is he now?'

'They're holding him at the Staybridge Suites in McLean.'

'A hotel?' Miriam could not believe what she was hearing. 'Is that the best they could do? What security does that place offer?'

'We've used it before, usually for low-level assets. We have people with him.'

'Okay,' Miriam said, unconvinced. 'Look, I need to get some papers together. Shall I meet you in the parking lot at four o'clock?'

Booker nodded and returned to his office. Meanwhile, Miriam picked up the phone on her desk and spoke to an assistant in the library.

'I need the file for the last Mexican elections and photos of all the people involved on both sides. And I need it yesterday.'

***

Booker drove Miriam the two miles to the hotel.

On the way, she asked him, 'Why is he being moved to Seattle?'

'Two reasons: there is a high Latino population and there are also several Turkish cafés. So, it should satisfy him on two counts. Plus, Seattle satisfies our normal criteria on the location of safe houses.'

'Make sure the house is not next to a McDonald's.'

Booker laughed.

***

When they entered Santos's suite, Booker and Miriam saw him spread out on the couch.

'Oh no,' Booker groaned. 'He's not still sleeping.'

Santos heard Booker's voice and sat up.

'Good to see you again, *Senor*. I wondered if you would visit before they took me away.'

Santos wore a pair of Levi's and a purple University of Washington sweatshirt with a capital W spread across his chest.

'I see you have new clothes, Santos; you look good.'

'Yes, your CIA men went shopping for me. It's not what I would have bought, but they assured me it is normal to wear such clothes where I am going.'

'You'll fit in very well,' Booker agreed.

'Mister Santos, my name is Miriam Snape, I work for the CIA and there are some questions I would like to ask you.'

Miriam stood in front of Santos, waiting for his reply. Santos looked thoughtful.

'More questions, yes, yes, I will answer. I understand this is the payment I must make for my new life.'

'Good,' Miriam said. 'Shall we sit over there?' Miriam pointed to a table by the window of Santos's room, which had a view over the courtyard.

Miriam opened her bag and spread several photographs on the table.

'Mister Santos, I want you to look at the photos and tell me if you recognise any of these people.'

Santos studied the photos for a few seconds and then looked up.

'Why, these are all people involved in the Mexican elections.'

'Good, that's what we hoped you would say. Now, I want you to look a little closer and tell me who, of these, were more closely involved with you in the election.'

Santos picked out a few photos and handed them to Miriam.

'These people dealt with data mining and sending e-mails. They were small people, not important.'

'Did you meet any of them before this election?'

Santos smiled. 'No, they were new to me and were novices. I had to train each of them, and now they are skilled enough to work for themselves.'

Miriam removed the photographs Santos highlighted and moved on to the next question.

'On the day of the election, you said they persuaded the locals to vote for the right people, are any of those persuaders shown in these photographs?'

'Of course,' Santos said, selecting some people. 'These were bad people; their methods were cruel. I had nothing to do with them.'

Miriam's method impressed Booker with the way she highlighted various groups involved in the rigged election. But she didn't end there.

Next, Miriam took out a photograph of Henrique Jimenez.

'Is this the man who asked you to be involved in the election?'

'No, but I recognise who he is. Henrique Jimenez is the Mexican Minister of Culture, a powerful man. He controls the money.'

'Then is this the person who hired you?'

Miriam showed Santos a photo of Jimenez's son, Francisco. Santos saw the photo and pretended to spit.

'No, but I know him as well,' Santos said with a sneer. 'He was in charge of the bullies persuading the peasants. He likes to hurt people.'

This left Miriam with no photographs, and she wondered who contacted Santos. Then Santos volunteered the information.

'The man who hired me was Antonio Segura, a friend of Henrique Jimenez.'

It was a lightbulb moment for Miriam.

'Antonio Segura?' she said, surprised at this revelation. 'Was he any relation to Pablo Segura?'

'Yes, I think Pablo was his grandson. An intelligent young man. It surprised me Pablo was not in your photos.'

'What did Pablo Segura do? Was he involved in helping you?'

'No, not me, specifically. He was young and had only just left college. But he was extremely useful, running errands and taking messages.'

'Is that all?'

'I remember he was idealistic and angry at some tactics Francisco used. He didn't like violence. He thought the anti-corruption policy was the reason the people should vote for the new president, who would respect them more than the previous president. There would be arguments between Pablo and his grandfather, who he insisted should tell Henrique what was happening.'

Miriam turned to Booker. 'Why don't we have any photographs of Antonio Segura?'

'I don't know. I'll phone the library.'

'You may not recognise him as Antonio Segura,' Santos said.

'Why not? How would we recognise him?' Miriam asked.

'He goes by the nickname of The Professor.'

'I've heard of him,' Miriam said; it was another lightbulb moment. 'He lives in Hawaii. We suspect him of being part of the Jimenez drug-running outfit.'

'Yes, he taught chemistry at the university in Mexico City. After the election, Henrique said the president wanted him arrested for his drug expertise, but Henrique arranged for him to escape.'

'So, why did Pablo go to London?' Miriam asked.

'First, he went to Hawaii with his grandfather, but he was still angry with the Jimenez family.'

'And you know this, how?'

'I kept in contact with Pablo. He said he needed to go to England because part of Jimenez's organisation was there. I told him I knew some people, and I helped him enter the country while avoiding the police.'

'When was the last time you contacted Pablo?'

'When I was being held in Bogotá. On the day *Senor* Booker rescued me, I tried to call him, but there was no answer.'

'What day was that, Matt?' Miriam asked Booker.

'I picked Santos up last Saturday.'

'Mister Santos, when was the last time you actually spoke to Pablo?'

'It would have been two days before. Life in captivity is awfully boring, and I would speak to Pablo every other day. Talking to him would help break the monotony.'

'What did you speak about?' Miriam asked.

'Pablo wanted to visit London, because he was aware this was where Jimenez held his financial assets. He wanted me to help him break into the company's computer so he could find out how much Jimenez was worth.'

'How did Pablo intend to find this information?'

'By getting a job with the hedge fund. He knew Jimenez's son, Emilio, worked in this company and Pablo asked Emilio for a job.'

'Wasn't Emilio aware of Pablo's feelings towards his father?'

'I think Pablo kept his feelings to himself. He was good at concealment.'

'So, you spoke to Pablo last Thursday, a week ago; at what time did you have this conversation?' Miriam asked.

'It was in the afternoon, maybe four o'clock? The sun was still high.'

'What time would it have been in London, Matt?' Miriam asked Booker.

Booker looked at his phone and pressed some buttons.

'Around ten o'clock in the evening,' he said.

'Were you actually talking to Pablo then?' Miriam asked Santos.

'Yes.'

'Do you know where he was and what he was doing?'

'Yes, he was in the computer room and he wanted me to tell him how to access some information. He was tremendously excited.'

'What did you do?'

'Based on what he was telling me, I suggested he should press certain keys, which should bring up the data he wanted.'

'And did he get the data?'

'I'm not sure, I don't think so. I heard Pablo cry, "Oh no!" followed by a noise. It sounded like the phone fell to the floor. I could hear a voice telling Pablo to go somewhere.'

'Did you recognise the voice?'

'No, but it sounded Mexican. It could have been Emilio, but I'm not sure. What has happened to Pablo?'

Miriam put her hand across the table, resting it on Santos's hand in sympathy.

'I'm sorry to tell you Pablo is dead. I don't understand the full details. Initially, the police blamed a contact of mine from England, but your evidence may help to clear him of this charge.'

Santos sat at the table with sad eyes, tears rolling down his cheeks.

'Do you still have Pablo's telephone number?' she asked.

Santos wrote it down on a piece of paper and handed it to Miriam.

'Mister Santos,' she said, 'you have been extremely helpful and we will note all of this in your file. I hope you have a pleasant journey to Seattle and that you can enjoy yourself in your new life. Stay safe.'

Santos managed a half smile and nodded to her.

'Oh, and by the way, when you are in Seattle, make sure you go to the Istanbul Café. Tell them Miriam sent you. The food is excellent.'

Santos's smile grew wider.

***

Miriam and Booker walked silently across the hotel car park. Once inside the car, Miriam broke her silence.

'I think I know who Pablo Segura's killer is.'

'Who?'

'Well, we need proof, but I don't think Pablo's phone broke when it fell.'

'How does that help us?' Booker asked.

'I'm assuming they kept the phone and that whoever answers it is our killer.' Miriam said.

***

Back at CIA HQ, there was a message for Miriam to call the local police in Kona. Following her last conversation with Pika, she was expecting this. Before returning the call, though, she dialled Pika's number.

'Hello Miriam,' Pika said, sounding depressed.

'Hi Pika, what's the situation? Where are you now?'

'I'm at home, nursing the baby, and there's a police officer outside my door, so I can't leave the house. Have you talked to anyone?'

'Not yet,' Miriam replied, 'I wanted to see how you were first and to see if there have been any developments.'

'I gave them your number, as you suggested, which is why you have the message. Our boy is still in the hospital, but he is under police guard. They know he's a druggie, and they wanted to understand how he came to be at my brother's house. Also, they wanted to know where he got the drugs.'

'OK, that's fair enough, but why are you under house arrest?'

'Because, until they talk to you, I'm the prime suspect.'

'Understood; how's your brother?'

'They haven't arrested him and he is free to move around as he pleases. Keko has a regular job and they can see he is not involved. It's just me they're not sure of as I run a stall at the farmer's market. They're threatening to investigate my suppliers, which might be a problem.'

'I'll see to it, Pika,' Miriam confirmed. 'You take care of your family. How's your wife coping?'

'She's fine. My wife understands what I'm like, and worries, but it's no big deal.'

'OK, Pika. I'll call the police now and be back to you shortly.'

Miriam put the phone down, reflecting on her conversation with Pika. He was a very useful contact, and for all their sakes, she didn't want him to be in any trouble.

She dialled the number for the Kona police and spoke to the detective handling the case.

'Hello Detective, I'm Miriam Snape. I had a message to call you.'

The detective outlined his end of the story, threatening the arrest of Pika and the English thug in possession of illegal drugs.

'I understand what you're saying, Detective, but I can assure you Pika has no interest in drugs. He was helping me in an investigation.'

The detective responded negatively and with such fury, it hurt Miriam's ear.

'I know the CIA does not operate in the US, but this involves international issues and you also understand that the man in hospital is from the United Kingdom. Added to that, I have discussed the situation with Captain McCarthy at FBI headquarters here in Washington. He promised me somebody from your local FBI office will be in touch with you shortly.'

The detective seemed to calm down when Miriam mentioned the FBI.

'Right,' Miriam continued. 'I'm glad you're willing to assist. I would like you to keep the Englishman under guard in the hospital and I would like you to remove my Hawaiian friend from house arrest. He is a good friend of Hawaii and the United States of America.'

The detective grudgingly agreed to Miriam's wishes and put the phone down.

At her end, Miriam redialled Pika and told him the news. Pika confirmed the police officer had already left his grounds. Then, as an afterthought, she asked Pika an important question.

'Do you still have the Englishman's phone?'

'Yes, shall I hand it over?'

'No, definitely not,' Miriam said, being quite emphatic. 'it holds key information, which the FBI doesn't need to have. I'll contact you when I have made the arrangements for a drop.'

Next, Miriam phoned Frank McCarthy to make certain the Kona FBI was on the job and to request they call her.

Within five minutes, her phone rang, it was Agent Reed.

'Agent Reed, thanks for calling me. I just wanted to appraise you of the situation. It involves the Englishman at the hospital. He is a prospective witness in a case on which I am working. He is only a minnow, but he has information which will enable us to convict the leaders. I would like to find out where he got the drugs that were in his possession. This is likely to be local, but the information is vital as it could unlock several doors—not just involving drug running, leading to prosecutions at the highest levels.'

Agent Reed understood Miriam's point of view and reassured her he would handle the situation personally.

'Thank you, Agent Reed,' Miriam said. 'keep in touch.'

Next, she needed to inform the UK authorities of the situation, as it involved British subjects, and she would want their help. She put a call into the British Government Communications Headquarters (GCHQ). Even though it was in the middle of the night in the UK, she knew somebody would answer her call.

CHAPTER EIGHTEEN

Patrick Covington sat in the departure hall at Zurich Airport, where he had spent the night after the ridiculous episode with that American woman and her husband. His back ached, his neck was sore, and he felt cold. Even though he checked in last night, the lounges closed at eleven o'clock, so there were no comfortable seats available, and once the final flight left, the management turned off the air conditioning.

Covington saw a few people in Departures now, all probably awaiting the six-thirty morning flight to Heathrow, but the check-in hadn't opened and neither had the British Airways lounge. The time for the flight had come and gone, but nobody understood why. This only aggravated Covington further.

He reflected on this relatively unsuccessful trip. He'd learnt that the Swiss banking authorities were going to relax their privacy laws, the person he knew as Brian Jenkins did not exist, and the American woman's husband, who had chased him from the hotel threatened unnamed injuries. On the bright side, the new bank account was now open, which meant the relationship with the Mexicans could continue unabated.

A man pushing his all-purpose cleaning machine passed nearby. On the off chance he might help and because he simply wanted to talk to somebody, Covington asked him a question.

'Why is there a delay to the London flight?'

The man stopped, scratched his head and looked at Covington.

'Sorry,' he said, in a thick Germanic accent, 'something about fog on route.'

Covington cursed his luck. He could have left Zurich yesterday lunchtime and enjoyed a good night's sleep in his comfortable bed. But he'd fancied his chances with the American woman, and the demands of his crotch overruled the rationality of his head.

He looked at his watch. It was just after eight o'clock. He realised Herr Fischer had not called him with the true identity of Brian Jenkins. But how could he? All yesterday afternoon and evening, he romanced this American woman, and then he fled the hotel for the airport to avoid her husband's potentially bruising intervention.

Covington phoned Fischer.

'Hello, Herr Fischer, have you been trying to contact me?'

'Yes, I tried several times at the hotel, but they did not know your location. However, my friend who recommended him said his name was Brian Roberts. Apparently, a problem occurred, and he was blamed, but my friend recognised his innocence and suggested he work abroad for a while.'

'Can you tell me about the problem?' Covington asked.

'No, my friend would not say, but he said it had been resolved and Brian Roberts was no longer a person of interest. He also said he would arrive in Zurich today from America. He looked forward to seeing the young man again.'

This news caught Covington totally by surprise.

'What is the name of your friend? I should like to speak with him.'

'Sorry, Herr Covington, I'm not at liberty to say. I promised him anonymity.'

'But you must,' Covington said, pressing strongly.

'Why, Herr Covington? Why is it so important to you?'

'I can't say, but it is very important I speak to him. Roberts knows something about my business and I need to understand the extent of his knowledge.'

'But of course he knows about your business. He used to work for you. Why do you forget who you are talking to, Herr Covington? I understand things about your business. Is this how you treat people who know your secrets?'

With that, Herr Fischer ended the conversation, leaving Covington to reflect on his last comment. *What did he mean? Was he going to be a problem?*

As Covington considered Fischer's comments, he looked up and saw a line of people walking through to the exit from the Arrivals Hall. He noticed one person, in particular, carrying a backpack, with no large luggage. Although far away, Covington recognised him. It was Brian Jenkins, or Brian Roberts, as he now realised.

A message over the tannoy announced the BA departure for London was now boarding. The announcer apologised for the delay to services caused by fog, but in an effort to get back on schedule, they asked passengers to board as quickly as possible.

What should he do? Covington realised he'd paid for his ticket and his luggage had been checked. He couldn't simply leave the airport without causing a fuss. He would have to answer many questions. It would take too long, by which time Brian Jenkins would have disappeared.

He phoned his lawyer, Franz Josef Haas. The result of the phone call, though, was negative. Haas had no photo of Brian Jenkins, and he did not know where Brian might go after he left the airport. Covington did not know the name of the Banker's friend. It represented an impossible situation, which only left Covington even more frustrated.

Then, after a last call to board the BA flight, Covington realised he was in danger of missing his plane altogether. He ran to the departure gate, showed his passport, and the air hostess greeted him with a comment he didn't like.

'Caught this just in time, sir. You really must get to the airport earlier.'

Covington snarled at the young lady as she checked his passport.

She smiled as she saw he was a business class customer. She would serve in that cabin today, and Covington would come to regret his attitude. She had ways of dealing with unappreciative customers.

***

Brian exited the airport ahead of the other passengers, grateful because he only carried hand luggage. The flight was uneventful, with only him and a dark-haired woman who was visiting Zurich for the first time.

During the flight, they had a brief conversation about Zurich. He said he knew the city well but wasn't from Switzerland. With a name like Bernd Muller, she guessed he must be German, but with his long, dark- brown hair, he did not look like the normal German male.

She introduced herself as Daphne Mitchell. Brian suggested they share a cab to go into the city, but she said someone would meet her. From the conversation, though, it transpired they were staying at the same hotel so, probably, they would meet again.

***

Daphne collected her luggage and forty minutes after the plane landed, she exited the airport. She looked around. Joe recognised Daphne from the photo he received.

'Hello,' he said, greeting her in the European way with three kisses, much to Daphne's surprise. 'I'm Joe Thompson.'

'Good to meet you, Joe, I'm Daphne Mitchell,' she said, looking a little flustered after Joe's over- familiar welcome. 'You're here nice and early.'

'I was already in Zurich on other business. We tracked somebody who's just left on the early London flight.'

'You received a call from Miriam Snape about Brian Jenkins?'

'Yes, she called GCHQ very early this morning, UK time. They contacted my wife, Helen, who also works at the Circus, and she contacted me.'

'So, you expected me, but not necessarily Brian?'

'No, did you see him?' Joe asked.

'Yes,' Daphne said. 'He's going under the name Bernd Muller.'

'Do you know where he's staying?'

'Yes, we're both at the same hotel, I confirmed that when we talked.'

188

'He has no suspicion you work for the CIA and that Miriam sent you?'

'None whatsoever.'

'That's good,' Joe said. 'I have a taxi waiting; 'let's check you into your room and we can update each other.'

'Is it a pleasant room?'

'Oh, the best. And I've had a bit of fun in it already.'

Daphne was not sure how to take Joe's remark.

***

In London, Kylie sat at her desk as the morning meeting finished. She heard her mobile phone ring, and she bent down to retrieve it from her bag. It was Helen.

Kylie moved away from her desk and into the corridor outside her office, so she could speak freely.

'Hi Helen, I'm at the office,' Kylie said.

'Is Jeremy with you?' Helen asked.

'No, Helen; I said I'm at the office. We've just finished the morning meeting and I've work to do. What do you want?'

'Sorry, Kylie, my head's all a tizz today. They woke me in the early hours and Joe's not here.'

'Who woke you, Helen? What's going on? Where's Joe?'

'Kylie, I need to speak to you urgently. Can you get away? It concerns Brian.'

If Helen wanted to catch Kylie's attention, she knew now she only needed to mention Brian's name. It worked, but Helen wasn't lying, it did concern Brian.

'OK,' Kylie said. 'I can probably get away shortly. Where shall I meet you?'

Helen gave Kylie the address of her Kensington flat. This impressed Kylie, as she'd never been to Helen's home previously. She made her excuses at the office and rushed outside, where she hailed a passing taxi.

On the way, she wondered if Jeremy would be there and whether he told her the latest developments, which they talked about yesterday evening.

The taxi dropped Kylie off at Helen's apartment. Kylie recognised the location as she'd been shopping on Kensington High Street many times. She pressed the button to Flat 34, and Helen immediately responded.

'Who is it?'

'It's Kylie.'

'Come on up,' Helen said.

A buzzer sounded; Kylie pushed the door and entered the building. Of late Victorian design, the elegant block of flats had a large lobby leading to the lifts, which looked like they were last updated in the 1930s. Kylie took the lift to the third floor, and Flat 34 was directly opposite as she exited.

She entered Helen's flat and any evidence of an historic period disappeared completely. These were modern flats with spacious rooms, ceiling lights and a wall-hung television. Helen led Kylie into the living room and she saw Jeremy was already there, drinking a coffee. Helen went into the kitchen and came back with another coffee for Kylie.

'Right,' Helen said. 'We need to talk. There has been much happening, most of which I have only found out in the past twelve hours. I'm aware, Kylie, that you didn't understand what Joe and I do, even though Jeremy blurted it out accidentally.'

Jeremy hung his head in shame.

'But that doesn't matter. When we met at the pub and you said you were looking for Brian, I didn't realise where this would lead. Jeremy claimed he was also looking for a Brian but didn't admit to it being the same Brian. First mistake.'

Kylie looked askance at Helen. Annoyed at Helen's attitude, she hit back.

'Helen,' Kylie said heatedly, 'this is no good. You said we need to talk and we do, but we don't need you to lecture us about the mistakes we've made. The biggest mistake, so far, is that you and Joe have not been honest with us, with me. If you had, I might have come to you sooner for your help.'

Helen gave Kylie a look, which would frighten Joe in an instant, but Kylie's expression of anger remained unchanged. This shook Helen, who meekly sat on the nearest chair and put her hands on her knees.

'What do you propose we do then, young lady?' Helen said, with a bitterness Kylie hadn't experienced before.

'Well,' Kylie replied, 'we know Brian is travelling, but is he coming to London or going to Switzerland?'

'I can help with that,' Helen said. 'He landed at Zurich this morning. The message I received extremely early this morning was from the woman, Miriam Snape, who helped him in Hawaii. A colleague of hers travelled with Brian, and Joe met her off the plane.'

'Excellent, so is Brian with Joe as well?'

'No, Brian rode into town on his own.'

'That doesn't sound very sensible,' Kylie said.

'But he is staying at the same hotel,' Helen said.

'I still don't understand,' Kylie said.

'Maybe they want to see what Brian will do before they get involved. They can keep him safe from afar,' Jeremy offered.

'To be honest, Kylie,' Helen said, 'we're still not sure about Brian. He's travelling under the assumed name of Bernd Muller, but we also realise Brian Jenkins is not his actual name. We think it's Brian Roberts.'

Kylie exhaled loudly.

Jeremy intervened.

'When the police interviewed me, the detective sergeant said they could not be certain Brian Jenkins had left the UK. Well, if he left using his proper name, then that explains why they couldn't find him. Does it also mean he might have killed this security guard?'

'Quite,' Helen said.

'But Brian's not a killer, whatever his name is. I know him,' Kylie said, exasperated.

'But if he is, it's a good reason Joe has not intervened,' Jeremy said.

'No, I don't believe you,' Kylie said. 'I won't believe you.'

'There is something else,' Helen said.

191

'What now?' Kylie said, feeling exhausted.

'When the security guard died, he made a phone call to somebody being held by the police in the States. Apparently, the phone may still be active and be in the hands of the killer.'

'Do you have the number?' Jeremy asked.

'No, the CIA woman has it,' Helen confirmed.

'Why, then let's ask her to make the call to see who answers.'

'It's not as simple as that,' Jeremy said.

'Why not?' Kylie asked.

'First,' Helen replied, 'could we identify the killer if they answer? And would it give the culprit too much forewarning? Secondly, how do we prove it if the killer answers? He might just throw the phone away and then we have no proof. No, we need to have eliminated all possibilities.'

'Who could it be? It has to be Covington,' Kylie said.

'Unlikely, because he said he was at home at the time of the guard's death. And even if it is, he is on his way to London at the moment. We can't phone him.'

'It can't be Brian,' Kylie said.

'We haven't eliminated him yet, which is why Joe has not contacted him.'

Kylie turned around, away from the other two, and gave a loud snort of annoyance. Turning back to Helen, she said, 'Well, what do we do now?'

'We wait.'

After a moment's silence, Kylie spoke again.

'Why did Covington go to Zurich and why was Joe following him?'

Helen answered.

'Apparently, he went there to open a new bank account. Joe found out Brian might have compromised the original account. So, Covington took no chances and opened a new account.'

'What did Brian do?' Kylie asked.

'Hasn't he told you?' Helen asked.

'No, only that they suspected him of murder. What did he do?'

'He downloaded some sensitive information from the firm's computer,' Jeremy said.

'Also,' Helen said, 'Joe mentioned Covington was livid when he found out Brian Jenkins wasn't his actual name.'

***

Covington arrived at his office in the early afternoon. His anger had not dissipated as he stormed past reception and on to the trading floor, where people looked up as he entered. Emilio was already in Covington's office, unaware of his return until the door slammed. Emilio quickly closed the drawer in which he was looking and acknowledged Covington's presence.

'What are you doing?' Covington asked in anger.

'I needed to look at some papers,' Emilio said.

'You will not touch those drawers unless I give you permission!' Covington shouted.

'So, do you think you give the orders now?' Emilio asked.

'This is my company and my business. You have no right to interfere.'

'As it happens, I do,' Emilio responded. 'My father is concerned about any clients who might have left recently, because of the market weakness. You only have this business because he set you up initially. He expects a return on his investment and worries you may not fulfil your end of the bargain.'

Outside Covington's office, Ron saw the argument developing and becoming heated. Whilst his boss was away, Emilio had acted poorly, walking around like a wounded beast and berating the traders to get them to work harder. Ron did not understand what was happening, but he could see it wasn't good.

Even though Brian warned of deteriorating stock market levels and advised the traders to liquidate portions of the firm's portfolio, performance had worsened and the latest news revealed several clients wanted to withdraw funds. Ron wondered about the reason for the

193

argument between Covington and Emilio, or was it that Covington had been absent from the office at a crucial period?

***

Ron left the office feeling very unsettled. The argument between Covington and Emilio lasted for over an hour. Emilio stormed out of Covington's office looking furious. Covington left shortly afterwards. He tucked a slim briefcase under his arm, but Ron could see the shape of a gun clearly, as the briefcase pressed against Covington's body.

Ron was not the only employee to witness this, and after he left, wild conversation between the traders erupted. They all realised something cataclysmic had happened and feared for Covington's sanity as well as their jobs.

On the street, Ron did not know what to do. He felt he should tell somebody, but who? He walked towards Tower Bridge and realised the person he should give this information to should be Kylie. Ron did not fully appreciate Kylie's purpose in investigating Covington. It had something to do with Brian, but he did not understand the full extent. Although Covington blamed Brian for the security guard's murder, he didn't think he did it, and neither did Kylie.

On an impulse, he returned to the office. The receptionist was still there. He asked her if he could look at the register of people who signed in on the night the security guard died. At first, she would not let him, saying this was privileged information. But after a little persuasion, she conceded, also upset by the argument between Covington and Emilio, the news of which had travelled through the firm.

Ron looked at the register and what he saw surprised him. He noticed a line with no writing on it, but somebody had obviously removed their name. He remembered an old childhood trick where you found out the writing underneath by rubbing a pencil over the area. Sure enough, a name appeared.

Ron rushed out of the building a second time. He understood where he was going now.

Ron reached the Pont de la Tour restaurant in record time as he brushed past the crowd walking over Tower Bridge. He was out of breath as he walked up to the reception at the restaurant. Thankfully, they recognised Kylie from Ron's description and from the fact this was a regular haunt of hers.

They would not give Ron her address, but they did telephone Kylie to advise that somebody was looking for her. She came down to the restaurant immediately after the call and saw Ron waiting.

Kylie sat Ron down and offered him a drink. Ron didn't realise he was so thirsty as he drank his pint of Guinness in one go. He blurted out his story about the argument and how he'd found that name on the register.

Kylie leaned back and exhaled sharply.

'Ron, thanks for coming to me. Now, I must pass this message on, where it can do some good.'

'Do you know where Brian is?' Ron asked.

'Yes, and he is safe, but he doesn't realise what's happening here. This information will definitely help.'

***

Kylie bought Ron another pint and left the restaurant.

Outside, as she stood by the entrance to her lobby, a figure emerged from the shadows.

'What do you want?' she asked, with a tremor in her voice.

CHAPTER NINETEEN

FRIDAY 11TH APRIL 2008
KONA, BIG ISLAND (LOCAL TIME 08.00)

Pika drove to the Kona Farmer's and Crafts market to set up his stall, which was his normal daily routine, except Tuesdays, when the market closed. As he drove past the Jimenez hotel, Pika noticed several people outside, sweeping the paths, watering the flowers and putting up bunting. This was not a holiday weekend, and he wondered why there was so much activity.

Also, there were more people on the street than normal and he thought he must have missed something. Shops were opening earlier than usual, there were more police cars in evidence; what was going on?

When he arrived at the market, most of the stallholders were already there, and now Pika was certain something was happening. On the way to his stall, he passed one of his oldest friends.

'Hey Liam, what's happening? Why are there so many people here?'

'Haven't you heard? Pika, we are being visited by royalty today.'

'Is Princess Kawananakoa coming to the Big Island?' He asked with eager anticipation.

'No, silly,' Liam laughed. 'She's probably still sitting on her throne at the Iolani Palace. No, *Senor* Henrique Jimenez, the Mexican Minister for Culture and the owner of the worldwide Jimenez hotel chain is arriving for a brief stay. He'll be here for the weekend.'

Pika was astounded.

'Why is he coming to the Big Island?'

'Don't know. Probably, he wants to visit his son.'

Pika wasn't so sure of this. He had to find out more information.

***

At his stall, Pika began removing the materials from the various artefacts he kept there to show that he was open for business. Although the stall contained many Hawaiian relics and treasures, these did not bring in the bulk of his income, but they made a useful front for his proper business.

A nondescript man arrived, dressed in pale slacks and a blue short-sleeved shirt, so he wouldn't stand out in a crowd. His blond hair, military haircut and general demeanour, though, would give him plenty of attention from the locals.

Pika recognised him as a CIA agent.

'I've a message from Miriam,' he said. 'You have a phone for me.'

Pika had been expecting him and reached into a pocket for the phone, which he handed over.

'I want to get a message to Miriam,' Pika said.

'Oh, yes?'

'Henrique Jimenez is arriving today and will stay for the weekend.'

'Right,' he said. 'I'll make sure she hears about it.'

Pika did not like the agent's casual attitude. He grabbed the man's shirt and said tightly, 'No, you will tell her now. This is important.'

'Okay, OK, I'll phone right now.'

The agent dialled, a voice answered, and the agent forwarded the message.

'That's good,' Pika said. 'Now get on a plane and take that phone to Miriam.'

***

At CIA HQ, it was early afternoon, Miriam became animated following this phone call. She stood out in the corridor and shouted, 'Matt, I need you. *Now!*'

197

Heads turned as the rest of the staff wondered what had got into Miriam. Matt Booker, though, heeded her call and ran the twenty yards from his office as if his life depended on it.

'What is it, Miriam?'

'I've just had a phone call from our runner in Hawaii. He said Henrique Jimenez is arriving on the Big Island today.'

'Do we know why?'

'No, possibly it's just to visit his son, but maybe there's something else involved.'

'Jimenez is taking a risk coming on to US soil. He knows he's suspected of various infractions, not the least relating to events surrounding the election, but probably considers he's safe from prosecution because of diplomatic immunity.'

'For the time being, he is safe, but we need to make the case against him and ask the Mexican President to lift his immunity.'

'Do we have enough evidence for that?'

'I'm not sure, but we need to review the situation.'

'How much time is there?'

'Two days. Jimenez leaves the island on Sunday.'

***

Miriam closed the door to her office and sat down with Matt Booker. Time was now of the greatest importance, as they couldn't say when Henrique Jimenez would visit his son in Hawaii again.

'It's not just about Henrique Jimenez,' Miriam began. 'We should coordinate our actions with Zurich and London.'

'OK, but is there enough evidence to arrest Jimenez, assuming we can get the President to waive his diplomatic immunity?' Booker asked.

'Santos is our witness to the election fraud and the physical pressure on the local population,' Miriam said, 'and his friendship with young Pablo now becomes even more important, because we suspect his death is linked to the bullying of the peasants.'

'Santos mentioned Pablo's grandfather, Henrique's friend. Where does he fit in to all of this?' Booker asked.

198

'My God, The Professor!' Miriam said. 'I'd forgotten about him. He lives on the Big Island. We need to contact Pika.'

Miriam and Booker stopped their discussion as Miriam dialled Pika's number in Kona.

Pika's phone rang, and he answered.

'Hello?' Pika said, uncertain it was Miriam calling.

'Hi Pika, I've got Special Agent Booker with me, you're on speaker phone.'

'Yes, Miriam; you've heard the news?'

'Yes, Pika. Events are happening fast at this end and I need you to do something for me.'

'What is it?'

'Do you know a man they call The Professor?'

'Yes, he's Mexican. He keeps himself very quiet, but he's rumoured to be involved in drugs.'

'It's not a rumour, Pika,' Miriam said. 'We need you to keep track of him. He and Henrique Jimenez are old friends and The Professor may try to contact Jimenez whilst he's on the Big Island.'

'Pika, Matt Booker, when is Jimenez arriving on the Big Island?'

'There's a private plane due early afternoon.'

'OK, tell us when he arrives and anything you can find out about The Professor.'

'Will do,' Pika confirmed.

***

Miriam and Booker resumed their discussion.

'While we are on the drug situation, we need information from the FBI on how the investigation into the English guy is going. What have they found out?'

'Right,' Miriam agreed. 'I'll speak to Agent Reed to see what they've learned. I'll also tell him the news about Henrique Jimenez so they can observe him as well.'

'We want to keep the FBI presence low key.'

'Agreed.'

'What about your initial contact, Brian? Do we need him any more?'

'Definitely. Even though I downloaded the information from his USB stick, there may be more he knows about the London operation. Anyway, I don't want to drop him now, in case the other side became suspicious. I don't want to put him at risk. We wouldn't have uncovered any of this without him and the various links involved, had we not met by accident on that plane to Kona?'

'OK, so we keep him under Daphne's protection?'

'For the time being, but Daphne has also met up with a British agent, so we should bring him in on what we know.'

'That makes sense; the Brits are involved with the money-laundering operation and we should bring everything together at the same time.'

'When we speak to them, with Daphne, Brian should also be there.'

'Why?' Booker asked.

'As I said, he provided the impetus, and even though he is way out of his depth, he wants to get home eventually and we should help him. Also, he has this girlfriend who phoned him when we were in Kona. She helped with information from the firm at the centre of the money-laundering operation. She may also have vital information. We should tell the Brits about that.'

'Is that it?' Booker asked. 'It's quite a complex situation.'

'There is one last piece of the puzzle. The murder of Pablo Segura, The Professor's grandson. It was the reason my relationship with Brian developed initially. I saw his face on a CNN news programme, but there was no sound, so I didn't understand what the story was about originally. Brian's girlfriend also saw the programme, and that was the reason she phoned him.'

'The phone from the English guy we are holding will arrive here tomorrow morning and it should also have info we can use connecting him with Miguel Jimenez and Brian's boss in London.

'We will need to coordinate with the Brits so that when we ring young Segura's phone, the person who answers will be the killer and the London police can claim the glory of arresting that man.'

***

Miriam dialled FBI Agent Reed's number in Kona.

'Agent Reed, it's Miriam Snape. I wondered what stage you were at with the interrogation of the Englishman?'

'It didn't take long to break him down, Miriam,' Agent Reed confirmed, 'and now he won't stop talking.'

'That's good news,' Miriam said.

'It appears that some guy, through Covington, used him to break into this other British guy's apartment in London and then Covington sent him off to Hawaii to spy on him. He never realised where he was going. When he got here, he had nowhere to stay, no money, and he was starving.'

'Tell me, did he go to the desk at the hotel the night he arrived? Pretending to be armed and asking for money?'

'Yes, how did you know?'

'It's a long story.'

'Where did he get the drugs?'

'He went back to the hotel and met one of the workers. They were told to put him in the workers' rooms, where they fed him. There was a message on his cell phone to prove this. Only now, he can't find his phone.'

'And one worker gave him the drugs?'

'He became friendly with this one guy, who said there was somebody who could supply him. But he also said he'd never taken drugs, if you can believe that,' the agent said.

'Where is he now?' Miriam asked.

'We've got him locked up in the local cop shop.'

'We'll need to get him off the island. I'll have a word with Frank McCarthy to arrange a transfer.'

'Fine by me. He'll be off our hands.'

'Oh, one other thing, Agent Reed,' Miriam said. 'Henrique Jimenez is coming to the Big Island today.'

'The owner of the hotel?'

'Yes, and the Mexican Minister for Culture. You'll probably see more activity around the hotel today.'

'The grapevine suggested a major figure is coming. The local cops are out in force, making sure there's no trouble.'

***

Miriam put the phone down and dialled Frank McCarthy at FBI HQ.

'Frank, hi, it's Miriam.'

Miriam explained the situation regarding the Englishman, and that she thought it best he should leave Hawaii. Frank agreed it might not be safe for him to remain in the custody of the local police if the situation was about to hot up there. He would contact Agent Reed and arrange for the thug to be brought to Washington.

***

Next, Miriam looked at the time and estimated it would be nine o'clock in the evening in Zurich. She dialled Daphne's number.

'Hi Daphne, it's Miriam. How's it going?'

'Hi, Miriam. Everything is fine here. I'm having dinner with Joe; he works for MI5 and we can see Brian eating dinner on the other side of the room.'

'Haven't you contacted Brian?'

'Yes, we chatted on the plane, but not since we've been in the hotel.' Daphne said. 'We wanted to give him some room, to see what he did.'

'Why did you decide to do that?' Miriam asked.

'Well, Miriam, Joe, and I agreed to play it cautiously. Do you realise his actual name isn't Brian Jenkins?'

'I know that. He travelled under the name of Bernd Muller.'

'But Brian Jenkins isn't his real name. It's really Brian Roberts.'

'How did you find out?'

'Apparently Joe was already here in Zurich. He was tracking Brian's boss, who came to open a new bank account. Joe had some help from a Swiss agent, called Emily, who was already investigating a situation which involved Brian at his asset management firm in Zurich.'

'Go on, Daphne; this is very interesting.'

'Apparently, one of the firm's wealthy clients accused Brian of fraud. Emily investigated and found the client had underworld contacts. Brian's boss was suspicious of his accuser and arranged for Brian to take a job in London after changing his name. The bank Covington used gave him the job.'

'From one crook to another,' Miriam said.

'Emily investigated the client and exposed him as the fraudster, not Brian, thereby clearing his name. The client is now in jail, serving a long-term sentence. Brian doesn't realise his name was cleared, but we weren't sure just how much we could trust him.'

'Okay, Daphne. I need to talk with you and Joe about what is happening here. Part of it involves Covington and his business in London. Also, we may find out about a murder the British cops are investigating.'

'When do you want to do this?'

'I'll have some more information tomorrow morning. I'm expecting a package from Hawaii, which should arrive on the red eye. You get in touch with Brian, perhaps at breakfast, let's allow him a good sleep tonight. We'll arrange the call for nine my time, which will be three in the afternoon your time.'

***

Daphne relayed Miriam's call to Joe, as he enjoyed his third large glass of red wine. As they were talking, Brian walked over and reintroduced himself to Daphne.

'Hello Daphne; I thought it was you. I'm not disturbing you, am I?'

Joe almost spilled his wine over his white shirt, as he was not expecting Brian to make contact.

'No, not at all, Brian. We saw you over there, but thought you preferred to be alone.'

'I've realised that I've been alone for too long. I've been trying to contact a friend, but she's not answering.'

'Brian, this is Joe,' Daphne said. 'Why don't you join us?'

'Yes, please,' Joe said. 'Would you like a glass of wine. It's very good.'

'Ah, a fellow Englishman,' Brian observed. 'Why not? It'll be good to have some company.'

'Who is this girl you've been trying to contact?'

'Oh, it's just a friend, but being in the US, the time difference made it difficult for us to speak at normal hours. Now I'm back in Europe, I thought it'd be easier. But apparently, it's not.'

Joe stretched his arms above his head and yawned.

'Look, you must excuse me, it's been busy these past few days, so I'm off to bed. We may meet again tomorrow, Brian.'

Brian nodded towards Joe.

'Goodnight, Daphne, sleep well.'

'Goodnight, Joe.'

Brian turned towards Daphne.

'Have you met Joe before?'

'No, he met me at the airport.'

'He seems like a nice guy, knows how to drink his wine, though.'

Daphne laughed.

***

Up in his penthouse room, where he met Emily, Joe sat on the bed and put in a call to Helen.

'Hi Helen.'

'Hi Joe,' Helen said. 'Are you having fun with these women in Zurich? Will you want to come home to poor little me?'

'Helen, be serious for a moment. I've just met Brian.'

'What, Kylie's Brian?'

'Yes.'

'What's he like?'

'Seems like a nice guy. Quite friendly. He had no clue who I was, or that Daphne was shadowing him. He seemed quite lonely, really.'

'That's interesting.'

'Ah, but you haven't heard the best bit yet. He said he's been trying to contact his girlfriend but can't reach her. He must have been trying to get in touch with Kylie. I wonder why she is not answering.'

'OK, Joe, you leave that to me. I'll try phoning her on some pretext, then if she doesn't answer, I'll get Jeremy to go over to her flat.'

CHAPTER TWENTY

Kylie stared at the man in front of her, one arm outstretched, holding a gun, pointing to her face just six inches away. She knew who he was, and she despised him.

'What do you want?' she asked. 'Police come down this street regularly, so I'd leave now if I were you.'

Kylie tried to sound stronger than she felt inside. Her body was trembling and she could feel her knees shaking. The sheer anger she had for this man allowed her to overcome the fear of what might happen next.

After his trip to Switzerland, Covington could not understand how his confidence had completely vanished. This was not something he had previously contemplated. If Kylie had appreciated how these events affected his mental state, she might have acted less aggressively towards him.

As a business owner and leader of men, Covington had always prided himself on his well-groomed appearance. While he was unmarried, or even without a partner, Covington believed he could have any woman he wanted. He could use his natural charm and he would succeed. But that hadn't worked with Emily. He wasn't used to failure.

Now, his hair was unkempt and his tie loosened against his unbuttoned shirt. If Kylie had taken notice of his physical appearance, she might have seen his scuffed shoes where he had kicked in anger against the wall outside her apartment, whilst waiting for her to appear. She could have seen the bloodstained knuckles from when he had punched the bricks of her building in exasperation. She would have recognised that here was a man at the end of his tether. A man who was very dangerous.

Kylie stood there as Covington continued to hold the gun at her head, not saying a word. His eyes were fierce, his mouth shaped into a snarl. She didn't know what to do, other than to repeat the question.

'What do you want?'

Covington grabbed an arm and twisted it behind her back, causing Kylie to cry in pain.

'Inside,' he ordered.

Kylie used her other arm to reach into her pocket for a key to open the door. Roughly, he pushed her forward, kicking the door shut behind him. They walked up the stairs to her apartment. Kylie thought of knocking on the doors of the other flat owners on the way up, but she was uncertain anyone else was home and his grip on her arm was too tight.

At the door to her apartment, Kylie stood, daring him to harm her. She didn't believe he had the guts to force her to open the door, but she was wrong.

Covington's grip on her arm tightened behind her back, forcing out another scream, which she hoped might bring somebody out of their flat. It didn't. Kylie had no choice but to open the door, but as she did so, Covington pushed her so forcefully that she fell forward, hitting her head on the floor, causing blood to flow.

He closed the door and grabbed Kylie underneath her armpit, yanking her up from her prostrate position, making her cry out again. Tears were now rolling down Kylie's cheek as her inner fear overwhelmed her dogged determination to remain steadfast against this brute.

Covington pulled Kylie into the lounge and sat her on one of her favourite Wishbone dining chairs. He looked around the room, searching for something with which to secure her. Kylie saw an opportunity and leapt towards the hallway and the exit, but Covington was quicker. He still had the gun in his hand and swiped it across her face, knocking Kylie to the floor.

When she came to, with arms tied behind her back and feet secured to the legs of the chair, there was blood trickling down from the gash in her forehead where Covington's gun had hit her. Kylie raised her face, sitting there, looking at him, now turned away in contemplation. Her fear had disappeared, to be replaced by sheer terror.

How dare this monster do this to me? she thought. The blood dripped down her cheek and onto the collar of the satin blouse she bought recently. It cost a fortune, now it was ruined. *You will pay for this!*

The phone rang. Both Covington and Kylie immediately turned their attention to the ringing of the landline, and to the message that followed.

'Kylie, it's me, Helen. Can you call me as soon as you get this? We're trying to reach you and worried that nobody can get in touch with you. Brian has said he had difficulty in contacting you. Call me, Kylie, I'm at home.'

At the mention of Brian's name, Covington became alert.

'Where is Brian?' he spat at Kylie, slamming his fist into her ribs.

One for Emily, he thought.

'I don't know,' she said, pleading with him.

***

'Hi, Jeremy, it's me Helen.'

'Hi Helen, how are you? Can I help with anything?' Jeremy asked.

'Yes, I've just tried to phone Kylie at home and she's not answering. I'm worried. Apparently, Brian also tried to contact her without success. Can you go to her flat and see if she's there, and that she is all right?'

'How do you know Brian's tried to contact her?'

'Long story, but Joe's in Zurich and he met Brian at the hotel. It came up in conversation.'

Jeremy wasn't aware that Brian knew Joe, but somehow, he did.

'Okay, Helen, I'm on my way.'

***

Jeremy drove to Kylie's flat as fast as legally possible, and luckily, there was a parking space immediately outside. A rarity.

If Kylie wasn't answering her phone, she was probably in the Pont. He walked in to the bar through the Shad Thames entrance, which was right next to the front door of the apartments in which Kylie lived.

As he entered, he saw Ron Mathis downing the pint Kylie bought him and preparing to leave. Jeremy walked up to him.

'Hi Ron,' Jeremy said. 'Do you remember me?'

'Yes, I saw you in the coffee bar with Mr Covington.'

'That's right, I was doing some business with him. But I'm also a friend of Kylie.'

Ron wasn't certain he should trust Jeremy.

'She's just left. She bought me this pint.'

'Do you know where she was going?'

'I think she was going to her flat. She said she had to forward the message I had just given her.'

'What message was that?' Jeremy asked.

'I don't know if I should tell you.'

'Ron, this is very important. I'm her friend and we have been working together to help Brian. Her life may be in danger.'

Ron told Jeremy about the fight at the office and how he'd gone back and found the name on the register.

'Right, Ron, come with me, I may need your help.'

Jeremy and Ron rushed out of the Pont and turned left towards Kylie's apartment. The door was open.

'Quick, something's wrong. This door was not open a few minutes ago.'

They rushed upstairs as fast as they could. Jeremy was panting by the time he was only halfway to Kylie's front door, but Ron was much fitter and leapt up two steps at a time.

'The door's shut,' Ron shouted back at Jeremy.

'Can you hear anything inside?' Jeremy asked, puffing heavily.

'No, I don't think so. Wait, there is something. It sounds like groaning.'

'Bash the door down; we can deal with the consequences later.'

Ron was strong, even though he was wiry in appearance, but the door would not budge. Eventually, Jeremy caught up with Ron, and together, they broke the door down. Inside, they found Kylie, still tied to the chair, face slumped on her chest. She was making a whimpering sound.

She had been beaten senseless. There were bruises on her face; her hair had blood matted on it where the gun had hit her and there were deep gouges on her ankle where the rope was tied too tight.

'Shall I untie her?' Ron asked.

'Wait a minute, we should probably do it together. She may fall otherwise. First, I'll phone for an ambulance.'

Gently, they untied the ankles from the chair legs. The horrendous red weals almost made Ron vomit. Next, Jeremy went round the back of the chair, instructing Ron to catch Kylie when she fell as they freed her wrists. As expected, Kylie fell forward, but Ron was strong enough to support her.

Ron held Kylie by her shoulders as Jeremy reached for her feet. Together they moved Kylie, and eased her gently onto the floor, laying her on her side. Jeremy fetched a cushion and placed it under her feet to help with the circulation, whilst making sure not to block her airways.

Jeremy heard the ambulance siren outside. The door buzzer rang and voices shouted upwards.

'Is everything all right up there?'

'We're on the top floor,' Jeremy said, 'we have a young lady badly beaten.'

There was a rush of noise on the stairs as three burly ambulancemen arrived in Kylie's flat.

'It would be the top floor,' one man said.

'Crikey, somebody's done a job on her,' another commented.

The third ambulanceman knelt by her side to check the pulse in her neck.

'The pulse is weak,' he said, 'and she's lost some blood. We need to get her admitted as soon as possible.'

Whilst his colleagues carefully lifted Kylie onto a mobile stretcher and slowly took her downstairs to the waiting ambulance, the third of the crew took notes from Jeremy.

'No, we're not related to the victim, just friends.'

'Who might have done this?' the third crew man asked.

'I have an idea and I'm going to phone Detective Sergeant Mortimer at the City Police. Where will you be taking her?'

'The nearest A&E department is at St Thomas's. We'll also inform the police and meet you there.'

***

After the ambulancemen left, Jeremy sat Ron down.

'Right, Covington is on the loose, and if I'm correct, he is very dangerous.' Jeremy said.

'What should I do?' Ron asked.

'Go home and keep quiet. Don't go near your office in case he returns. I don't know how he got Kylie's address. Chances are he followed you to her, so that makes you a potential target.'

'Can I come with you?' Ron asked. 'If Covington is as dangerous as you say and he knows I met Kylie, then he will be after me. If you're going to talk to the police, they'll want to talk to me as well. I'll need protection.'

Jeremy agreed and then dialled Detective Sergeant Mortimer.

Mortimer said that he, personally, would meet him at the hospital and asked Jeremy to bring Ron along, who he considered vital to the case. He would station two men near Covington's office, in case he returned.

***

At the hospital, Jeremy phoned Helen to tell her the news.

'I was afraid something bad had happened,' she said.

'I contacted Detective Sergeant Mortimer, of the City Police, and he should be here any minute. Do you want me to mention your involvement?'

'You could do, although I'm not sure he'll be happy about it, but he will soon realise that this is a complicated case. I'll phone Joe to give him the news.'

As he was talking to Helen, a doctor came out of the emergency room, where she had been looking after Kylie.

'Hold on, Helen, I have the doctor here. There may be more news.'

'Mr Crichton-Smith?' the doctor asked. 'Are you a relative of Miss Griggs?'

'No, just good friends,' Jeremy replied.

'Me too,' Ron said.

'Does she have any relatives?'

'I'm not sure,' Jeremy replied. 'None she's mentioned. Is it important?'

'We need to contact a next of kin. It is extremely important. I should not tell you this, but under the circumstances, I will. The blow to the head has caused a slight crack in the skull, which has bled. We need to be very careful and the next forty-eight hours will be crucial to her recovery.'

'She will recover, though, won't she?' Ron asked.

'We can't be sure.'

'I'll contact her office,' Jeremy said. 'The HR department should provide me with details.'

'That would be good,' the doctor said. 'In the meantime, I must get back to her. We need to make sure that her vital signs remain stable.'

As the doctor prepared to return to Kylie, a nurse rushed out of the room where they were treating her.

'She's crashing!' the nurse cried out.

Immediately, five people hurried towards Kylie's room, including the doctor, trying to stabilise her.

'Did you hear that conversation, Helen?' Jeremy asked.

'If not all of it, I understood the meaning. I'll phone Joe now. Have the police arrived?'

***

Jeremy looked around and saw DS Mortimer strolling down the corridor, accompanied by two police officers in uniform. As he reached Jeremy and Ron, his notebook was being prepared for their statements.

'Right, let's sit down over there.'

Jeremy gave DS Mortimer the basic story about Kylie being beaten up, probably by Covington, but there were no witnesses to prove that.

'It must be him. Who else would have done it?' Ron asked.

'Excuse me, sir,' DS Mortimer said, addressing Ron. 'You'll have your chance to speak in a minute.'

Jeremy did not tell DS Mortimer about Ron's message to Kylie but thought that should come from Ron himself. He did, however, mention that he worked with Helen and Joe, from MI5, trying to prove that Covington was employing foreign citizens, in this case Mexicans, without proper immigration papers.

'Ah, you forgot to mention that when we spoke previously, Mr Crichton-Smith.'

'Yes, I'm sorry, Detective Sergeant, but at that stage, I didn't feel I could. I have now informed my MI5 contacts, Helen and Joe Thompson, I am speaking with you about this incident and they will contact you shortly.'

Ron's mouth opened wide when he heard Jeremy talking about MI5.

DS Mortimer scratched his head.

'I said I don't like loose ends,' he said. 'Is there anything else you're not telling me?'

'For the record, I knew that Brian Jenkins had left the UK. He was in Hawaii. His actual name is Brian Roberts, and he is currently in Zurich.'

'So, Mr Covington was correct in his assertion that he had left the country, maybe he was also correct that this Brian Jenkins, or Roberts, killed the young Mexican.'

'I don't believe he did. Brian was in Hawaii, trying to prove his innocence,' Jeremy stated.

'According to you,' DS Mortimer said, not believing Jeremy. 'Now, what is your part in this story, Mr Mathis.'

Ron, who was extremely nervous, told the detective sergeant everything he knew concerning the fight between Covington and Emilio Jimenez, the name he saw on the register and how Kylie thought this was an important message to forward.

'Did she say to whom the message was to be forwarded?' DS Mortimer asked.

Ron could only say, 'No.'

Jeremy interrupted, 'I'm sure she wanted to tell Helen Thompson.'

'Your friend also works for MI5?'

'No,' Jeremy said, exasperated with DS Mortimer. 'She knew her because Helen tried to set up a relationship between me and Kylie. She only found out later that Helen worked for MI5. Brian was the guy she fancied, not me!'

'Talk about loose ends. Is there anything else?'

'Since you ask, Brian left the country because he had information that Covington's company was guilty of money laundering.'

'Is that true?' Ron asked.

'Yes, Ron,' Jeremy said, 'but somebody killed Pablo Segura and blamed Brian, although he is totally innocent.'

'So you say,' DS Mortimer said.

'But in Hawaii, Brian met a woman who worked for the CIA.'

'The CIA are involved now, are they?' Mortimer asked, incredulous at this latest offering.

'Yes, Miguel Jimenez is the brother of Emilio Jimenez, and he runs the hotel in Hawaii where Brian stayed with the CIA woman.'

'OK, stop, I can't take any more. My notebook is not big enough.'

***

Sweat was oozing from Detective Sergeant Mortimer's brow as he tried to digest Jeremy's long-winded story. He was sure there was more to glean, but for now, his primary task was to secure this young woman's safety.

Mortimer instructed his men to wait outside Kylie's room to make sure nobody tried to attack her again. The doctor emerged, and Mortimer informed her what was happening. She nodded in agreement.

Jeremy went over and talked to the doctor.

'Is she OK?'

'She seems to be stable for now, but as I said earlier, the next forty-eight hours will be difficult.'

***

The detective's phone rang.

'Yes, I've just been speaking to him,' Mortimer said, 'and the girl is safe for the time being. She will be under observation, guarded by two of my best men.'

Jeremy was watching Mortimer's face intently, trying to find out who was talking to him and what they were saying.

'It appears to be a very complicated story,' Mortimer said, 'and I'm not sure I've got all the angles figured out. Yes, it would be helpful to have your input. I'm based at Bishopsgate. I'll see you tomorrow morning.'

Mortimer finished the call and turned to Jeremy.

'That was your MI5 friend.'

'I gathered,' Jeremy said.

'What will you do now?' Mortimer asked.

'I thought I'd wait to be here when she comes round.'

'Can I wait too? I'm scared to go home,' Ron asked.

'Sure,' Jeremy said, putting his arm around Ron's shoulder.

CHAPTER TWENTY-ONE

Joe always had trouble sleeping, especially when he was in a strange bed, so when he returned to his room, he put on the television and poured himself a Scotch from the minibar. He drifted off but awoke when his mobile phone rang. It was Helen.

'Hello, did you want to wish me good night?' he asked.

Helen sounded agitated.

'Joe, we have a problem.'

Joe sat ramrod straight on the sofa as he digested Helen's news.

'Where is she now?'

'In St Thomas's hospital. Jeremy is there and so are the police.'

'Where is Covington?'

'We don't know. They have police stationed by his office. He's not at his home address. Local police have checked. We need to find him.'

'Okay, Helen, calm down,' Joe said a little too casually. 'Let me think.'

'You need to come home.'

'You're right, but first I need to tell Brian and Daphne.'

'Why?'

'So that she can inform her people in the US. This may affect the timing of their investigation.'

'When will you be back?'

'The first flight is due to leave at six thirty, so I should be with you by mid-morning.'

Joe ended the call and then dialled Daphne. She had already been sleeping but was fully alert when she heard the news. She agreed to go to Joe's room immediately.

Next, Joe phoned the front desk, saying he needed to contact Brian urgently, or Bernd Muller as he registered at the hotel. The hotel agreed to connect Brian to Joe's room.

'Hello,' he said sleepily.

'Brian, I need you to concentrate. You must come to my room now. I have some news about Kylie.'

'How do you know Kylie?' Brian asked suspiciously.

'It's a long story. I'll tell you when you get here. It's room 401.'

***

Daphne arrived at Joe's room first and was making coffee when Brian arrived. He smelled the rich aroma as he walked through the door. Joe was still in his robe as he opened the door to Brian, who was slightly suspicious when he saw Daphne already there.

'What's going on?' he asked. 'What's this about Kylie?'

'Sit down, Brian, there's a lot to take in,' Daphne said.

'You sound like a woman I met in Hawaii,' Brian said. 'She always sounded like she wanted to take care of me.'

'Miriam,' Daphne and Joe announced in unison.

Brian blinked in utter disbelief and with a growing sick sensation in his stomach.

'Okay, this is strange.'

'Brian,' Joe said, 'let me tell you about Kylie first and Daphne can fill you in afterwards.'

He sat back in his seat with his arms crossed, nervous.

'Kylie is in hospital. She's been badly beaten. She has a cracked skull and is under observation.'

'How?' Brian asked. 'What happened?'

'We think Patrick Covington, your boss, did this.'

'Oh fuck!' Brian said, holding the knuckles of his hand to his mouth. 'When?'

'A few hours ago. Jeremy is with her, so is your colleague, Ron.'

'Where is Covington now?'

'No idea. The police are still searching for him. Do you know where he might be?'

'Me? No, I only saw him at the office, but you might try his head of security, Emilio Jimenez.'

'That's a good point. I'll phone Helen now so she can give a message to the police. Why don't you take over, Daphne?'

'Okay, Joe,' Daphne said. 'Brian, I work with Miriam at the CIA and she asked me to keep track of your whereabouts in case anything happened to you.'

'Why, what might happen?' Brian asked.

'It's very clear this is a global case, as you are well aware. She said you assumed originally it was a domestic problem, which your authorities could easily handle. But you noticed the impact in the US, Mexico and Switzerland, which made it an international operation.'

'I was right. Your job is to look after me.'

'Partly,' Daphne confirmed. 'Miriam asked me to meet with the British Secret Service to inform them of our knowledge so we can combine our efforts. The fact that Joe was already in Switzerland working on another case was a coincidence.'

'Hang on! So, Joe works for the Secret Service?' Brian asked.

'That's correct,' Joe intervened.

'This is really weird,' Brian said. 'How did you meet Kylie?'

'Funnily enough, we met in a pub by Hammersmith Bridge, when she tried to avoid the attentions of an overenthusiastic male friend. Now, my wife Helen tries to introduce Kylie to people she thinks might be suitable, such as Jeremy.'

'Jeremy?' Brian laughed. 'She's too fussy for Jeremy.'

'We realise that now. Ever since you disappeared, it's been obvious that you are the one for her.'

'Me? Now you are joking.'

Brian had not considered the possibility before.

'Did Kylie realise you worked for the Secret Service?' Brian asked.

'Not initially, but I worked on this case involving money laundering and Jeremy helped me on some aspects.'

'But I went to Jeremy and said I had evidence of money laundering at my firm. He was no good. He said he'd get back to me, but he didn't.'

'Ah, yes,' Joe acknowledged. 'That was my fault. He tried to tell me about you, but I was unavailable and he wasn't sure how much he could disclose to you at the time. You then rushed off to Hawaii.'

'After my flat was burgled, and an enormous lump of a guy threatened me with a knife.'

'Agreed, but we didn't understand where you were and so couldn't help you.'

'That's where Miriam intervened.' Daphne said.

'Was that planned?' Brian asked.

'No,' Joe said. 'It was a complete fluke, but it helped break the case. This happens all the time. You see these movies on television and they all persuade you that the police, or the CIA, are super-efficient because of their methods, but mostly it's luck.'

'Because we have all sides of the story, we are experts at putting the pieces together,' Daphne said, trying to defend her organisation.

'But it wasn't until Miriam worked out that the Jimenez family had to be organising the drug running from Mexico that she realised they controlled the money laundering in London as well. They were using a small bank here in Zurich to manage the money flow. That was the point where we completed the entire picture.'

'When we found out that Pablo Segura's death at your office was murder, and not an accident,' Daphne said, 'we realised we had to act quickly.'

'Kylie getting injured was unexpected, but this has made us move even faster and we need to get back to London on the first flight tomorrow morning,' Joe said.

'What happens then?' Brian asked, grateful for the reviving effects of the coffee.

'Daphne and I will contact the police and help them in their investigations.' Joe said.

'What about me?' Brian asked. 'Am I allowed to return to the UK?'

'We think so,' Joe said, not totally sure. 'We believe the police have cleared you of the murder allegation. However, Border Control may wish to interview you on your return to the country. But don't worry, Daphne and I will be there to assist.'

'What passport will you be travelling under?' Daphne asked.

Brian hadn't considered that his name would make any difference. He realised he no longer needed the Bernd Muller passport.

'Why, Brian Jenkins, of course.'

'Why don't you enter under your proper name?' Daphne asked. 'Brian Roberts.'

'You know about that?' Brian asked. 'Of course you do. Why am I surprised?'

'Don't worry, Brian,' Daphne said. 'I understand you're cleared of your problems in Switzerland and you can safely use your actual name.'

'No more subterfuge,' Joe said. 'Tell the truth.'

***

SATURDAY 12TH APRIL 2008

Joe, Daphne, and Brian met in the hotel lobby at five o'clock. The sky was still dark, but there were the beginnings of a sunrise. The desk clerk thought it strange how many people checked out early in the past week. However, as requested, he arranged for a taxi to take these three to the airport to be in time for the early morning departure to London.

The absence of conversation between his passengers did not surprise the taxi driver. It was very early in the morning and they appeared very serious. There was minimal traffic to the airport and the journey only took forty minutes. Fog can be a hazard for early morning flights from Zurich, but not on this day. The BA flight arrived on time and reached Heathrow as scheduled, at seven o'clock UK time. The Swiss would appreciate the efficiency of this flight.

At the airport, queues to enter the UK through Passport Control were light. Joe and Daphne went ahead of Brian with no problem.

However, the official noticed Brian's passport photograph did not match the name the police had submitted for them to review. He asked Brian to step aside as he closed his channel.

Police arrived and escorted Brian to a nearby room. Joe and Daphne talked to one of the police officers, and after showing their credentials, assured him Brian should be able to leave freely.

Nevertheless, the police insisted on questioning Brian. Joe and Daphne insisted on being present whilst the questioning took place. After less than an hour and various phone calls, the police allowed Brian to leave, but Joe had to provide assurances he would be responsible for Brian until they could resolve the matter.

Upon leaving the airport, Joe suggested he and Daphne should meet Helen and discuss what they needed to do next. Brian, though, wanted to see Kylie urgently.

***

At Joe and Helen's apartment, Helen wandered around in her dressing gown, wearing fluffy pink slippers and dark glasses. When Joe and Daphne arrived, he laughed at Helen's outfit, especially the slippers. Daphne turned away, embarrassed, and walked towards an adjacent window.

Helen was agitated and extremely angry with Joe for not warning her he was bringing Daphne as well.

'I have not slept a wink all night, worrying about Kylie and thinking about what happens next,' she said.

Joe walked over and put an arm around his wife.

'Sorry, Helen, I didn't think,' he said. 'Helen, I want you to meet Daphne.'

***

Brian took the underground from Heathrow to Westminster, where he alighted and crossed the bridge before walking the short distance to St Thomas's Hospital. At the front desk, he asked for Kylie.

A police officer arrived and asked him for some identification.

'I'm Brian Roberts—no Jenkins,' he corrected himself. 'I'm a friend of Kylie Griggs.'

'Wait here, please,' the officer instructed. He walked away and spoke into his personal radio. After nodding a few times, he came back to Brian.

'We've been alerted of your return to the UK, and Detective Sergeant Mortimer wants to talk to you. He is coming to the hospital now. But in the meantime, you have clearance to see Miss Griggs.'

Brian breathed a sigh of relief. He hadn't expected there to be police here, or for them to be interested in talking to him. He just hadn't understood the situation, but it seemed reasonable. At least he could visit Kylie.

In the corridor outside Kylie's room, another police officer stood on guard, while Jeremy was in a chair, asleep with his head slumped backwards. As he walked towards Jeremy, there was a cry behind him.

'Brian, I'm so glad you're here.'

It was Ron Mathis, smiling and walking towards him with a cup of something hot in his hand.

'Hello, Ron, what's going on?'

'Well, you know Covington beat up Kylie; we've been here waiting in case she awoke.'

'Did she?'

'No, but she seems to have had a stable night. Earlier, there was a big rumpus when she crashed, but the doctors and nurses came running and fixed that. Since then, it's been quiet.'

'Have you both been here all night?'

'Yes, well, we couldn't leave her on her own, could we?'

Brian hugged Ron, who was bemused by this action.

'You're a good man, Ron.'

Ron blushed.

'I see Jeremy's unconscious. Have you had any sleep?'

'Nah, I can't sleep when something like this is happening.'

As Brian and Ron were talking, Jeremy awoke, turned his head towards them and smiled.

'Hello stranger,' he said. 'Welcome home.'

The police officer on duty must have heard a noise, for he opened the door to Kylie's room and put his head in slightly. He then walked to the nurses' station and two nurses, together with a doctor, hurried to Kylie's room.

Brian walked over to the police officer.

'Did you hear something?' he asked.

'Yes, there was a slight noise and so I informed the nurse.'

The nurse came out of the room and looked at the three men. She was smiling, which made the worried trio feel better.

'Miss Griggs has come round. She's asking for Brian.'

'That's me,' Brian said, looking at the other two.

'You can go in now,' the nurse said, 'but be careful not to upset her and don't stay too long. She's been through a lot. Too much.'

***

At Helen's apartment, Joe made a call to Detective Sergeant Mortimer but he was unavailable. Daphne informed Joe she wanted to phone Miriam, but as it was only six in the morning in Langley, she would leave it for an hour.

Helen had finished dressing and came back into the room.

'Right, what do we do now?' she asked.

Joe's phone rang. It was DS Mortimer.

'We have secured Emilio Jimenez. He is at the City Police station but he is not talking and not assisting us to find Covington.'

'I'll go to the station and see if I have better luck,' Joe said.

'You'd better be quick; he's asked for a representative from the Mexican Embassy to be present.'

'I'll leave right now,' Joe said, then turned to Helen. 'Daphne needs to phone Miriam in an hour. I'm off to the police station. Can you wait here and coordinate everything? Try to get hold of Jeremy to find out what's happening at the hospital. Brian should be there by now. I'll keep you in touch with what's going on at my end. Ta-ta.'

And with that, Joe was off, running down the stairs rather than taking the elevator, and hailing a taxi outside the apartment.

***

DS Mortimer strode along the corridor at the hospital. He replaced his mobile phone in his breast pocket as he approached Jeremy and Ron.

'Where is he?' DS Mortimer asked sharply.

'If you mean Brian,' Ron said in similar fashion, pointing to Kylie's room, 'he's in there with Kylie.'

'I need to speak with him now,' DS Mortimer said.

'Give him a few moments,' Jeremy said. 'She's just come round and asked for Brian. He won't be long.'

DS Mortimer was used to having his own way and felt uncomfortable when not in control.

***

Inside the room, Brian looked at Kylie with her head in bandages, bruises around her eyes and cheek bones, looking far less beautiful than he remembered. His fists clenched at the realisation of what happened to her and the pasting he would like to give Covington right now.

But instead, he whispered her name, ever so gently.

Kylie opened her eyes and tried to smile, but only grimaced when she sensed the pain from the injuries she received.

'Brian, what happened to me?' she asked.

'You've had a rough time,' he said, realising his answer was totally inadequate. 'Do you remember anything?'

'It's all very hazy,' she said. 'I remember I needed to tell you something. The next thing I know is I'm in here.'

'Don't worry, Kylie. You don't need to remember a thing. You just need to get better.'

'Am I dreaming, Brian?' Kylie asked. 'Are you really here?'

Then Kylie experienced a sharp pain, and she was unconscious again. Her heart was racing. The nurse rushed in, followed by two doctors, one of whom injected something into her. He turned to Brian.

'You'd better leave, sir,' he said. 'We'll deal with this.'

Brian's face had lost all colour as he rushed out of the room.

'Toilet, toilet,' he said.

Jeremy pointed in the lavatory's direction and followed him.

Brian emerged from the gent's toilet, having vomited in the cubicle. The smell was disgusting, but Jeremy still cleaned up after Brian's mishap and tidied himself before leading Brian back into the corridor and the seats outside Kylie's room.

Brian panted heavily and puffed hard as he tried to regain his normal breathing. Jeremy had wet his handkerchief and applied it to Brian's forehead, which helped soothe him.

DS Mortimer came over and asked Brian if he would answer some questions.

Jeremy was angry with the detective, as it seemed unreasonable after what Brian had experienced. Jeremy wanted him to give Brian some more time.

The nurse came out of Kylie's room and addressed the men, looking at Ron.

'We've sedated Miss Grigg to calm her. We need to do some tests to check the extent of Miss Griggs's injury. I suggest you all leave. She needs rest.'

'There doesn't seem to be anything anyone can do here,' DS Mortimer said. 'We should go to the station.'

'I'm coming,' Jeremy said.

'Me too,' Ron echoed.

CHAPTER TWENTY-TWO

Miriam had just reached her desk when the phone rang; it was Daphne calling from London.

Outside her office, the mailman was making his first delivery of the day.

'Overnight package for Mrs Snape,' he called.

Miriam waved her hand for the mailman to enter her office as she spoke to Daphne.

'Hi Daphne, what news from London?'

'Well,' Daphne began. 'Joe Thompson and I are with his wife, Helen, who has updated us on the condition of Brian's girlfriend. It doesn't sound good, as she's taken a hell of a beating. Brian is at the hospital with her.'

Miriam choked when she heard that news.

'Joe's going to the police station. They have Emilio Jimenez, Covington's security chief, but they haven't found Covington yet. He needed to get there before the Mexican Embassy intervenes and see if Joe has any better luck getting Emilio to talk than the police did.'

'Aren't you going with him?' Miriam asked.

'Oh, that's all right, Miriam. Joe doesn't need me for that. What's been happening at your end?'

'The mailman has just made a delivery, which should be the phone that Pika retrieved from the young English man when he caught him at the airport. The FBI doesn't have a clue about that and I want to see what information it holds.'

'You're looking for a link between Covington and Miguel Jimenez?'

226

'Correct, and also we've just found out that Henrique Jimenez is arriving in Kona today.'

'What!' Daphne exclaimed. 'That's interesting, it couldn't have been better timing for you.'

'We'll see. With Miguel's father in Hawaii, the FBI are flying the English thug up to Washington to avoid any problems.'

'Sensible,' Daphne agreed.

'Matt Booker and I are planning to fly down to Kona to confront the older Jimenez, if Matt can secure a plane.'

'Will that work? What do you hope to achieve?'

'Well,' Miriam said, 'we understand Henrique Jimenez is only in Hawaii for the weekend and we don't know when we'll have a similar opportunity again. We appreciate he has diplomatic immunity, but we're working on getting that lifted. In the meantime, if we can reach his old friend, Pablo Segura's grandfather, we may get further evidence against Jimenez, which will help us persuade the Mexican President to be on our side.'

'If you can get the link between Covington and Miguel, you can hold that against Henrique Jimenez and if the Brits can secure the money laundering charge, that will strengthen your case.'

'Yes, but there's a lot that can go wrong if we don't get those facts.'

Matt Booker rushed into Miriam's office.

'Time to go, Miriam, put the phone down. I've got the Gulfstream, if we leave straightaway, we can be there in time for lunch.'

'Right Daphne, I must go. I'll talk to you on the way to Hawaii.'

***

LONDON (00 LOCAL TIME)

Daphne ended her call with Miriam and turned to Helen.

'That was very interesting,' she said. 'Henrique Jimenez is going to Hawaii for the weekend and now Miriam is flying down to confront him.'

'Is that wise?' Helen asked cautiously. 'Has she made her case against him yet?'

'Not a hundred per cent, but she is hoping for some success here in London, which is why it's so important to find Mr Covington.'

'Let's hope Joe has success in persuading Emilio to offer some information.'

'Yes,' Daphne agreed, 'and she has also received the phone used by Covington's fall guy, which should confirm links between Covington and Miguel.'

'Henrique must be very sure of himself in going to Hawaii.'

'That's part of Miriam's plan. By going there to confront him, she hopes to surprise him. Also, if she arrests Miguel, and maybe Emilio in London, it may weaken his position with the Mexican President, sufficient to lift his diplomatic immunity.'

'That's a big if,' Helen said.

Daphne nodded. 'But she's done this before. Never underestimate Miriam.'

***

Joe arrived at the City of London Police Station in Bishopsgate, just ten minutes' walk from Patrick Covington's office, near Leadenhall Market. The desk sergeant escorted Joe to an office, where he met with a colleague of DS Mortimer, lounging in his chair with his feet on the desk.

The desk sergeant gave Joe a look which showed he didn't approve of the young man's attitude.

'Has anyone arrived from the Mexican Embassy?' Joe asked, also not impressed with the young man in front of him.

'Not yet,' the plain-clothed detective said, sitting up straight.

'I take it Emilio Jimenez hasn't spoken?'

'Not to my knowledge.'

'Where is he?'

'Downstairs in an interview room.'

'Is he alone?'

'No, there's a uniformed police officer with him.'

'Have you offered him any tea or coffee?'

'No, of course not.'

'Why not? Is he under arrest?'

'No.'

'Does he realise he is not under arrest?'

'Well, we haven't accused him of anything yet.'

'But you want him to help you. You're not making him feel comfortable, are you?'

'He's a person of interest.'

'Have you explained that to him?' Joe asked. 'Good Lord, no wonder he's not assisting you. I wouldn't if I were him. He's from a foreign country and he's concerned that you think he's done something wrong. He may have, but if you want something from him, get him on your side. Don't act like an idiot.'

'But DS Mortimer said we were to hold him until he returned.'

'So, have you even asked him any questions?'

'No, he just said he wanted someone from the Mexican Embassy to be present.'

'My God, this gets worse. You haven't asked him any questions, so he doesn't have any idea what information you want. No wonder he wants a friendly face to be present.'

The young officer's face turned from pink to puce as Joe quizzed him. He recognised Mortimer would take a similar stance, and he would be in serious trouble when his boss returned. The officer considered he'd better improve his attitude.

'I'll go ask him if he would like some tea or coffee,' he said.

'That'll do for a start. I'll join you shortly.'

***

Joe entered the interview room and asked the uniformed officer to leave. He walked over and held out his hand to Emilio, who declined to respond.

'Hello, *Senor* Jimenez, my name is Joe Thompson, MI5. Please accept my apologies for the poor treatment you have received so far.'

Emilio looked at Joe with a blank face and nodded.

'I believe you requested a black coffee. It should be here soon.'

Emilio muttered a 'thank you.'

Joe sat down opposite Emilio and grinned broadly, effusing the warmest of welcomes. He brushed the shoulders of his jacket, still smiling, and looked Emilio directly in the eye. Joe was doing what he did best, being totally British.

The uniformed officer brought in two cups of coffee, placing them in front of the two men. Joe took a sip and then made a sound of pure enjoyment, as if this was the best coffee he had ever tasted. Emilio looked at Joe curiously.

'I expect you must wonder why you are here?' Joe asked.

'Where is my representative from the Mexican Embassy?' Emilio responded.

'Oh, he should be here soon,' Joe said, 'but we don't really need him, do we?'

Emilio sat there in total silence.

'Unless you have anything to hide, of course,' Joe said. 'No, I'm sure you haven't.'

Joe let that comment hang in the air.

'You understand, we are having a bit of a problem in locating your boss, Patrick Covington, and we thought you might help us find him?'

Emilio's face registered Covington's name, but still he said nothing.

'You do work for Mr Covington, don't you?'

'*Si,*' Emilio responded.

'Yes, you do. You're his head of security, aren't you?'

'*Si.*'

'Good, now we're getting somewhere,' Joe said, smiling broadly. 'I thought we would. I expect you're an excellent head of security.'

Emilio responded grudgingly to this compliment.

'I expect Mr Covington has total faith in your abilities.'

Emilio nodded.

'So, what would happen if something went wrong and had to be dealt with immediately?'

'I would be responsible,' Emilio said.

'But what if something happened that you couldn't deal with and you needed to contact Mr Covington, what then?'

'Then I would contact him. But that is a very rare situation.'

'How would you contact him?' Joe asked.

'I would go directly to his office.'

'But what if he wasn't in his office and this problem occurred after office hours? What would you do then?'

'Sorry, I don't understand. My English is not very good.'

'Well, do you phone him at home? Or does he belong to a club, where you can contact him?'

'No, he doesn't belong to a club. I phone him at home.'

'When he isn't at home? Where then?'

'I don't understand what you mean.'

There was a knock on the door, and the uniformed officer poked his head in.

'Sir, the gentleman from the Mexican Embassy is here.'

'Ah, that's good,' Joe replied. 'Ask him to come in. I'll leave for now.'

'Can I go?' Emilio asked.

'Not yet. I'll be back in a minute.'

Joe returned upstairs and was about to walk outside for some fresh air when DS Mortimer arrived with Brian, Jeremy, and Ron.

After the mutual greetings, Mortimer took Joe aside.

'Has he said anything yet?'

'I think we were getting close when the man from the Mexican Embassy arrived.'

Ron butted in.

'Ask him why he was in Covington's office going through his drawers.'

'When did this happen?' DS Mortimer asked.

'Just before Covington returned. We believed Covington was still in Switzerland as he said he would not return until today.'

'What was Covington's reaction?' Joe asked.

'He went wild. They fought, and it looked really nasty. The entire office witnessed it. The argument lasted for some time, with both men shouting at each other.'

'What happened next?' DS Mortimer asked.

'Eventually, Emilio left, looking furious. Covington left a little while afterwards. He tucked a briefcase under his arm, but it was very slim and I could clearly see the outline of a gun in the briefcase.'

'Did you notice either Covington or Emilio again that evening?'

'Well, Covington had left Kylie's flat by the time Jeremy and I arrived.'

'But you didn't see him there?'

'No, but we are certain it was him who hurt her.'

'No, we aren't,' Jeremy intervened. 'We suspect it was, but we have no proof.'

***

Joe returned to the interview room downstairs, accompanied by DS Mortimer, who agreed reluctantly to let Joe lead the questioning.

The representative from the Mexican Embassy said that unless they planned to arrest *Senor* Jimenez, they had no reason for holding him. However, Joe suggested he might ask a few more questions. This time Emilio agreed.

'*Senor* Jimenez, do you get on well with your boss?'

'I don't understand. What do you mean?'

'Well, is he a good boss? Do you respect him?'

'I suppose so.'

'Well, that's a damning statement if ever I heard one.'

'Yes, I respect him as a boss.'

'Is that all? Do you like him as an individual?'

'I do my job. He does his job. That's the way we work.'

'Are you honest with him? Would you go behind his back?'

'Don't answer that question,' the representative from the embassy said.

'Why were you searching his drawers in his office?'

The embassy representative was about to tell Emilio not to answer when Emilio waved his hand in defiance.

'Mr Covington told me I was in charge when he was away. I needed some information, and I tried to look for it.'

'But he came back too soon, didn't he?' Joe said. 'And found you.'

'I thought he was in Switzerland!' Emilio shouted.

'What information were you looking for?'

'And why put you in charge? A head of security is not normally the man in charge when the boss is away.' DS Mortimer asked, 'Did it have anything to do with your father?'

Then the Mexican Embassy representative put both hands up to bring proceedings to a halt.

'*Senor* Jimenez, do you know the whereabouts of Patrick Covington?' Joe asked.

'No,' Emilio replied.

'Was the information you were looking for anything to do with the agreement between your father and Mr Covington to make payments to the International Bank of Ireland and South America in Zurich?'

Emilio looked aghast when Mortimer asked that question. A look which wasn't lost on the Mexican Embassy representative. They stood up and left the room, leaving Joe and Mortimer smiling at each other.

'I'm sure that shocked them,' Mortimer said.

Joe patted him on the back in agreement.

Upstairs, Jeremy asked the two men how the interview had gone.

'Well, we still don't know where Covington is, but Emilio now understands our knowledge is greater than he assumed.'

The phone rang and the desk sergeant answered it. After a couple of 'hmm' and a few other acknowledging noises, he looked over towards DS Mortimer.

'They picked him up a few moments ago, sir. Outside his office. He should be here any moment.'

DS Mortimer collected himself and took a deep breath.

'Right, you lot, in that room over there. I don't want him to see you, especially you two,' pointing towards Brian and Ron, 'when he arrives.'

***

Outside, in the street, the Mexican Embassy representative, Felipe González, faced Emilio.

'What was that comment about an agreement between your father and the man they are after?'

'It is nothing. My father provided the money for Covington to set up his business and in return he would receive an income.'

'Is that all? You seemed shocked that they knew about this agreement. I hope there is nothing that will harm the Minister's reputation.'

'No, of course not. I was just surprised they were aware of it, that's all.'

While they were talking, a police car arrived, from which Patrick Covington emerged. Felipe González ushered Emilio aside so that Covington wouldn't recognise him. But Covington saw him and his eyes blazed in anger as they pushed him inside the building.

***

Covington sat alone in the interview room, with no uniformed officer present and without being offered any tea or coffee.

Upstairs, DS Mortimer was organising the next interview. Joe was preparing to accompany him again, but Mortimer didn't want this to happen at the moment. He looked over at Jeremy.

'You've met Covington before, so would you like to attend this time?'

Joe complained about his absence.

'This is just an initial sortie, Mr Thompson, all in good time,' DS Mortimer responded.

Jeremy wasn't sure what he could contribute, but he was used to Mortimer's methods and went along with him.

Downstairs, the two men entered the room. Covington stood up and demanded to know why he had been brought to the station.

'Have I been arrested?' he asked.

'Sit down, Mr Covington,' DS Mortimer said. 'All will become clear in a minute.'

Covington sat down again.

'Now, Mr Covington, do you recognise this man with me?'

'Yes, of course I do, he's Mr Crichton. He is helping me with staffing matters.'

'And do you know why he might be here today?'

'No, apart from the fact that we have been doing business together.'

Covington felt uneasy as he answered the question. It was not something he thought they would discuss.

'And what business is that?'

'You'll be aware that I own a business which employs overseas personnel, and he was helping me with a new appointment.'

'I am mindful of that fact, and in which particular role would that be?'

'There are several people I might look to employ in various roles.'

'Would one of those be as a replacement investment strategist?'

Covington felt a chill go through him as he recalled his former investment strategist.

'Possibly.'

'You employ several Mexicans in your organisation, don't you?'

'Yes,' Covington replied, unsure about this change of tack.

'All the Mexicans are part of your security team, aren't they?'

'They are. Is there a law against that?'

'Unfortunately, no. Unusual but not illegal.'

'Mr Covington,' Jeremy said. 'I can't remember when we last spoke, but how many Mexicans do you have in your security team?'

'Five or six... no I'm sure it's five.'

'And you have the correct immigration papers for all of them?'

'Yes, of course.'

'We'll come back to that in a minute, Mr Crichton-Smith,' DS Mortimer said. 'Mr Covington, is the fact that you employ Mexicans for your security team anything to do with your arrangement with the Mexican Minister for Culture, Henrique Jimenez?'

'What arrangement is that?' Covington asked.

'Didn't *Senor* Jimenez finance your operation in London, in return for a regular income?'

'No, who gave you that idea?' Covington said, suddenly remembering he'd seen Emilio outside. 'Was it my head of security? He knows nothing.'

'OK, that's all for now, Mr Covington.'

'Can I go?'

'Oh no, we have more questions for you,' DS Mortimer said with relish. 'I'll be back shortly.'

Mortimer and Jeremy left the room. Covington sat there, perspiring slightly. He realised there was a problem, but how much of it could he blame on Emilio?

Mortimer reviewed the meeting with Joe, who he wanted to come in with him next time.

'That was useful,' Mortimer said. 'We asked him how many Mexicans were in his security team. He said six, then corrected himself to five, obviously not wanting to include Pablo Segura. We'll get him on the lack of immigration papers and work visa. We also asked him about the arrangement with Henrique Jimenez, which Emilio mentioned, but he said there was no arrangement.'

'So, he's not got his story straight,' Joe said.

'Nowhere near,' Mortimer replied. 'Now I want to tackle him on his fight with Emilio and see where that gets us.'

'We need him to confess to Kylie's beating,' Joe said, as DS Mortimer walked away.

'Correct.'

CHAPTER TWENTY-THREE

The Gulfstream was five hours out of Langley, halfway to Hawaii, and Miriam had been in deep contemplation about the next few days. Matt Booker guessed she might be asleep, but he was wrong. Her eyes opened and Matt realised his error. Miriam considered all angles, and many times she fooled people who would pass by her office. They would see this little old lady seemingly asleep at her desk, leaning back in her chair, and they would smile. If only they could perceive the plots that were running around in her head.

'Right, Matt,' she said. 'I need to speak to Langley. Can you ask the steward to patch me through?'

Booker stood up and walked to the galley at the back of the Gulfstream, where the steward prepared a light breakfast of eggs Benedict on sourdough toast. The yeasty aroma of the toast caught Booker's nose and made him feel immediately hungry. As he returned to his seat, the steward brought headphones for Miriam's use so that she would not concern herself with extraneous aeroplane noise. It was a good connection, as if Miriam were back in her office.

After a brief conversation, she took off the headphones and looked at Booker. Her face beamed with joy.

'Good news?' Booker asked.

'The best,' Miriam replied,. 'And I can't believe it. The techies were having trouble getting into the phone, thinking they would need to break the passcode, but there wasn't any security, no encryption.'

'No?!' Booker exclaimed in disbelief.

'Apparently not. They have found conversations between the English thug and Covington, who sent him to Hawaii. They also found conversations between the thug and Miguel, but the best bit was when they secured a conversation with Miguel in which he mentioned Covington by name and by the order he gave.'

'Fantastic!'

'Yes, so we have the link between Covington and Miguel, which they cannot deny. I must tell Daphne.'

A few minutes later, Miriam again took off the headphones.

'How is Daphne?' Booker asked.

'Oh, she's fine, enjoying the transatlantic lifestyle. The Thompsons are taking her to a fancy restaurant, somewhere in Chelsea, she said. Didn't you have a fling with her once?'

'That was a long time ago,' Booker replied, 'but we parted as friends. What did she say?'

'Apparently, Covington is in a mess. He hasn't admitted to beating up Brian's girlfriend and his statement disagrees with something Emilio Jimenez said. They're keeping him locked up overnight and will question him again tomorrow.'

'Hasn't he asked for a lawyer? He'd get him released in an instant, especially if they're not charging him.'

'As I said, Covington is in a mess and they are confident he'll start talking in the morning.'

***

The layer of thick clouds mesmerised Booker as he looked out of the aeroplane's window, Miriam looked over to see what fascinated him. She stood up and walked towards the pilot's cabin, holding on to the seats as she wandered. Once inside the cabin, the co-pilot rose to give her his seat, which Miriam gratefully accepted.

'Hello, John,' Miriam said. 'it's been a while since I've had the pleasure of your company.'

'That's correct, Mrs Snape, but it's always good to have you on board. How can I help you?'

'First, by calling me Miriam; we've known each other better than you needing to stick to Mrs Snape.'

238

'OK, Miriam, what do you need?'

'I wanted to know the time in Hawaii, as I've just made a couple of calls and need to speak to my contact in Kona. Is it too early?'

'Well, we've been flying for six hours, which makes it eight o'clock in Hawaii, breakfast time. We are due to arrive in Kona in under four hours, in time for lunch at your favourite restaurant.'

'You remember, John? It's always been my favourite. I use it all the time.'

'Do they still have that server who thinks he's a Russian revolutionary?'

'Oh, yes and they still make wonderful Mai Tais.'

'Ah, yes, the Mai Tais, what a way to watch the sun go down.'

Miriam laughed at the pilot's comment. It was many years ago that she'd spent a wonderful evening with John; she was only a young woman then. Bert was out of the country on a mission, but John helped her fill the time in his absence. She regretted that Bert never found out about her liaisons, but she was sure he would not mind. She also suspected Bert had his own romances around the world.

**

Back in her seat, Miriam put her headphones on and the steward connected her to Pika.

The conversation was brief. Miriam only had to inform Pika of her arrival time and to make sure he had booked two rooms at the hotel, the usual one for her and the one that Brian had occupied for Booker.

Pika confirmed he had done this small task. He also informed her that FBI Agent Reed was available as required and that life at the hotel appeared normal.

'How was Henrique Jimenez?' Miriam asked.

'Relaxing around the pool with a beer,' Pika said, 'with some of his men in close attendance.'

'How many?' Miriam asked, slightly surprised. Maybe this was not just a friendly visit?

'Two that I could see,' Pika said, 'but there may be more inside.'

239

'OK, Pika,' Miriam said, 'comprehensive as ever, exactly as I expected.'

'Thanks Miriam; see you in a few hours.'

'Oh, can you tell Agent Reed I would like an FBI presence around the hotel, whilst I'm there, but to keep it subdued. I don't want Henrique's bodyguards to get twitchy?'

'It's done. See you, Miriam.'

***

Miriam relaxed back into her seat, took a deep breath and smiled as the Steward brought the breakfast and a pot of coffee for two. Booker watched Miriam as she tucked into her eggs Benedict with gusto and he laughed.

'You know, Miriam,' he said, 'for such a small lady, you have an enormous appetite. We'll be having lunch soon. How do you fit all that food inside you?'

'I have an excellent metabolism, and anyway, lunch is over three hours away.'

The rest of the journey was uneventful. Miriam settled in her seat and closed her eyes.

But Booker wondered, was she sleeping or merely plotting her next moves?'

He would find out in time.

***

At the airport, Miriam rented a white Thunderbird convertible. Before she left the plane, though, she put on a wide-brimmed straw hat, tied under her chin. Also, Miriam wore a red Hawaiian shirt over tight white shorts, complete with a Hermes scarf and gold-rimmed sunglasses.

'Just as well you didn't want to look conspicuous,' Booker laughed.

'I want to make an entrance,' Miriam said.

240

'You certainly will, Miriam, you certainly will.'

***

Whilst checking in at the hotel, Miguel Jimenez came running down the corridor, shocked at seeing this figure at the front desk.

'Mrs Miriam! Why it *is* you,' Miguel gasped. 'What are you doing here?'

'I've come back to complete my holiday, of course, Miguel. Are you surprised to see me?'

'Why no, of course, it's always a pleasure to see you. How is your friend?'

'My friend? Oh, she died,' Miriam said, waving her hand nonchalantly. 'Oh, and I've brought another young man with me. He'll be staying in the room next to mine. You know, the same room as the last young man used.'

'Of course, of course,' Miguel gabbled, totally confused.

***

Henrique couldn't help but hear the noise coming from inside the hotel. He rose from his sun lounger, one of his men draped a towel around him, and walked towards Miguel.

'Who was that my son? I have never seen such poor taste in a woman. That was a woman, wasn't it?'

'Yes, father. I've never seen her dressed like that, either.'

Miguel was so exhausted after his experience with Miriam that he had to sit down and wipe the sweat from his brow.

'Who was she?' Henrique repeated.

'She is a regular visitor, but she had to leave recently because her best friend was very ill, and apparently she died, so the lady has returned.'

'What kind of woman dresses like that?' Henrique asked. 'Especially one in mourning. I will never understand American women.'

'Oh, and she works for the CIA,' Miguel said casually.

'What!' Henrique said, shocked. 'Are you sure?'

'Well, not a hundred per cent, but she used to come here with her husband and he died.'

'Did she dress like that after he died?'

'No, of course not, but I looked up his name, and they reported he was a CIA agent.'

'And you did not think to tell me this?'

'I didn't realise she would return so soon.'

'How many years has she been coming to your hotel?'

'*Our* hotel, Father. Oh, about the last ten or twelve years.'

'Since I have been in government?'

'That's about right.'

'You fool, Miguel, she could be working for the CIA right now, trying to investigate me.'

'Be serious, Father. I told her nothing. She likes to bring young men to the hotel. She has brought another one with her today.'

'When was the last time she brought a young man to your hotel?'

'That was different; she met him on the plane and he had nowhere to stay on the Big Island. He was the man who worked for *Senor* Covington, in London and…'

Miguel's jaw dropped as the realisation of what he had said hit him.

'And?' Henrique said, persistently.

'And who escaped the island?'

'What about the man you sent to catch him?'

'That was Covington's clown. He ended up in hospital.'

'Is he still in hospital?'

'I don't know, I'll find out.'

'Miguel, I know I did the right thing by not bringing you into the organisation, but I thought you could run hotels,' Henrique said sadly.

'I can, Father, I can,' Miguel replied, his head hung in shame.

***

'Well, Miriam, you certainly made an entrance,' Booker said, holding his hips, laughing.

'Shh, Matt, listen to this.'

Miriam and Booker sat in Miriam's room, listening to the conversation between Henrique and Miguel. They could not believe what they were hearing.

'How did you do that?' Booker asked.

'I slipped a bug under the desk at check-in. They'll never find it, but we can remove it when we next go downstairs. It's linked to my phone.'

'That's amazing.'

'What's more amazing, but understandable is that Miguel is not part of Henrique's operation and we now have proof his organisation exists.'

'Yes, we do and it all fits with the evidence we got from Santos.'

***

When Miriam and Booker returned downstairs, Henrique was still admonishing Miguel. Their eyes, though, remained drawn to Miriam's outfit. Although Booker did not want to look as outlandish as Miriam, he wished he was more appropriately dressed, as the temperature was now over 80 degrees Fahrenheit. CIA regulation jacket, tie and slacks, specified for the headquarters staff, are not suitable in Hawaii.

They walked out of the hotel and across the road to the Kona Village Shopping Centre, knowing they were the centre of attention, but this was part of Miriam's plan. Once inside the shopping centre, they followed the boardwalk around to the Kona Inn restaurant.

Gregor came running out of the restaurant as soon as he saw Miriam.

'Mrs Miriam, you have returned. I was so worried.'

'Well, Gregor, there was nothing for you to worry about. I had to go back to Washington, but now I'm back.'

'Yes, and with a nice young man. He looks much nicer than the last one you brought here.'

'Now, Gregor, don't be judgemental. The last young man was perfectly OK. He was just troubled.'

'Even so, Charlie and me, we didn't like him. But we like you,' Gregor said, flashing his full set of teeth at Booker.

Miriam turned towards Booker.

'Matt, this is Gregor; he is the senior server at this fine restaurant.'

Booker held out his hand to Gregor, who grasped it firmly and shook it several times.

'Shall I show you to your normal table? You're much earlier than usual.'

Booker turned to Miriam. 'Do you mind if we eat inside? I'm not dressed for this heat and I would prefer to sit in the area where there is aircon.'

Miriam nodded to Gregor, who turned about and marched Miriam and Booker to the front door, which Charlie was holding open for them.

'We have our second-best table upstairs, overlooking the bay and very air conditioned,' Gregor announced, pointing towards the flight of glossy pine stairs leading to the second floor.

'Where is the best table?' Booker asked.

'Oh, that is outside, facing the beach and we reserve this permanently for Mrs Miriam.'

'OK, lead on Gregor, second-best it is.'

They sat down, and immediately, Charlie brought a carafe of iced water, promptly filling their glasses.

'The menus appear enticing, but I don't want to eat that much. How long do you think we'll be here?' Booker asked.

'Well, I am expecting some visitors, but only friendly ones. We'll be perfectly secure up here. They never open the top floor at lunchtime, it's always reserved for me when I'm on the Big Island. So, we can talk freely with whoever appears.'

This seemed mysterious to Booker.

'Do you own shares in this place?' Booker asked. 'You have the best table on the beach, which nobody else can reserve and you have this complete floor upstairs for your own purposes. What have you done to warrant such an amenity?'

'Matt, I'll let you into a little secret, but you mustn't tell anybody.'

Booker was fully attentive.

'Gregor pretends to be a Russian revolutionary, but he was a Russian spy who defected. We set him up in this restaurant with the owner's approval.'

Booker whistled his surprise.

'Charlie is a former weightlifter who won the Hawaiian Iron Man contest many years ago. He's in a relationship with Gregor. The two boys have been together for over ten years and they kind of adopted me. They are my protection, but I also protect their secrets and now you will also protect them.'

Booker held up his hands in defence.

'I most certainly will. I would not want to get on their wrong side.'

Gregor returned to take their orders.

'Gregor, sit down for a moment, will you?' Miriam asked.

Gregor did as Miriam asked.

'It's OK, we are not very busy downstairs and Charlie can cope.'

'I'm sure he can, Gregor,' Miriam said. 'There is something I need to tell you.'

Gregor's face turned serious, his mouth closed, and the teeth disappeared.

'Matt works with me at the Farm, Gregor, and I told him about you and Charlie.'

He took a moment to digest the news and looked upset when he heard Miriam had told Booker their secret.

'But don't worry, he is perfectly responsible and will not divulge anything I told him.'

Gregor nodded, whilst Booker fixed his eyes firmly on him for any reaction to Miriam's words.

'We are on a case involving the owner of the hotel where we are staying and his son. We want you to use your contacts to provide any information you can and to let us know what you find.'

Gregor nodded more enthusiastically this time, just as Pika arrived upstairs and walked to their table.

'Ah, Pika, I'm glad you arrived now. I was telling Gregor about our case. You can fill in some blanks and let Gregor know how he can help.'

Pika sat down at the table, filled a glass of iced water, as Miriam's phone rang. She showed this was an important call and that there should be silence. Nobody said anything.

Miriam listened and her face dropped. She interrupted a couple of times, but it became obvious she was unhappy.

As she cut the call, expectant faces all around waited for Miriam to speak.

'Well,' she said, 'that is disappointing but not surprising. The Mexican President is unwilling to lift Henrique Jimenez's diplomatic immunity.'

There was a collective sigh of dissatisfaction around the table as they all believed Miriam when she said the Mexican President would have no choice but to lift the immunity, such was the weight of evidence against Henrique. Clearly, that was not the case.

What hold does Henrique have over the President? Miriam wondered.

After a few seconds, Miriam realised there was still work to be done. More evidence to gather and other arrests to be made. Maybe there was still a way to get Henrique.

'Right, Pika, we still need to find The Professor. He holds the key now. If we can get him to provide the evidence on Henrique's drugs operation, not even diplomatic immunity can save Henrique Jimenez whilst he is on US soil.'

'OK, Miriam,' Pika said. 'I'm on to it, although he has been conspicuous by his absence over the past few days.'

'Gregor, see if your contacts can give Pika any help. Ask Charlie.'

'OK, Mrs Miriam, we'll search high and low for The Professor.'

As the meeting finished, Charlie came up the stairs with a large tray of fresh fish sandwiches and a clubhouse sandwich for Booker. FBI Agent Reed followed close behind.

'Ah, Agent Reed,' Miriam said. 'Please sit down and eat some lunch with us.'

'Lunch on the CIA? How could I refuse?'

'This is Agent Matt Booker,' Miriam said, making the introduction. Agent Reed acknowledged Booker.

'We've just learned Henrique Jimenez remains protected by diplomatic immunity.'

Agent Reed nodded but said nothing.

'However, we can still arrest his son, Miguel Jimenez, for drug operations.'

'Can you?' Agent Reed queried. 'You have no evidence that he, personally, was in charge of selling drugs.'

'We don't have any evidence that he did,' Miriam agreed, 'and we are sure that he didn't, but we know that members of his staff provided drugs for Covington's thug. Also, there is no evidence of the relationship between Miguel and Covington, who runs the money-laundering operation in the UK and who conspired to catch the Englishman, Brian Jenkins. Hopefully, this might force Henrique to say something in defence of his son.'

'It's a little flimflam,' Agent Reed said, and Booker nodded in agreement.

'It's the best we have for the moment and you never know what might happen.'

'What about this Professor?' Agent Reed asked.

'No luck, at the moment,' Booker said, 'but we have people working on the situation.'

'What people?' Agent Reed asked.

'Don't ask and I can't tell a lie,' Miriam said.

Agent Reed shook his head in amusement as he bit into a fish sandwich.

***

After lunch, Miriam and Booker walked back to the hotel, accompanied by Agent Reed with three other FBI agents. Walking up the ramp towards the swimming pool, they could see Henrique Jimenez still lying on his sun lounger, with a cold beer on the table by his side. There were three men nearby, dressed in suits and looking uncomfortable in the heat. Miriam guessed they were his bodyguards.

Miriam walked over to Henrique, who looked up at her as she stood over him. The bodyguards approached, but Henrique waved them away.

'What do you want?' he asked in a harsh voice.

'I would like to introduce you to FBI Agent Reed.'

'So, what can you do? You can't arrest me. I have diplomatic immunity. I understand you tried to have it lifted.'

'We don't want to arrest you, Henrique, not at the moment, at least. It was your son we were after. Do you know where he is?'

This was unexpected, and Henrique sat up on his lounger.

'My son? What do you want with him. He has done nothing. He is useless.'

As his father raised his voice, Miguel came out of his office.

'What is it, Father? What is happening?' Miguel asked.

'Don't say a word, Miguel. It is nothing.'

'Miguel Jimenez, you are under arrest for operating a drug ring in Hawaii,' Agent Reed said, then, turning to one of his men, he added 'Read him his Miranda Rights, Officer.'

'You can't do this,' Miguel pleaded. 'I'm not a drug operator.'

'I told you to say nothing,' Henrique repeated, standing up from his lounger.

'But Father, tell them you said I was not in your operation.'

Henrique turned purple with rage.

'You fucking idiot of a son, keep quiet!'

Agent Reed continued.

'You are also charged with attempting to harm a foreign individual, a resident of the United Kingdom.'

Miguel could not believe what was happening. As he looked towards his father, his eyes begged for help.

'Finally, you are charged with knowledge of a money-laundering operation in the United Kingdom and Switzerland relating to funds from the said drugs operation.'

'What!' Miguel said in total shock. 'Father, help me!'

Whilst this was happening, nobody took any notice of people moving around them. Pika and Charlie were running up the ramp towards Miriam and the others. They did not shout, because they did not want the others to be aware of who else was in front of them, striding towards the group.

It was The Professor.

Suddenly, Henrique saw him.

'You!' he said. 'What are you doing here?'

Everybody turned round to The Professor, who was a few feet away. Pika and Charlie stopped where they were, a few feet further back, their mouths hung open and not believing what was happening in front of them.

They saw The Professor reaching into his shirt, pulling out a gun and pointing it directly at Henrique Jimenez.

'You were my friend,' he announced. 'I trusted you when you told me I had to leave Mexico because the President wanted me arrested for organising those fake elections.'

The Professor continued.

'But you only wanted me to use my knowledge to produce the drugs you needed to supply to the United States. You are not my friend. You are a fraud. My grandson told me he had evidence that you were laundering money from the drugs, so he went to the United Kingdom to find the proof and you had him killed.'

Henrique Jimenez held out his hands in supplication towards The Professor.

'This is not true,' he said. 'Pablo was your grandson, but he was like a son to me. I loved him. I would not wish any harm to come to him. Believe me, Antonio.'

But his words fell flat.

Everybody seemed frozen in time as The Professor denounced Henrique Jimenez. The world went silent. They could do nothing but watch as the bullet sped in slow motion from The Professor's gun and plugged into Henrique's forehead.

Henrique was dead in an instant and fell to the ground where he stood.

The Professor turned the gun onto himself, into his mouth, and fired once more. The bullet smashed though his brain, as his head exploded,

Somebody switched the sound back on as everybody rushed around. There was pandemonium, with phones ringing, people shouting and ambulance sirens sounding.

Miriam could not believe what had just happened.

CHAPTER TWENTY-FOUR

This was not what Miriam wanted.

She had two men dead, lying on the ground at her feet. The local police arrived and were arresting all the hotel staff. The FBI sheltered the residents inside the hotel and soon they would take their statements and offer them alternative accommodation.

This was now a crime scene and the normal processes would ensue. The pathologist arrived and she would examine the bodies, although everybody present saw what happened.

Statements would be taken, but that would take time, and Miriam had none to spare. She pulled Booker aside.

'Matt, we need to leave *now*. Get hold of John, tell him to ensure the Gulfstream was ready for take-off in thirty minutes. I need to get to London as soon as possible. This is the worst possible thing to happen.'

'Will do, Miriam,' Booker said, taking his cell phone and putting a call into their pilot.

Miriam beckoned FBI Agent Reed to speak with her.

'Agent Reed, I have to leave. I can't speak to anyone, but there are enough people who saw what happened. I want you to keep a lid on the back story. As far as anyone should be aware, this was an unfortunate meeting between two old enemies from the revolutionary days in Mexico. We must stop the Mexican President from finding out too soon or there will be an international incident.'

'Where are you going?'

'Back to Langley for now to see my director, but can you tell Frank in Washington what went on here? He'll need to brief his bosses. There'll be international ramifications, I'm sure, if we don't manage the story correctly. We don't want Henrique Jimenez to be painted as a martyr. He was no hero, but he was his country's Minister of Culture. We need to drip feed information to the press.'

'I'll do my best, Miriam.'

'Oh, and I wasn't here.'

'Of course not,' Agent Reed said, smiling.

Next, Miriam went over to Miguel, who was on his knees, sobbing near the body of his father. He looked up as Miriam approached.

'I do not do drugs,' Miguel said, holding Miriam's hand.

'I understand, Miguel, but your father did, and you knew that, didn't you?'

'Yes, I did, but he told me he was glad I wasn't a part of his organisation. This pleased me, too. But I am good at managing hotels. You have always enjoyed your stays here, haven't you?'

'Yes, you've always looked after me excellently.'

'Will I go to jail?'

'Yes, because you assisted Covington in his harmful pursuit of Brian Jenkins. Also, you knew about the drugs operation and the money laundering. We may require you to be a witness when we close the cartel, which your elder brother runs.'

'Francisco is an evil man,' Miguel agreed.

'Just like your father, but without his personality,' Miriam said.

***

The Gulfstream was waiting and the engines revving when Miriam and Booker reached the airport. No other flights were due to leave at that time of day, so their departure would be uncomplicated.

On board, they met the pilot and settled into their seats.

'I was expecting more rest time in Hawaii, Miriam,' John said, scolding her.

'We appreciate that, John; it didn't work out as we thought.'

'I'm out of hours, so Jeff will fly this leg, while I get some shuteye in the back of the cabin.'

'That's understandable. We'll try not to disturb you.'

'I've spoken with Langley,' Booker said, as the co-pilot began the take-off. 'We should arrive by two a.m. and they will put you on a flight to London, landing at RAF Northolt by mid-afternoon.'

***

After a brief stop at CIA HQ, where Miriam informed the Deputy Director of Operations what went on in Hawaii, she was on her way to London, courtesy of another CIA operated flight.

Miriam looked at her watch, it was approaching three a.m. She put a call in to Daphne.

SATURDAY 12TH APRIL 2008
LONDON (08.00. LOCAL TIME)

Daphne stood by the window of Helen and Joe's smart apartment in Kensington, looking down on the street below. She'd heard about the weather in the UK and it was definitely true. Rain showers from a grey sky. She preferred her home town in Florida, even though the weather could be turbulent. At least it was warmer.

Joe saw her gazing and looking glum.

'Don't worry, this will soon pass and the sun will be out later,' he said.

'I'm sure you're right. You Brits talk about the weather so much, you must be familiar with what you're talking about.'

'I wouldn't be so sure,' Joe said. 'Now, Helen will have your toast ready soon, are you sure that's all you want?'

'Oh yes,' Daphne said. 'After that wonderful meal last night, I'm not even sure I could eat the toast.'

'The restaurant did us proud, didn't they?'

'Oh yes, it was fabulous.'

'Mind you, I think I preferred it when it was Tante Claire. I was a regular there, but I don't go so much these days.'

Helen came into the room, holding a phone in her hand.

'Somebody's phone's ringing,' she announced.

'Oh, it's mine,' Daphne said. 'I'd better take it.'

'Hi Miriam,' Daphne said, turning to Joe and Helen. She said, 'It's Miriam.'

Joe looked at Helen and said, 'It's Miriam.'

Continuing in the conversation with Miriam, Daphne said, 'You're coming to London?'

Joe turned to Helen and said, 'She's coming to London. She sure gets around, that girl. I thought she was in Hawaii.'

Helen laughed and slapped Joe on his chest.

'Let her get on with her conversation,' Helen said. 'She'll tell us later.'

Daphne could not believe what she was hearing from Miriam.

'No! Really? 'I can't believe it,' she said. 'I'm still at the Thompsons' flat. We're going to the police station after breakfast. It's only just after eight here.'

Then there was a pause before Daphne finished the conversation.

'I'll see you later this afternoon. Bye, Miriam.'

***

Daphne sat down at the breakfast table and picked up a piece of toast.

'Well?' Joe asked. 'It's unbelievably frustrating only hearing one half of a phone conversation.'

'Then you shouldn't listen,' Daphne said, teasing Joe mildly. 'Miriam's on her way to London.'

'That much was obvious,' Joe said.

'She'll be here by mid-afternoon.'

'Nothing new there.'

'What Joe and I want to know is what did she say that excited you so much?'

'Well,' Daphne said, taking a deep breath. 'I can't believe it, really.'

'Can't believe what?' Joe asked.

'Apparently, Henrique Jimenez is dead.'

'No!' Joe said.

254

'Yes, apparently, his old friend, The Professor, shot him.'

'Really?' Helen said, taking turns with Joe.

'Then, he shot himself, after blaming Henrique for the death of his grandson, Pablo.'

'That's unbelievable,' Joe said. 'This is all falling into place nicely. We only need to prove Covington killed Pablo and we have a slam.'

'That's why Miriam's coming to London,' Daphne said. 'She has the number of Pablo's phone and so she will dial the number and whoever answers it, we've got him.'

***

Patrick Covington sat in the interview room, looking dishevelled after a long night in his cell and with no washing facilities. His one-day stubble revealed his natural reddish colouring, which he hid with the use of chemicals. The bags underneath his grey eyes clearly showed his lack of sleep.

Covington sat there, listless, with his hands, on the table in front of him, cradling a cup of black coffee, which he had no energy to lift, or inclination to drink even though the smell filtered into his brain.

A single uniformed police officer stood between Covington and the door to the corridor, but the latter had no thought of escape and was reconciled to his fate.

DS Mortimer entered the interview room on his own. He bade the officer leave the room so there would be no witnesses to what he was about to say.

'Mr Covington, you realise you committed crimes for which you will be punished? Would you like to confess?'

Covington looked at DS Mortimer with a blank expression.

'There is nothing to which I need to confess. You have me here under completely false pretences.'

'Do you deny beating Miss Kylie Griggs on the afternoon of Thursday 10th April at her premises at around six o'clock?'

Covington said nothing.

'Do you also deny an altercation with your Head of Security, Emilio Jimenez prior to this?'

Covington said nothing.

Following a knock on the door, the police officer, previously in the room with Covington, handed DS Mortimer a piece of paper and exited the room.

DS Mortimer looked at the paper and then at Covington. His expression turned grave as he spoke.

'Mr Covington, I have this piece of paper informing me that Miss Griggs died in hospital at six o'clock this morning from the wounds inflicted by you.'

The news shocked Covington out of his silence.

'She can't be dead!' he exclaimed. 'I hardly hit her. She wouldn't tell me what I wanted. If anyone is to blame for what happened, it's her. She left me with no choice.'

'What did you want?'

'She could have told me where that bastard Brian Jenkins was. I only wanted to find him. He is the culprit in all of this.'

'But Brian Jenkins is not the criminal.'

'Yes, he is; he killed Pablo Segura.'

'No, Mr Covington, *you* killed Pablo Segura. We have a witness who says that you had not left the office on the night Pablo Segura died.'

Covington shook his head vehemently.

'You killed Pablo Segura for what reason, we do not yet understand, but we will find out, you can be sure. Is that why you had the altercation with Emilio Jimenez?'

'What? No, he was rifling through my drawers, looking for information with which he could discredit me.'

'What information was that, Mr Covington?' DS Mortimer asked. 'Was it anything to do with a money- laundering scheme you operated on behalf of his father?'

'Money laundering? No, I have never been involved in money laundering. That's illegal. It was to do with an agreement with *Senor* Jimenez, where I guaranteed a return on his original investment in my company.'

'Were you unaware of the source of the funds which came into your business?'

'Of course not,' Covington replied. 'It was from his friends who wanted a secure investment, but who wanted the information kept from the Mexican tax authorities. That's not a crime in this country.'

DS Mortimer stood up and told Covington he would be back later.

'Oh, silly me,' he said. 'I didn't turn on the tape machine.'

***

Upstairs in his office, DS Mortimer decided he needed to talk to all three of the young men involved in this situation, all of whom would be witnesses when they brought Covington to trial.

Ron Mathis worked for Covington. He saw the fight with Emilio Jimenez and also the register where Covington erased his name, to remove proof he was in the office the night someone killed Pablo Segura. But what else did he know?

Jeremy Crichton-Smith worked for the FSA, and nominally, monitored the Hedge funds although they were unregulated in the UK. He also assisted Joe Thompson, from MI5, who investigated Covington's immigration records. Could he use any information on that score against Covington?

Then there was Brian Jenkins, or Brian Roberts? There was a strange fish. What information was it that Mortimer did not know about? How did he get the job at the hedge fund in the first place? If he was British, why was he working in Switzerland and where will he go when this is all over?

DS Mortimer did not like loose ends.

He started by phoning Brian's number.

'Hello?'

'Mr Roberts? Or is it Mr Jenkins? How do I address you?'

'Jenkins will do, although I suppose my correct surname is Roberts. Why don't you just call me Brian?'

'Okay, Brian, we have your boss, Patrick Covington, in the interview room here at the station. He's not very forthcoming and I'm

257

trying to tie up some loose ends. Can you come down to the station so we can have a few words?'

'I don't really want to, Inspector. There are some arrangements I need to sort out regarding Kylie.'

'It's Detective Sergeant, Brian. There are more pressing requirements which you can help me with, so I'd like you to come here now. You can deal with Miss Griggs's matters later.'

It didn't sound like a request.

'As I said, I don't like loose ends and you can help me fill in some gaps,' DS Mortimer reiterated.

'Okay, Detective Sergeant, I'll be over. It shouldn't take long, you're close to my old office, aren't you?'

'That's correct.'

***

First Brian called Jeremy.

'How are you, Brian?' Jeremy asked. 'Tough times, eh?'

'I'm going to catch a cab to meet Mortimer. He wants a few words with me. Apparently, he doesn't like loose ends.'

Jeremy chuckled.

'I've heard that one before. Just be careful what you say. Where's Covington?'

'In the interview room. Mortimer probably wants some background information on the business. I won't discuss anything else.'

'Best of luck. Do you want a word with Ron?'

'Why, is he there with you?'

'He doesn't want to go home. He's still afraid of Covington and Emilio, so I said he could shack up with me until this is over.'

'Okay, put him on… Hi Ron, how are you doing?'

'I'm OK, Brian. Jeremy's flat is way better than mine.'

'Jeremy will look after you, but you should go home eventually.'

'I will, soon.'

'I'll come over after I've been to see DS Mortimer.'

***

DS Mortimer was about to phone Ron Mathis when his Sergeant opened his office door.

'There are two people here to see you, sir, a Mr Thompson and a Miss Mitchell.'

DS Mortimer had met Joe Thompson, but not Miss Mitchell.

'Ask them to come in and bring some coffee will you?'

Joe and Daphne stepped into DS Mortimer's office and sat down.

'May I introduce Miss Daphne Mitchell?' Joe said. 'She is an American and has an involvement in this affair.'

'CIA?' DS Mortimer asked.

'Yes,' Daphne said.

'Why am I not surprised?'

The sergeant brought in three cups of coffee and handed them around.

'Miss Mitchell,' DS Mortimer started.

'Call me Daphne,' she said.

'Daphne, I'm investigating a murder and a severe beating of a young woman. Do you have any information that is relevant?'

Joe interrupted.

'She doesn't have any specific information on the murder or the beating, but her boss is flying in from the US and will be here this afternoon. She will have some information which may apply to the murder. So, I suggest we delay any further interrogation of Covington until she arrives.'

'I hear what you say, but I've not interviewed Mr Covington sufficiently at present. There are also aspects to this case which may relate to money laundering.'

'And to drug running,' Daphne said.

DS Mortimer smiled wistfully.

'I love these simple cases,' he said with a sigh.

Daphne brought DS Mortimer up to date with the events in Hawaii, involving Brian's escape after they burgled his flat. The burglary was news to DS Mortimer. She confirmed that Brian, and now Miriam, had

259

concrete financial evidence of irregular money payments, which pointed to money laundering.

DS Mortimer sighed loudly.

Joe then told DS Mortimer about the Swiss bank which Covington used to channel funds to the UK, to facilitate the money laundering.

By the end of their stories, DS Mortimer's coffee cup slipped out of his hands onto his desk, spilling coffee everywhere.

'*Sergeant,*' DS Mortimer shouted, 'come here and clean up this mess.'

As the sergeant cautiously poked his head around the door, he told them that Emilio Jimenez had arrived.

'What's he doing here?' DS Mortimer said in exasperation.

***

DS Mortimer came out of his office to meet Emilio.

'You don't have your Embassy representative here?'

'No, I came to talk to Mr Covington.'

'He is currently undergoing an interview. You may not speak to him until after I've finished.'

'Who is with him? Does he have a solicitor?'

'He has waived his rights to a solicitor,' DS Mortimer informed Emilio.

'Then it is most important I see him,' Emilio said. 'He must have legal representation.'

'Why do you say that, Mr Jimenez? What do you know that I don't?'

'There is information which puts Mr Covington's business in jeopardy. As Mr Covington's Head of Security, I insist he has a solicitor.'

'What information is this?'

'I am not at liberty to discuss it without a solicitor being present. It is not relevant to your investigation.'

'I'll decide what is and what is not relevant, Mr Jimenez. Would you like to enlighten me?'

'I've said enough. I'm not saying anything else without a solicitor present.'

'*Sergeant,*' DS Mortimer called, 'can you take Mr Jimenez to interview room two? He'll want to call his solicitor, somebody from the Mexican Embassy, I presume?'

As the sergeant escorted Emilio downstairs, Brian entered the police station.

'You wanted me, DS Mortimer?' Brian asked. 'I'm here.'

DS Mortimer turned around to face Brian. He was running out of interview rooms, he thought, as he mopped his forehead.

'Go into my office,' DS Mortimer said. 'You'll recognise the people in there.'

Brian opened the door to DS Mortimer's office and saw Daphne and Joe were present. They stood up to acknowledge his presence. Daphne put her arms around him to give him a hug and Joe touched Brian's shoulder, as a sign of support.

DS Mortimer wondered who he should talk to first. Covington could sweat for a little while longer, Emilio Jimenez wanted his solicitor, he would talk to Brian first.

'Sergeant, can you locate the details of a burglary in Ealing on Friday 4th April?'

CHAPTER TWENTY-FIVE

SATURDAY 12TH APRIL 2008
LONDON (3.00 LOCAL TIME)

DS Mortimer had let Patrick Covington stew in the interview room for the rest of the morning. Emilio remained in interview room two, waiting for his Mexican Embassy official. Neither could communicate with the other, but they were both increasingly frustrated. Emilio, in particular, seemed near boiling point. He stood up to pace around the room. The uniformed officer on duty asked him to sit down.

'Where is my embassy official?' he asked. 'How long are you going to keep me waiting here?'

The officer did not say a word and looked straight ahead, just as the guards do outside Buckingham Palace.

'I insist on speaking to your detective.'

Still, the officer didn't respond, leaving Emilio steaming.

***

Upstairs, DS Mortimer spoke to Brian in the presence of Joe and Daphne.

'Brian, I have some questions for you. Are you happy to talk with Mr Thompson and Miss Mitchell present?'

'Sure,' Brian replied, in a noncommittal tone.

'I understand there was a burglary at your flat on 4th April; you apprehended the attacker, but he escaped.'

'That's correct.'

'At the time, did you recognise the man who burgled your flat?'

'No.'

'Do you know if he had any associates?'

'Not at the time he looted my flat.'

'But you do now?' DS Mortimer asked. Joe and Daphne leaned forward with growing interest.

'Yes, he came to Hawaii and tried to attack me at the airport as I left the Big Island.'

This was news to DS Mortimer.

'What happened?'

'I was being driven to the airport by an associate of Miriam Snape, who works for the CIA, and he stopped this thug from attacking me.'

'Continue, please.'

'We found his phone and his call log showed he was in contact with both Covington and Miguel Jimenez.'

'So, Patrick Covington sent him to Hawaii?'

'That would be my guess.'

DS Mortimer looked down at his papers. A loose end no longer loose, but still not proven. The likelihood, though, there was a connection between Covington and the thug.

'Where is this person now? Still in Hawaii?'

'I presume so, but I'm not sure.'

'I can help with that, Detective Sergeant,' Daphne said. 'He was in hospital on the Big Island, but Miriam, Mrs Snape, felt he should move to Washington given Henrique Jimenez arrived for a stay at his son's hotel.'

'Why was he in hospital?' DS Mortimer asked.

'He overdosed on drugs, which we believe the hotel staff supplied,' Daphne said.

'So,' DS Mortimer said, 'he's in Washington now?'

'Probably,' Daphne said, 'but it's not confirmed.'

'Okay, now the father joins the son on the Big Island?' DS Mortimer repeated.

'Yes, but he's been shot,' Daphne said.

'*What?* When were you going to tell me?' DS Mortimer said, going red with rage.

'Sorry,' Daphne said, apologetically. 'I planned to tell you, but you insisted on questioning Brian.'

This news threw DS Mortimer into a panic.

'Is there anything else you want to tell me?'

'Only that he was shot by Pablo Segura's grandfather.'

If the previous news shocked DS Mortimer, he was positively apoplectic with the latest revelation. Brian sat there with his mouth wide open as he tried to digest the news. Joe sat there calmly, with the hint of a smile on his face.

'Getting kind of interesting, isn't it?' Joe said.

***

DS Mortimer stood up and walked out of his office, leaving Joe, Daphne, and Brian alone. He had to have time to think. He needed fresh air. The sergeant at the desk saw the open door of Mortimer's office and wondered what had just happened. Whatever it was, it didn't look good.

Inside the office, Joe and Daphne were arguing.

'Why did you have to tell him?' Joe asked.

'He had to know because of his investigation,' Daphne said vehemently.

'But why then?'

'I don't know, it kinda slipped out.'

'Slipped out?' Brian asked. 'Anyway, how did you find out?'

'Miriam told me on her way to Washington.'

'Where is she now?' Brian asked.

Daphne looked at her watch.

'She must have arrived in London by now.'

'Is she coming here?' Brian asked again, querulously.

'That's what she said,' Daphne said. 'I told Joe and Helen over breakfast.'

DS Mortimer returned to his office. He still had questions for Brian, but they could wait until he digested this latest news and what it meant for his investigation. DS Mortimer asked Brian to sit outside while he spoke to Joe and Daphne.

'Miss Mitchell, is there any proof Henrique Jimenez was in charge of a Mexican drug cartel?'

'Suspicion, yes, but no proof as far as I am aware.'

'If you can't prove the drug running, then it is more difficult to prove the money laundering,' DS Mortimer said.

'But we have details of deposits and payments made by the hedge fund through Switzerland. That should be sufficient to question the legality of the operation,' Joe said.

'But Mr Covington said to me these payments arose from friends of Mr Jimenez who didn't want the Mexican tax authorities to notice them. That's not illegal in the UK, but it is up to the Mexican revenue authorities to question the fact.'

'The UK is not a tax shelter,' Joe said.

'I agree, but we are not discussing anything other than the Mexican tax system. Where it came from is another matter and it still has to be proven it is drugs related,' DS Mortimer said.

'He's correct,' Joe said. 'We can provide back up evidence, but until your government can prove this is drug money, our case against Covington on money laundering is on hold.'

'I'm sure they'll be working hard to prove it is drugs related,' Daphne insisted.

'Until then,' DS Mortimer said, 'we will have to park this to one side. By the way, why did Pablo Segura's grandfather shoot Henrique Jimenez?'

'Miriam said he blamed Henrique for having his grandson shot,' Daphne said.

'Now, that's interesting,' DS Mortimer replied. 'Do we have any additional proof Pablo's death was not an accident but murder? Who are the likely protagonists?'

'Ron Mathis said he found Covington's name on the register, which he had removed, so that proves he was there,' Joe said.

'What about Emilio?' Daphne asked. 'If Henrique wanted Pablo dead, he could have organised it through Emilio.'

'Possible,' DS Mortimer said, 'but I'm still not sure about Brian. It's clear now he left the country and there's more to his story than he's mentioned.'

'There is one foolproof way, and that is through Pablo's phone. If it's not broken and still in the possession of the murderer then, if we dial the number, whoever answers will be the killer,' Joe said.

'Miriam has Pablo's phone number and she will be here soon,' Daphne said, 'so we can find out when she arrives.'

***

Miriam's plane arrived at RAF Northolt on schedule at three o'clock. A police car waited for her at the bottom of the steps as she exited the aircraft. She'd enjoyed her recent flights in the Gulfstream, but she understood this was an expensive way to travel and she'd have to justify the cost in due course.

The car, a black Jaguar XF, was one of many makes used by the British police as an undercover vehicle. Miriam admired its smooth, elegantly rounded shape, and thought it stylish. The female police officer guided Miriam into the rear of the car whilst she sat in the front passenger seat, to the left of the driver. Miriam had never got used to the fact the Brits drove on the wrong side of the road. She would never become used to driving on the left-hand side and sensed she would be dangerous to pedestrians if she did.

'Comfortable Ma'am?' the driver asked.

'Very,' Miriam replied.

'Traffic's heavy on our way into the city, there's a cup semi-final on at Wembley. We may have to use the lights and siren to get us there on time.'

'Exciting,' Miriam said. 'Try your best, but I'm not looking to break the speed limit.'

'Okay, Ma'am, it should take just over an hour.'

Miriam settled back in the comfortable leather seats and looked forward to the drive.

***

Meanwhile, at the police station, DS Mortimer had asked Jeremy to come in and answer some questions. When he arrived, he saw Joe sitting on the bench with a woman he didn't recognise. He'd met Brian outside the station, pacing around. With his face pointing to the ground. He appeared to be concentrating and didn't acknowledge Jeremy as he walked up the steps into the station. A sense of unease came over him.

'Ah, Mr Crichton-Smith,' DS Mortimer greeted Jeremy as he arrived. 'I've had a very busy morning, so let's get going.'

DS Mortimer showed Jeremy to his office. Joe looked up and gave Jeremy an awkward grin. Again, it made him feel uneasy.

'Sit down, Mr Crichton-Smith.'

'Please, call me Jeremy.'

'Now, I want to investigate your relationship with Mr Covington.'

'Carry on,' Jeremy said.

'You said your work for the FSA involves monitoring hedge funds, even though they are unregulated, but I understand you have another relationship with Mr Covington. What is that?' DS Mortimer asked.

'Mr Thompson, who I see is sitting outside, asked me to help him investigate Mr Covington in the employment of his staff, particularly his security staff.'

'You didn't mention that previously.'

'You didn't ask me, and in any case, it wasn't relevant to the murder of Pablo Segura.'

'Are you certain?'

'Not in my view,' Jeremy said.

'I already mentioned Pablo Segura did not complete any immigration papers in gaining employment with Mr Covington, did I not?'

'You did, and I said at the time it did not concern me.'

DS Mortimer looked at his notes and smiled.

'At the time, Mr Thompson had already asked you to help him investigate the employment of Covington's security staff, yes?'

'You're probably correct.'

'Why then did you say this did not concern you, when clearly it did?'

Jeremy looked flustered and felt unsure how to answer without compromising himself. He remained silent.

'Did Mr Thompson investigate the illegal entry into the UK of foreign nationals, one of whom was Pablo Segura?' DS Mortimer said, persisting with this line of questioning.

'Yes,' Jeremy said, mumbling into his beard.

'Sorry, Mr Crichton-Smith, I didn't hear you?'

'Yes,' Jeremy said, speaking louder.

'How then can you say this had nothing to do with you?'

'I acted on behalf of the security services and was unsure what I could say to you.'

'You can say anything you like to me, Mr Crichton-Smith,' DS Mortimer said. 'I told you I hated loose ends and this would have provided another avenue of questioning to help me solve his murder.'

'I didn't realise who had the primary responsibility in this issue.'

'That's for us to resolve amongst ourselves, not for you to guess, and guess wrongly, I might add.'

Jeremy felt duly admonished.

'How did you plan to proceed with your investigation of Mr Covington?' DS Mortimer asked?

'Joe suggested that I talk to Mr Covington about any staffing issues he had,' Jeremy said. 'my plan was to become closer to him and he might allow me to talk to his personnel chief. In that way, I might see what records he kept on his staff and whether they used the business as a route for illegals to come into the country.'

'How far did you get?'

'Not far at all,' Jeremy replied. 'I had coffee with him and then he saw Kylie Griggs in the coffee shop with Ron Mathis, whereupon he rushed outside and grabbed Kylie. He was mad as hell.'

'So, the beating which we presume he gave Miss Griggs and which put her in the hospital was not the first time he had acted violently towards her?'

'No.'

'Did Mr Mathis witness this act of violence?'

'No, he was quicker than Kylie and had raced inside the office before Covington saw him.'

'What did you do?'

'I left quickly, so Kylie wouldn't see me, but she did anyway.'

'You didn't think to help her?'

'No, I didn't want to blow my cover.'

'Not very gentlemanly, Mr Crichton-Smith,' DS Mortimer said.

'It upset her at first, but I think she forgave me.'

DS Mortimer stood up.

'Excuse me, I want to ask Mr Thompson to join us.'

***

The police car exited RAF Northolt onto the A40 arterial road into London but was caught in a severe traffic jam.

'Looks like this is worse than I thought,' the driver said, 'but we should be all right once we're beyond the North Circular slip road.'

Then, a few seconds later, he said, 'we've still a way to go. I'm not having this, let's turn on the sound and light show.'

The driver flicked a switch and blue flashing lights came on inside the car with the siren wailing loudly.

Miriam smiled as the adventure began. Cars in front of the Jaguar hurriedly moved aside to give the police vehicle space to move forward. On a two-lane highway, over a bridge and through a tunnel, vehicles squeezed together to make three lanes, wondering what happened ahead.

'It won't take long now,' the driver said.

The officer in the passenger seat laughed at her colleague's actions.

***

'Mr Thompson, I understand Mr Crichton-Smith assisted you in investigating Mr Covington regarding the possible illegal immigration of his staff?' DS Mortimer said, 'I have spoken with the Home Office and they confirm Pablo Segura entered the UK without completing the necessary papers.'

'Ah, that was you, was it?' Joe said. 'I knew somebody from the police had checked, but not who.'

'So, we can charge Mr Covington with employing illegal aliens.'

'Yes, but I tried to see if this was a route for illegals to come into the country. It led me to follow him to Switzerland, where I asked a member of the Swiss security services for support.'

'We'll explore that in a minute. Regarding Mr Crichton-Smith, do you often use non-Secret Service individuals to do your work for you?'

'When it's needed.'

'Right, moving on to your trip to Switzerland, what did you discover?'

'It had nothing to do with illegal immigrants; he had gone to Zurich to open another bank account.'

'Why did he do that?'

'Apparently, the fact somebody had gained access to the existing account meant he needed to open a new one.'

'So, your trip at the taxpayer's expense was not required?'

'True, but we didn't realise it at the time. In the event, I scared him and we thought it might lead him to make an error, which might benefit Brian.'

'It led to Covington putting Miss Griggs in hospital,' DS Mortimer said, looking at Joe severely.

Joe's face reddened in shame.

'I'm sorry,' Joe said in a very apologetic voice.

The three men sat in silence for a few seconds.

'Okay, that's all for now. I need to talk to Brian again.'

Joe and Jeremy exited DS Mortimer's office and saw Brian and Daphne in excited conversation.

'What do you mean, she downloaded my USB onto her tablet?' Brian asked, heatedly.

'Brian, it's of no consequence,' Daphne said. 'We needed to have our people look at the information on the stick.'

'But I said it was not for her to do.'

DS Mortimer walked out of his office and saw the two arguing.

'Ah, does the plot thicken?' he asked. 'Brian, can you come into my office?'

Brian stood up and slammed the chair against the wall.

'I hope you'll pay for any damage?' DS Mortimer said, cheekily.

***

DS Mortimer wanted to investigate Brian's Swiss background.

'Brian,' he began, 'are you Brian Roberts or Brian Jenkins?'

'I was born Brian Roberts, thirty-two years ago, in London, at St Thomas's Hospital.'

'But you have a Swiss passport.'

'That's because my mother married my stepfather, a Swiss resident, who adopted me. They moved to Switzerland when I was four years old.'

'So, you have dual nationality?'

'Correct.'

'Do your mother and stepfather still live in Switzerland?'

'They were killed in a car crash when I was thirteen.'

'But you remained in Switzerland?'

'I attended the international school in Zurich and went to university there.'

'Tell me how you came to work for Patrick Covington.'

'I was an investment strategist for a small asset management company in Zurich. I didn't realise my recommendations upset one of our clients, who then made an accusation against me. He could not substantiate the allegation, but it was enough to cause some difficulty with my firm as he threatened to withdraw his funds, which were substantial. My superior thought that if I left the company temporarily, he might smooth over the situation with the client. He knew, from one of his banking friends, that a position existed in London and he arranged for me to work there under an assumed name so the client could not trace me.'

'Are you aware of what happened to this client? Is he still with your old firm?'

'I have heard his accusation led to my old firm digging deeper into his background and they found he built his fortune on previous crimes he committed.'

'Would they not have been curious about his financial background before he became a client?'

'This is Switzerland you're asking about, Detective Sergeant,' Brian said. 'secrecy works both ways. If they don't ask, they can't be liable when somebody asks them.'

'It all sounds very dodgy,' DS Mortimer said.

'It is, but the world is changing and the incidence of dirty money arriving in Switzerland is disappearing fast. But these crooks will always find somewhere to put their money.'

'You have told me an interesting story, Brian, but I don't believe it is quite correct,' DS Mortimer said, looking Brian blankly in the face.

Brian looked back at DS Mortimer indignantly.

'Are you saying I've just told you a pack of lies?'

'Not entirely,' DS Mortimer said, 'but you have left out some important information.'

'Such as?' Brian questioned.

'My investigations show your move to London was part of an operation aimed at exposing Herr Fischer, the head of the bank, as a link to the illegal money operations.'

'Go on?'

'The Swiss security services were already suspicious of Herr Fischer. When he took on the banking operations for Patrick Covington and Henrique Jimenez, which was the same time as Covington moved his operations to London, they wanted somebody in London to gather evidence against him.'

'And you know this, how?'

'Are you not related to Emily Winterburn?'

Brian reddened in the face.

'Yes, she's my stepsister.'

'And is she the Emily Winterburn who works for the Swiss security services?'

'Yes.'

DS Mortimer sat back in his chair and smiled. As he enjoyed his moment, though, the door opened and the desk sergeant entered.

'Sorry to interrupt, sir, but the representative from the Mexican Embassy is here and wants to see you urgently.'

DS Mortimer was not pleased with this disturbance, but he knew he could not avoid talking to the man. He left Brian sitting in his office as he went outside to talk to the Mexican.

'Are you holding *Senor* Jimenez?'

'No, sir, we are not,' DS Mortimer said. 'He came here of his own free will, wanting to speak to Mr Covington. But as we had not finished interrogating Mr Covington, we asked him to wait in one of our other interview rooms.'

The Mexican representative was not happy.

'I have some urgent news for him,' he said.

'What is it?' DS Mortimer asked.

***

Before the Mexican representative spoke, Miriam entered the police station, to applause from Joe and Daphne.

'Miriam, hi, it's great to see you,' Daphne said, hugging Miriam, much to her embarrassment.

DS Mortimer reached boiling point, with this latest interruption.

'Who is this woman?' he asked.

'This is Miriam Snape of the CIA; she has come here with important information,' Daphne said.

'Ah, Mrs Snape, come into my office,' DS Mortimer said. 'There are a few issues I would like to discuss.'

'Certainly,' Miriam said, 'and please call me Miriam.'

DS Mortimer held his arm out, directing Miriam. Once inside his office, he closed the door.

Outside, Joe and Daphne, as well as Jeremy and Brian gathered, in anticipation of being included in the conversation.

Twenty minutes later, DS Mortimer came out of his room and spoke to his desk sergeant.

'Have everyone gathered in my office, and that includes the two men downstairs. Make sure there are enough chairs.'

The desk sergeant did as he was asked. Other police officers carried chairs into the room. Everybody entered DS Mortimer's office, nine, including the Mexican Embassy representative.

DS Mortimer stood behind his desk, with Miriam sitting on a chair to his left.

'This is a complicated case,' DS Mortimer said, 'involving drug running, money laundering, illegal immigration, grievous bodily harm and murder. It has too many loose ends. I am primarily concerned with arresting somebody for the murder of Pablo Segura, but I will also arrest somebody for the actual bodily harm of Miss Kylie Griggs.'

'You said she was dead,' Patrick Covington said, heatedly.

'I think you misheard me, sir,' DS Mortimer replied. 'I believe there are three people who might have murdered Pablo Segura. Brian, you had the opportunity, but no apparent motive. You exited the country under a false passport, or was it your true passport? For what reason? Because you were afraid of being killed? Why would you go as far as Hawaii? You must have been extremely scared to go that far, or was there another reason? There are many parts of your story that don't add up, but I don't believe you killed Pablo Segura.'

Brian heaved a sigh of relief at DS Mortimer's last words.

'Patrick Covington, I am certain your hedge fund business was used for the illegal purposes of money laundering, but that is not for me to prove here. However, you tried to hide the fact that you were at your office on the night Pablo Segura died. Why did you do this? It was your business. Surely, you could come and go as you pleased? Why hide the fact unless you were guilty of something? Was it that you knew Brian had stumbled on your illegal activities? Did Pablo Segura also try to find evidence of your illegal money-laundering operations? And was that why you killed him?'

Covington sat speechless, still in shock that the girl was not dead, as Mortimer had said, which previously led him to blurt out information he would not otherwise have mentioned.

'Emilio Jimenez, you are the Head of Security at the hedge fund and you are also the son of Henrique Jimenez, the Mexican Minster of

274

Culture and owner of the Jimenez hotel chain. Why would a man of your personal wealth choose to be a Head of Security of Patrick Covington's business? Was it because you were, in fact, your father's representative and the real person in charge, to whom Patrick Covington reported? How is your father? When was the last time you spoke to him? Was he aware Pablo Segura worked at Covington's firm? Did he tell you to kill him?'

'My father is dead,' Emilio said, staring at DS Mortimer.

'Ah, so you know this, do you?' DS Mortimer asked.

'Yes, I listen to the news programmes,' Emilio said, cursing at DS Mortimer, 'but even if I killed Pablo Segura, you cannot arrest me, I have the diplomatic immunity afforded to my family by the Mexican Government.'

It was then that the Mexican representative stood up and spoke.

'Senor Jimenez, that was why I wanted to talk to you. I have just heard from my government. Your diplomatic immunity was rescinded.'

Emilio looked aghast.

DS Mortimer then looked towards Miriam.

'Madam, I think it is time for you to dial the number.'

Miriam took out her phone and a piece of paper.

'On this piece of paper,' she said, 'is the number of Pablo Segura's cell phone. We have a witness in the US, Juan Luis Santos, who was a friend of Pablo Segura at the time they helped fix the Mexican elections, which brought the current President to power and which elevated Henrique Jimenez to the government. Santos and Pablo remained friends, even after Santos was arrested in Colombia. They spoke together on the night Pablo was killed, just as he was gathering evidence against the Jimenez family's money-laundering operations.'

DS Mortimer took up the story.

'By a complete coincidence, Brian also was working at his computer that night, and unknowingly, but at the same time, pushed certain computer keys, which put the systems under stress. First the system failed and then it returned, opening the account information relating to the Jimenez family. The killer, aware that Pablo now had the evidence he wanted, forced him to the back stairs. He knocked him down the stairs and this broke his neck, which killed him.'

Miriam returned to the story.

'We believe that Pablo, who had been talking to Santos at the time the computer systems failed, dropped his phone, which was picked up and kept by his killer. I will now dial the number given to me by Senor Santos.'

Miriam dialled the number. The room was heavy with silence as those gathered waited to see whose phone rang.

There was a dull ringing, Emilio reached into his pocket and took out Pablo's phone.

'I should never have recharged the phone to see who he had been talking to. I should have thrown this away a long time ago,' he said.

'Right,' Covington said, standing. 'You can let me go as I'm not the murderer.'

'No, but we will charge you with GBH.'

'You have no proof.'

'We will have when Miss Griggs comes round and we will also charge you with offences against the Immigration act for employing illegal aliens.'

DS Mortimer turned to Miriam. 'How did you know Emilio killed him?'

'Just before Pablo's grandfather shot Henrique, he accused Henrique of having his grandson killed. Why would Covington agree to do that? It had to be Emilio, doing his father's deeds.'

'Charge them and take them away, Sergeant.'

EPILOGUE

A sense of calmness prevailed after the recent turmoil, which had resulted in the arrest of Emilio Jimenez and Patrick Covington, but that was about to be broken.

It was Miriam's last day in London. She was due to leave for Washington on the five o'clock flight from Heathrow Airport, but she sat in a pub overlooking the River Thames, waiting for everyone to arrive. Miriam had checked out of her hotel after making a few telephone calls and taken a black cab, which dropped her nearby. She wasn't familiar with London yet, even though she'd been there a few days, and she made sure of being early. She needed to be there when everybody arrived.

Brian had been true to his word about showing her the sights. He'd taken her to Buckingham Palace, to see the changing of the guards, and the Tower of London. But the best was wandering around the streets by Covent Garden and Piccadilly Circus. She really enjoyed theatreland, Chinatown and Soho, which were exciting, but much smaller than their New York equivalents. Miriam didn't like the fact that the Brits drove on the wrong side of the road and she was nearly run over three times. Brian took her to some fabulous restaurants, but nothing compared to the Kona Inn, and she couldn't get any decent Mai Tais. Still, London was much older than anything in America.

She had a room at the Tower Hotel, by St Katherine's Dock, next to a cute little marina. Brian said that her room, from where she could see Tower Bridge, was right across the water from Kylie's apartment.

Brian left her when he visited Kylie, but he never stayed too long, as visits were still restricted. He said she looked well enough and the latest tests showed more stability in her condition. The doctors were hopeful she would make a full recovery, but it would take a while and she had to be careful.

Miriam was thankful that she only had hand luggage with her. Originally, she expected to be in London overnight, not for four days. If she'd packed as she did for Hawaii, it would have been much more difficult getting to this pub. Especially walking along those narrow, cobbled streets.

Helen and Joe were the first to arrive. They spotted Miriam, before she saw them, sitting outside on the terrace, looking at the river. Joe walked over and asked her what she wanted to drink.

'Do they serve Mai Tais here?' she asked.

'I'm not sure,' Joe said. 'I'll ask, but what if they don't?'

'Then I'll have an Earl Grey tea.'

Joe went to the bar, and Helen came over to sit down after fixing her hair.

'I find it's so windy by the river, don't you?'

'I don't know. I've never sat by a river,' Miriam said. 'I've sat by the ocean, but then it's much warmer in Hawaii.'

'That's true, but it's not a bad day for this time of year,' Helen said.

Joe returned from the bar with a tray carrying the drinks. This comprised a gin and tonic for Helen, a pint of Fuller's IPA for himself, and a cup of Earl Grey tea for Miriam. Also, on the tray was a small jug of milk and a small plate with slices of lemon.

Miriam took the tea and tasted it. Her face screwed up in disapproval.

'Don't you Brits know how to make a decent cup of tea? Surely you must, it's your national drink?'

'We don't drink Earl Grey normally, that's a specialist tea,' Helen said.

'Yes, the tea we drink we call builder's tea,' Joe confirmed.

'Builder's tea? What's that?' Miriam asked.

'It's our best-selling tea,' Helen informed her. 'It normally comes in tea bags and is not really tea; it contains tea dust rather than leaves.'

'My hotel made superb Earl Grey.'

'Yes, but your hotel caters for foreign travellers, mainly American,' Joe said.

As this discussion continued, Jeremy arrived and joined in the conversation.

'What are we talking about?' he asked.

'Hello, Jeremy,' Miriam said, acknowledging his presence. 'I've been looking forward to seeing you again. We're discussing the choices and merits of British tea.'

'Not my subject,' Jeremy replied. 'I prefer coffee.'

'Or beer?' Joe asked.

'Since you're asking, I'll have a pint of IPA,' Jeremy said.

Joe stood up and walked to the bar.

'Well, we're nearly all here. Does anyone know where Brian is?' Helen asked.

'He said he'd be here,' Miriam replied, 'but he had a surprise for us and would be late.'

'I wonder what the surprise is?' Jeremy asked, reaching out to take his pint from Joe.

'Well, you can ask him yourself. I just saw him on his way through Furnival Gardens,' Joe said, smiling, 'I won't spoil the moment.'

Then Brian walked around the corner, through the gardens beside The Dove, and as he did so, the group all hollered in unison.

'Kylie!' they screamed.

Brian pushed the wheelchair in which Kylie sat. She wore a heavy coat, with woollen gloves and a bright yellow bobble hat hid her hair. Kylie looked good for somebody who had experienced a severe beating and who was still recovering in hospital. Though thinner in the face than they remembered, she grinned when she saw all of her friends.

The one person she didn't recognise was Miriam, who stood and walked over to her.

'Hello, I'm Miriam. I'm very pleased to see you, young lady.'

'You're the lady with the gravelly voice,' Kylie said.

'I suppose so,' Miriam replied. 'Too many whiskies and too many cigarettes.'

'Well, it's good to meet you and thank you for looking after Brian,' Kylie replied.

'Oh, I think you've done your fair share of looking after him,' Miriam acknowledged, 'above and beyond the call of duty, I'd say.'

Joe stood up again.

'What would you two like to drink?'

'No alcohol for me, thanks Joe. I'm taking Kylie back to the hospital soon. She's only allowed out for a short while, and then I'm taking Miriam to the airport. Just a lime and soda for me.'

'I'm not allowed anything, either so I'll have to lay off the Merlot for now. A glass of water, please Joe.'

'Coming up, gorgeous and you Brian.'

Everybody laughed.

As he sat down, Brian looked at his watch. Jeremy noticed this and asked him if he expected somebody. Brian shook his head nonchalantly.

'Just checking how much time I have before I need to leave.'

***

Kylie sat next to Helen, safe in the knowledge that she wouldn't try to pair her off with anyone just yet.

'Kylie, what's the prognosis?' Helen asked.

'What she means, old girl, is how long are they going to keep you in the hospital?' Joe asked.

'I'm not sure,' Kylie replied, 'but they are happy with me, and Brian has said that when I'm let out, he'll come over and look after me.'

'But Kylie,' Helen asked, 'isn't there only one bedroom in your penthouse?'

Joe slapped Helen playfully on the knee.

'Helen,' Joe said, 'Kylie is beyond your boundary now. She has found her own man.'

They all laughed, except Jeremy, who wasn't satisfied with Brian's answer. He'd become close to him in the last few days. Jeremy thought he should prepare to leave—*and soon*.

'Not leaving us, are you, Jeremy?' Joe asked. 'You've hardly said a word. Is there something on your mind?'

'There might well be,' a familiar voice said, as DS Mortimer made his way onto the terrace from the inside of the pub.

'What do you mean?' Jeremy asked. 'It's all right for you, but somebody has to go back to work and keep this country running.'

'Is that what you do, Jeremy?' Brian asked. 'Do you keep the country running? Or do you look after yourself?'

'I don't understand what you mean,' Jeremy said. 'Why are you having a go at me? After all I've done.'

'Yes, Jeremy, what *have* you done?'

'I know some of what he's done,' Miriam said. 'We all assumed the person who burgled Brian's apartment and then followed him to Hawaii was Covington's thug, but he wasn't, was he Jeremy?'

'Of course, he was! Who told you differently?'

'I spoke to FBI Agent Frank McCarthy last night and he said that when the thug arrived in Washington, the FBI interrogated him,' Miriam said. 'He confessed to everything.'

'How could I think Covington had acted so quickly as to get this roughneck to my flat before I left the office unannounced?' Brian asked.

'Mr Covington said it was you that advised him, Jeremy, for this thug to burgle Brian's accommodation. Then, when he was unsuccessful, you convinced Covington to pay for him to follow Brian to Hawaii,' DS Mortimer said. 'We have all of this on tape.'

'You're not going to believe Covington's words, are you?' Jeremy pleaded.

Joe stood up.

'To think I believed you when you said you had evidence that Covington was employing illegal aliens and that I should let you get close to him so we could arrest him on anti-immigration laws. This only gave you regular contact with Covington, with no one becoming suspicious.'

'I was right, Pablo Segura didn't have the correct papers, he didn't have any papers,' Jeremy said, arguing his case.

'But your best lie was to suggest Covington had followed me to Kylie's flat, when you told him her address, Jeremy.'

Everybody turned round as Ron emerged from the pub.

'Covington couldn't have followed me. Because I had doubled back to the office to check the register and find out if Covington was there the night Pablo was killed, Covington had to be ahead of me. He was waiting for Kylie after she met me at the pub and said she had to tell somebody what I told her. I'm guessing that was you Jeremy. As she left to go outside, I noticed your car was already there and you were talking to someone. If not Covington, then who?'

'That's right,' Kylie said. 'I saw Jeremy's car, but I had no time to think it through and when I went outside, Covington pointed his gun in my face.'

Jeremy knew it was useless to run. Where would he go, especially with two uniformed police officers standing behind DS Mortimer?

'Cuff him, boys,' DS Mortimer said. 'Jeremy Crichton-Smith, I'm arresting you for aiding and abetting in connection with injury to Miss Griggs and potential injury to Mr Jenkins, or Roberts, or whatever his name is. Take him away.'

DS Mortimer turned towards Miriam.

'Mrs Snape, it's been a pleasure meeting you and thank you for your help in this case. I've never worked with the secret services before, whether on this side of the Atlantic or on your side, but it's helped me clear up all the loose ends.'

'Thank you, Ralph—may I call you Ralph? You may have different ways of working, to those on my side of the pond, but you have been most efficient.'

Helen and Joe stood up.

'Yes, DS Mortimer, Joe and I agree with everything Miriam has said.'

'Come on Miriam, time to get Kylie back to the hospital and you off to the airport. Bye everybody.'

And with that, Brian, Miriam, and Kylie left. DS Mortimer and his police officers took Jeremy away. Helen and Joe were on their own, with Ron, considering his potential as one of their contacts.

I'm sure I can find a girl for Ron, Helen thought.